EYE OF THE GATOR

Also by E. C. Ayres

Hour of the Manatee

EYE OF THE GATOR

E. C. Ayres

ST. MARTIN'S PRESS ❧ NEW YORK

This is a work of fiction. All the characters and events portrayed in this book are fictitious, and any resemblance to real people or events is purely coincidental.

Library of Congress Cataloging-in-Publication Data

Ayres, E. C.
    Eye of the gator / E. C. Ayres.
      p.   cm.
    "A Thomas Dunne book."
    ISBN 0-312-13490-8 (hardcover)
    1. Private investigators—Florida—Fiction. 2. Florida—
Fiction.   I. Title.
PS3551.Y72E94   1995
813'.54—dc20   95-34731
                                    CIP

First Edition: November 1995

10 9 8 7 6 5 4 3 2 1

Acknowledgments

The author wishes to thank the following persons for their support and assistance in the research and production of this book: my editor, Ruth Cavin, for her patience and tolerance; my friends, Bob, Bobby, and Becky Watson, who provided me with the idea of using the sinkhole; Susan Rose of The Snoop Sisters store and her Mystery Book Club members for their invaluable help; Robert Vanderslice of the Florida Department of Natural Resources; the research staff at the Florida Institute of Phosphate Research; my brother, Ed Ayres, editor of *Worldwatch;* my parents, John and Alice Ayres, for their unwavering support; and my dear friends, Rex Hearn and Kathy O'Shaughnessy-Hearn, who have given me so much over the years.

EYE OF THE GATOR

1

The sun was already low over Manatee Bay. The cellophane surface of the water glittered with slashes of pink and orange and purple, an artist's dream, reflected off the routine afternoon clouds out over the Gulf. It hadn't rained in nearly a month, despite the constant presence of moisture, but then that wasn't uncommon in the Florida spring.

The low light glinted off the glass of a blue-gray '89 Mazda 626 with Pennsylvania plates. The young man behind the wheel delivered a futile slap at an elusive preseason mosquito that had staked out a free lunch on his neck. He turned north on Route 41 out of Bradenton, where he'd been giving testimony at a petition hearing before the county commissioners. The petition was for an impending supermarina right in the path of the migration route for several extended families of manatees. A certain majority of the commissioners had listened politely, then drifted back into euphoric dreams regarding what sort of yacht they'd soon be acquiring, courtesy of the developers.

But they weren't his most present worry. He glanced again up at his rearview mirror for the third time in three minutes. A bead of sweat appeared above his right eyelid, then trickled down, momentarily blinding him on that side. He tried to blink it away, unwilling to take even one hand off the wheel. His grip was like that of a climber clinging to his last lifeline as the pitons driven into the cliff above slowly popped out, one by one. His skin was black, but his knuckles were pale, strangling the padded wheel.

The young man was twenty-three, a Yale graduate, and still new to Florida, having moved to the Tampa Bay area three months earlier upon graduation to accept what seemed like an outstanding career opportunity, at the time. He had been recruited heavily, by the government Civil Rights Task Force. Prodded by increasing anxiety over Florida's growing environmental interests and concerns, they were anxious to make a showing for their few remaining liberal constituents in Washington and Tallahassee. Florida no longer had any choice but to deal with this situation now, he had vociferously been informed by his briefing team. Or there would soon be no potable water for fourteen million people. There was essentially only one aquifer serving the entire state, centered beneath the Lake Wales Ridge, a prehistoric geological spine of limestone with water underneath it and spreading north, west, east, and south from there. Its only source for replenishment was rainwater, which, while falling regularly, fell at a rate that had now dropped to fifty percent of the rate of consumption, statewide.

The developers and their political cronies had no interest in hearing about this, of course. It was up to Swiftmud to pump in sufficient water to meet their needs. Consumers were only second, anyway, in water use: behind agriculture, and just ahead of the phosphates industry. The thing was, for the past few years, Swiftmud had been pumping water directly out of the aquifer, which wasn't going to get put back, ever. It was called "mining the aquifer," and as a direct result, the Florida water supply was, at this moment, in dire straits. Especially considering what he'd found only

2

yesterday in the county archives. The commissioners hadn't believed him, despite the impeccability of his research, which they'd politely shuffled off to one side. His work was headed directly, he supposed, for the cylindrical file upon his departure.

His name was Tim Cross, originally from Philadelphia, the City of Brotherly Love. Had he been born in the Sunshine State, ghettoed in the minority black culture—still kept sharply underfoot by vestiges of white supremacy that remain in control over much of Florida, (as in much of the South)—his parents, religious mentors, teachers, and even peers would have taught him to keep his head down, keep to the background, not "rock the boat." Not yet, anyway.

Instead, he, an outsider, had taken on several key elements of Florida's white power structure toe to toe, head to head. And now they were angry. He reached out and patted the brown file folder on the seat next to him. It was all in there: the twenty-year-old Environmental Impact Report, the test results which he knew were virtual liquid dynamite, and the revised Soil and Water Report he would now have no choice but to submit. It had only been a matter of courtesy, giving the company a chance to respond and propose reparations. Instead, they had tried to stonewall him. Well, it wouldn't work. He would do his job no matter what. There was far too much at stake.

The phosphate people weren't the only angry ones, though. That latest run-in with Cecilia's boyfriend—her self-proclaimed boyfriend—had been a close call. He was going to have to find a way to deal with that dude before something bad happened. She deserved better. She had found better, in fact, in him. It was just that she was too afraid to act on it. Tonight he was going to take matters into his own hands, and get her out of that situation. But first he had to attend the meeting. That was important, too. Vitally important, in fact. If only his life hadn't gotten so damn complicated, all in a matter of a few months. He had this "rescuer" trait, he knew. From his mother's side, probably. Anyone in need, especially a woman, he just couldn't help wanting to nurture, to assist. Too bad they usually didn't even appreciate it. He knew it was a compulsion that had done him little good in his short life.

He glanced at the illuminated clock on the dashboard, above the stereo. Seven-fifteen. He was going to be late.

Up ahead was a stop light. There was a county road off to the right that circumvented the ever-increasing congestion of Bradenton and cut across much of Manatee County. There was a little-used two-lane bridge above Manatee City, and another county road that shortcut twenty miles off the trip to Plant City. He could still make it. If he was lucky.

He glanced in his rearview mirror once more. Traffic was fairly light—just trucks, mostly—this being out of the mainstream for tourists. There were several cars and a pickup behind him, which had been there, he'd noted, since leaving Bradenton. But that was not necessarily cause for alarm. There were about a hundred motels and restaurants along this commercial strip of U.S. 41 that paralleled the coast from well north of Tarpon Springs all the way from Tallahassee south to Naples before cutting across the Everglades to Miami.

When he reached the light, he waited in the right lane. All the cars stayed in the left, or through lane. The pickup pulled up close behind him. He studied the dark outline of the two occupants in his rearview mirror and his feeling of uncertainty, apprehension, increased. He shook it off. The driver was obscured in the darkness, and he could, at a quick glance, determine nothing about him. His companion was a bit on the large side. Tim couldn't determine race just yet. Why did it even matter? He had been raised to be race conscious, though. And he never lost the dull, sinking sensation in his stomach—especially in the South—when he was confronted by white males, or flirted with by white females.

He turned sharply and accelerated onto the shoulder before the light changed. The pickup behind him followed suit, albeit more slowly. He was a quarter mile ahead before it began to gain ground. It held position about a hundred yards back for several miles until the scattering of auto repair shops, propane dealers, farm service shops, and occasional seedy motel gave way to thick pine woods.

Tim began to wish he hadn't taken this empty back road, shortcut or not. His pulse quickened, as the pickup behind him began to close the gap. He tried to speed up, but the pickup—a big American model—was more than a match, powerwise, for his Japanese coupe. Maybe they just wanted to pass him on an errand even more urgent, in their minds, than his. Probably out of beer or something. Except, he remembered, they'd passed the last 7-11 four miles back.

The woods were pitch dark now on either side, and Tim began to worry about deer, raccoons, and the like. A collision with a deer at high speed in a car like his could be fatal to both the deer and the driver. He slowed down, despite his concern about the pickup behind him. Hitting a deer in these woods was a very real, very imminent danger. Whereas, he supposed, the likelihood of any real threat from whoever was behind him was probably remote. A product of his increasingly paranoid fantasies, as of late.

The road straightened out, and the center line broke up into a passing lane. The pickup didn't pass, though. Instead it pulled up directly behind Tim's rear bumper, and put on its brights. Son of a bitch, thought Tim.

The pickup pulled alongside, and Tim tried to outrun it. He could not. The truck's big V-8 kicked in, and stayed with him. That's when he knew the race was over. They passed a closed service station as they tore through the darkness, and in the light cast from the parking area, he could see the driver's face clearly—white, and pasty, with a heavy five o'clock shadow. And at that moment, he recognized the driver. As the man gestured for Tim to pull over, his look seemed almost apologetic, Tim thought. That was when he knew he was finished, and chose not to resist. There was one thing he could do, though, in his final moments, as he pulled over onto the shoulder and braked to a stop. The man got slowly out of the cab and walked toward him, gun held at his waist, but pointed straight at Tim's head. Tim reached quickly for his shirt pocket, and found a pen. He reached down and started to write a message on the front of the car seat. But then the door was yanked open.

"Out," he was ordered.

The Old South is back, was his bitter thought, as he slowly obeyed. . . .

2

_____

Tony Lowell jibed and turned full downwind, trying to out-run the weather. Problem was, he was four miles down-stream, and a wind strong enough to drive him against it was also going to be capable of capsizing his sixteen-foot open-cockpit wooden sloop. The boat would have been com-parable to a Star class, but for the fact that it had been hand-made, by himself, to his own specifications.

He managed to clear the sandbar jutting out at the river bend using his old centerboard trick, and could just make out the shiny new spars of his schooner, The *Andromeda*, about a mile across the water. He should make it with no problem. Cleating the jib, he adjusted the downhaul, let out the main, put his feet up on the gunwale, and let 'er rip. This was the life: laying low, lying back, running before the wind, and minding his own business unless gainfully en-gaged to do otherwise. Which, he ruefully had to remind himself, had not happened for a little too long for fiscal comfort.

Right now, he was mostly engaged with avoiding respon-sibility. For his own feelings. Or maybe he was just avoiding dealing with them. Feelings weren't his specialty, other than when he listened to or occasionally played his music. He had an old Gibson J-45 guitar, left over from his college days, he'd taken out every few years or so to strum some long-forgotten blues or folk tune, or perhaps even jam along with the Wolf, or Muddy Waters, or Roger McGuin on one of his ancient platters or tapes.

Today he was trying to cope with a personal crisis. His daughter had just left, to go to another college. A whole new college this time. She'd transferred from Duke to Syracuse in midsemester. All over some boy she'd met who played basketball. Duke already had three good point guards, and Syracuse only had two, so they'd offered him a scholarship, and she had simply presumed that she was part of the package, and so had transferred along with him. Except that he'd dumped her right after the NCAA quarter finals for a prettier cheerleader. At least, that had been Lowell's bitter assumption. The worst of it was, Ariel had decided to go north anyway.

"I'll get him back," she had promised, tearfully.

Lowell just shook his head. What could he say? "You'll freeze your ass off, sweetheart," is what he'd said.

She'd blinked back the tears, laughed, and given him a tight hug—one of those ones, despite her diminutive size, that made him close his eyes, squeezing tight tears of his own from the corners.

She'd looked at him then. "Oh, Daddy. You're not all that tough, are you?"

"Never said I was," he said, and she kissed him.

That was when he'd given her the Gibson, as a good-bye present. That had led to more tears, more tight squeezes, and another kiss.

Then the plane had been announced, and she had waved good-bye, and headed north. To freeze her ass off, he felt confident. And also to learn some of life's tougher lessons.

Tony Lowell had learned a few of his own, during the past year. Such as that one man does not a shipyard make—

hence the unfinished schooner still drydocked on his beach—and also that sometimes crime does pay. He'd lost a case involving a husband who'd managed to spirit all his assets to the Turks and Caicos Islands, leaving a bereft wife— Tony's client—and four young children practically penniless. Tony had gone after him, only to be sidelined by armed militia. The husband, it seemed, had managed to acquire some clout. And small wonder, with seventeen million U.S. dollars behind him.

Another lesson Lowell had learned was that love was neither eternal, nor many splendored. It was mostly just difficult, time-consuming, gut-wrenchingly painful, and expensive. He had stayed out of the fray for most of his adulthood, until that incredible and unexpected reconnection with Caitlin Schoenkopf and his previously unknown daughter a few years back.

That reunion had not panned out, however, except that he had attached himself to his newly discovered daughter a lot more tightly than he knew was good for either of them. He'd tried to explain it to his friend, Perry, a local occasionally employed jack-of-all-trades, when they'd run into each other at the Clam Shack in Gulfbridge, where Lowell occasionally dropped by for shellfish and beer. Perry Garwood. Creek Indian. Black hair, some graying, in a tight bun at the nape of his neck. Lowell's sand-on-grime ponytail was back, from the time he'd cut it all off in Palm Coast Harbor, so they looked like at least social kin, except for the hair color. They were in fact brothers-at-arms, in a way. Both were Vietnam vets. Both decorated. Both trained for lethal combat. Both shared feelings of dismay at the violence now so rampant in their society, their country, their home state of Florida. Both were mavericks, both had sired children (Perry's were grown—a son doing time in Texas for a pot violation, and a daughter in med school at Tallahassee).

9

Both had left a large part of their lives back in the sixties and were still struggling to dig their way out of that bottomless foxhole. Both loved the blues. And frequently had them.

"Where's the mystery?" Perry was saying. "You never knew you had a daughter, then you run into your old lady—"

"Not so old," insisted Lowell.

"Fine, not-so-old lady. Only about your age, and you're ancient."

"If I'm ancient, you're an artifact," retorted Lowell. Perry had more crags and canyons in his deep mahogany tan than the Rocky Mountains.

Lowell was forty-eight, Perry fifty-one, and both were resisting middle age with all the diminishing power at their disposal.

"I *am* an artifact," agreed Perry, mildly. "A bundle of contradictions that make perfect sense. I'll be in a museum for sure, when I'm done. They'll stuff me and put me on one of them totems in some fancy Sarasota museum. 'Perry Garwood. Last of the Seminoles.'" That was half true. Or maybe only one sixteenth true. Perry had told Lowell his story over a six-pack on a dock on the Manatee River one harvest moonlit night. How he was half-Indian, half-English. How he had been fathered by a legendary British commando, who'd been brought in to train special forces during World War II—forces skilled at weaponless invasion, covert infiltration, silent entry, silent death, and successful escape by any and all means. Perry's percentage had resulted from a similar hit-and-run operation by his father on his Indian mother.

"Creeks," corrected Lowell.

"Whatever. Same thing. The government invented the Seminoles, actually, back around the Civil War. Some

10

government official decided it would be more convenient to take all those prisoners they had down here and give 'em all one name. Seminole was a local Indian word for 'farmer,' so he decreed that from now on, all Florida Indians would be Seminoles."

"He's probably the one who invented the tomahawk chop," noted Lowell.

"Do not jest, my friend. All those Florida Indian prisoners were from a lot of different tribes."

"Such as Creeks." Lowell actually knew the history at least as well as Perry. He'd studied it in college.

"Such as my mother's people." Perry's best and only source for all this knowledge was his Creek mother. Apparently a legendary storyteller in her own right. But true or not, Perry believed it, and Lowell liked it fine and accepted it. For his own part, Perry had gone into special forces in Nam, and had acquired survival skills at all levels—not just martial skills, but wilderness survival, urban survival, economic survival, and also (he asserted) emotional survival. He had, he sometimes claimed when especially into his cups, also killed some people. Specific people, not just random strangers, as in war. He seemed remorseful.

Lowell accepted him on his own terms. If he himself had killed anyone during Nam, he hadn't known about it. At least not for sure. It would have been done from a great distance. By artillery fire, long-range naval weaponry, a missile battery. Cleaner that way. You never had to look at the bodies. But he saw them anyway sometimes. In his nightmares. It had been when the nightmares had begun that he'd decided against use of weapons in his trade.

Perry claimed not to have nightmares. But he had plenty of day-mares, usually involving women. He smoked a lot of Jamaican ganja, and then tended to level it with a shot of rum, or a beer. Which tended to level him. Lowell usually

11

joined him for the beer part, but sometimes a toke as well. Lowell had used plenty of weed in the sixties, but seldom since, except for the rare social occasion. He'd once found a plant at the edge of his mangrove thicket. He suspected one of Ariel's boyfriends who'd been hanging around for a while, fascinated with the schooner, occasionally helping out. That had been during summer vacation last year. He could have planted a few seeds for the hell of it. Lowell knew Ariel wouldn't have. She was down on drugs, and he was careful never to allow any traces on the property. (He wondered at times and with some grim amusement what his friend Lena Bedrosian would do if she found any pot on the premises. Lena, the hard-nosed police detective from Manatee City, would probably feel some kind of moral obligation to bust him on the spot, and politely explain the facts of moral turpitude with a cool righteous apology sometime later, while getting him off. Usually in return for one favor or another.) He was glad Ariel was so straight. Maybe she could become his role model or something. On the other hand, that was before she fell in with the basketball crowd. God knows what they were into.

"Love sucks," Perry was saying, taking a long pull at his joint. Lowell shook his head, refusing the automatic offering. "Never again will I fall in love. Just like Nam, man. You can never win."

Love was the trickiest battlefield of all, they both agreed, and parenthood the second trickiest. Both of which were the topics of the current conversation.

"The problem with women," Perry decided, "is that they are hormonally challenged. Always out of chemical balance, all the time. It's what makes them so damn difficult."

"Ariel was not hormonally challenged. Well, maybe partially. At times."

"Like clockwork," said Perry.

12

"Okay, but she was very levelheaded, which is why I just can't figure this Syracuse thing."

"Hey, man, you're a detective. You can't figure out something right under your nose? It's called love."

"Mine for my daughter, or hers for this basketball player?"

"Both. When it comes to Ariel, you are like some little baby clinging to his favorite new toy," interpreted Perry. "Lighten up. You got no choice. You have to know, a woman, even your own daughter, is only gonna stay in your life for so long."

"Well, it worked anyway," said Lowell. "We're pretty close now, and I'm glad about that."

"Except now she's gone," commented Perry, never too prone to subtlety. "And for a fucking basketball player. Jesus. Syracuse only made the finals but once, and lost. Besides, she'll freeze her ass off."

Lowell had sighed, shrugged, and sipped his beer. It was true. He and his daughter Ariel had remained close, and would probably continue to do so, Syracuse or no. And he felt a deep sense of satisfaction at that.

Tony's other lessons in love had been, to a considerable extent, a lot less gratifying—mostly catching up to reality in the love world. Like the two-week affair with the stunning woman client who owned half of a winning lottery ticket (the ex-boyfriend had the other half). The ex-boyfriend had been a karate champion, and wanted to practice on her. That had been a bundle of laughs. Or the single-mother tourist from Indianapolis, who'd picked him up at the Clam Shack, when all he'd wanted was clams. All she'd wanted, it seemed, were minor things like a lifetime arrangement with a basic hunk of a guy to take care of her every whim. Plus take out the garbage, feed the cats and kids, get rid of her no-good ex-husband, pay the bills, and support her in the

13

manner to which she'd always dreamed of becoming accustomed.

The wind on the bay was picking up now rapidly. Lowell was beginning to wish he hadn't been so foolhardy today. The morning reports on marine weather had been explicit. Afterrnoon small-craft warnings from Clearwater south to Venice. He was smack in the middle of things. And one thing he really hated, in the early spring, was to get wet. Despite what the Chamber of Commerce might be saying, to his way of thinking it was still cold. But then, to a native Floridian, anything cooler than seventy degrees was frigid.

On the other hand, after dropping Ariel off at Tampa and racing home, he'd felt strongly that there was nothing he'd rather be doing at this particular moment than be out on the water. Alone, face in the warm breeze, just he and the birds and the mullet. And on those rarest and most special occasions, the manatee, which had started to return. A middle-aged couple of them, in fact, had taken winter residence near the power plant discharge at Manatee City, and then migrated to more sheltered, less trafficked, waters, downriver in the bay. His waters. His bay. They'd be heading north soon, to God knows where.

Besides, what had been the point of taking six months off from his life project, the schooner, in order to build this little runabout, if he wasn't going to sail her?

Lowell piloted the boat straight into his own narrow channel without mishap, brought it full about, dropped the sails, and slipped backward, almost perfectly, into his mooring. One of these days, he vowed, he'd build a dock. Meanwhile he'd have to wade ashore through the chop, as usual. No big deal. The bottom was shallow and sandy, the water relatively clear. True, there were occasional stingrays and jellyfish to consider. But not too often. As for the gators, they usually stayed well upstream, in the fresh waters they pre-ferred.

He moored the bow and stern lines, folded and packed the main and jib, and contemplated whether or not to drop the mast. He decided the hell with it, tightened the stays, and went into his bungalow for some sun tea. And maybe a joint. Perry had given him some Jamaican a while back, which he'd dutifully stashed in a coffee can. He had a firm rule, of almost thirty years standing, of never smoking alone. But what the hell, he'd thought to himself. A joint wouldn't hurt. And this was an emergency: One didn't lose one's only daughter every day.

He stopped by to look at the schooner. Hull and super-structure were finished now, and refinished, and refinished, to a bright polished mahogany-and-teak glow. The spars were up and also finished. It looked like a brand-new, first-class wooden sailing yacht. The only problem was, there was nothing belowdecks but a hollow, empty space. The interior still remained to be done, and at this rate would take years. He had thought about launching, and working on it in the water. But there were too many complications: accessibility of power, tools, and materials while on the water being the main ones. Also, he was still impaired by his old injury, which slowed him down considerably. Plus, there was the matter of getting around to building a dock. His real dream, of course, was to build a boathouse: big enough for a pho-tography studio (all his old works, and some new ones), as well as to house the two sailboats. He'd probably add a power runabout for errands, eventually. When he won the lottery. Or got a rich client who actually liked spending money.

3

The phone was ringing as Lowell entered the house. And that was not all. Detective Lena Bedrosian was sitting there, her prim duff making barely a dent in his white leather love seat. She looked as impeccable and sour as ever. He let the machine pick up the phone call.

"Afternoon, Detective. What brings you downstream this soggy afternoon?" he inquired, perching on his desk. Lena, he was thinking. Now, here's a woman who is never hormonally challenged.

"You got any of that weird hippy ice tea of yours?" she wanted to know, first of all. As usual, she was overdressed, in a black twill jacket and skirt, and white ruffled blouse. "Iced coffee. I'll even take a Coke. Something." Not surprisingly, she was perspiring. As was usual when he went sailing, he was wearing cotton running shorts, and little else. She seemed a little uncomfortable about that, but didn't comment.

"You off duty?" he asked. "I don't want this to turn out to be some kind of setup, like for luring a police officer into a career of iniquity, all for a—"

"Just get me a cold drink, would you?" she demanded. "And then maybe I'll tell you what I dragged my butt all the way down here for, when I coulda stayed home and done something I like."

Lowell grinned. "It boggles the mind, trying to imagine what that might be." He fetched himself a beer and her an herbal sun tea. He actually thought he deserved credit for introducing her to that little pleasure, a couple of years back. Before then, all she knew about was Coke and Pepsi. She was still pretty clean-cut, all in all. And still basically a pain in the ass. But what the hell. She was a good cop, they'd worked together successfully at least once since the Folner affair, and were even friends, of sorts. Of course, underneath that patina of courteousness was plenty of good old cop-versus-PI rivalry. Not to mention the man-woman thing. Relating to which, one thing that never got in their way—despite the fact that by the standards of popular culture both could pass for good-looking—was romance. She was married, he knew it, and that was fine with both of them. They didn't mess around. Plus, both knew neither was the other one's type, and were content about that. It actually helped.

"So. What's up?" Lowell asked conversationally while playing back his antiquated Radio Shack phone machine. It was the kind you had to carry around this little battery-powered beeper for that was bigger than a lot of computers these days, if you wanted to retrieve messages. Which, luckily, he rarely did.

"We found a body this morning," she told him. "Or rather somebody found a body, in an alligator pond up towards Plant City."

Lowell twisted off his Kirin beer cap and tossed it into the fireplace. "Isn't that out of your jurisdiction? Plant City is way north, in Hillsborough."

"Yeah. But the pond is in Manatee County. And there's—"

"Hello? Anybody there?" an aging male voice called out on the tape. "Tony, this is Ernie Larson," the voice went on. "My nephew, Timothy, he seems to have disappeared, over on your coast? We haven't heard from him for a week, which ain't like him, and his mother's havin' a fit. We were wonderin' if you might check him out, see that he's all right. Hello? Just give a call, will you?" There was a fumbling sound, and a click.

Lowell looked at her, a sinking sensation in the pit of his stomach. "I get the feeling there's a connection here."

Bedrosian got up and paced the room. "That was your black friend over at Palm Beach?"

"The latest term is 'African-American.' "

"How the hell am I supposed to keep up with that crap? Where I grew up, it was 'Negro.' Then they went 'black.' Okay, fine. Now it's 'African-American.' Great. I'll write a report. What's next, 'person of dark complexion with an attitude'?"

"How about 'human being'?"

She threw up her hands. "Gimme a break. Your friend, Larson. He's a nice man. I met him on the Folner case, am I right?"

"You cased him out, at least," Lowell sighed. "And you think that was the nephew you found?"

" 'Fraid so. We found his wallet," she informed him. "The victim's name was Timothy Cross. Age twenty-four. Also, there was this." Bedrosian reached into her jacket pocket and pulled out a plastic envelope. Inside was a small, soggy-looking brown leather personal phone book. "Your friend's name was in this book. Which was on the body. It sounds like it might be him. I'm sorry."

18

"Oh, man." Lowell made a face and waved the envelope away. The fetid smell of death and decay was still clinging to it. "You got a positive ID? Before I call Ernie back with the bad news?" This was going to be hard, he was thinking. Ernie's family was very tight. And Ernie was a good friend.

"I'd rather you hold off on that part," said Bedrosian. "There are a few loose ends we'd like to look into before going public."

"This was a homicide, then?"

" 'Fraid so. The body was pretty badly chewed by the time we got to it. But it was a homicide all right."

"Chewed?"

"Gators. A ranger picked it up from the state forest. There was a gunshot wound to the head."

"Jesus. Chewed?" Lowell thought about that.

She sat down again, crossed and uncrossed her legs, careful not to reveal even the slightest glimpse of thigh, and leaned forward. "We have reason to believe he was headed for Plant City," she went on. "There was a map in the car, and Plant City was circled. Also, he had a note in his pocket that said 'Meeting, Plant City.' "

"Was that all there was? In the car, I mean."

"That was it."

"Was the car nearby?"

"No. And yes. We found it in this little burg called Orange Blossom. Halfway between here and Plant City."

Orange Blossom. The name triggered a few old memories, none of them pleasant. It was a small town in the midland, a place where no one went, if they could help it. He wondered why a young black man with prospects would ever want to go there.

"It's where the deceased was staying," Bedrosian continued, "based on a receipt we found. The car's still being gone over by forensics, down at the sheriff's lab, if you're interested," she went on. "The apartment's been sealed off, but I haven't been over there yet. Want to come along?"

Such an invitation, especially to him, coming from her, was unheard of.

"You got any clue as to a motive?"

"Not yet. But I'd like to know what your friend knows. About why he was here, stuff like that."

"I never knew Ernie had a nephew over on the East Coast. Where was he from, any idea?"

"Philadelphia, according to the license. We're working with the sheriff's department, which has jurisdiction in Orange Blossom. They've agreed to wait for me, though, before going over the apartment where he was staying."

Lowell put the beer down and reached for the phone.

"Who're you calling?" she demanded nervously.

He looked at her. "Hey, Bedrosian. Last I noticed, this was my house, and you are here on a social visit, since, to the best of my knowledge, you are not paying me. I'm calling my friend."

She considered pressing down the lever, and reconsidered.

"Relax," he told her. "I won't mention the homicide. But I'm going to have to give him something. This is family."

"Okay, okay, but no mention of deaths, or homicides, or this investigation. Absolutely. Tell him the nephew went camping or something. Buy some time. Meanwhile, try to find out what he knows about this guy."

"That's what I was about to do in the first place." Lowell checked the number in his book and dialed. The phone rang six times before a weary voice that sounded like tires on a crushed-oystershell driveway answered. "Larson's Boatyard."

"Ernie? This is Tony Lowell. How's it goin', man?"

"Tony, thanks for calling back. You remember my sister, Marsetta, up in Philly? Marsetta Cross, her married name was. She's the one wanted to be a dancer, way back when, works in a bakery and weighs three hundred pounds?"

"I remember her well." Lowell sighed. She had visited the harbor a couple of times, when he was a teen, and had taken up large quantities of space everywhere she went, much to the outrage of the city fathers. Ernie was fond of her, and Lowell had liked her a lot himself. This was going to be hard.

"Anyways, she called me all frantic this morning. Seems her son, Timothy, been workin' on some government project over your way, and he up and disappeared a week or so ago. He always called her Sunday mornings before church, she said. He was a good boy, by all accounts, and I was wonderin' if you could look around. I could pay you somethin'—"

"Forget the money part, Ernie. But to be honest, I've already heard mention of him." Lowell glanced over at Lena, watching him sharply. She shook her head. He ignored her and turned away. "The news isn't good, I'm afraid, I've gotta tell you."

"What? He in trouble?"

Bedrosian was making all kinds of threatening gestures, most having to do with garroting. "He's my friend," mouthed Lowell, and turned his back on her. "I can't say any more than that yet, Ern. But you better begin to prepare Aunt Marsetta."

Lowell had called her his aunt. She'd been to visit a number of times, but the kid he didn't remember at all. Probably born right after Lowell had left home, left his girlfriend, left a child of his own—in other words, this boy, Tim Cross, he was Ariel's age! The realization stung him.

He heard the sigh of someone who was old and tired, accepting the possibility of the inevitable bad news that life brings, at the other end of the line. "That bad, huh?" Ernie asked softly.

Lowell nodded, to no one. "That bad. But look, you hang in there, the missus and Marsetta, too, tell them both I love 'em. And I'll get back to you with more information, just as soon as I can. Okay?"

"Okay." Another sigh.

Lowell glanced at Bedrosian, whose hands were on her hips, an expression of incredulity at his audacity all over her face. "Oh, by the way, Ernie: You have any idea who he was working for, or what kind of project?"

"Somethin' to do with civil rights, or the environment," the old man replied. "One of them causes that always gets black folks in trouble."

"Yeah." Tony hated this. "You all right, Ernie?" he asked.

"Yeah. I'm all right." There was a pause.

"Okay, then, you take care of yourself, hear me?"

"Yeah, yeah," said Ernie. "See you, Tony."

"See you. Oh, Ernie? Look, I don't have too much to go on here. Can you give me anything else, who he was hangin' with, anything at all?"

"Well, I heard he had a girlfriend," ventured Larson after a moment. "Marsetta mentioned that, he'd talked about her a lot. Another one of his rehab projects. He was always trying to save the world or somethin'. I think he was in love with this one, though. Name something like Cecily. Somethin' like that. He mentioned a place called East Manatee."

"Cecily. In East Manatee. I'll check it out. Thanks Ernie."

"You let me know, soon's you hear something. Marsetta's havin' a heart attack up there."

"I will, Ernie." Lowell reached to hang up. He heard a sharp call:

"Tony?"

He put the receiver back to his ear. "Yes?"

A pause. "You be careful."

"I will." Lowell hung up, thinking about Aunt Marsetta. She would very likely have an attack, when she got the news. He turned, and arched his eyes at Bedrosian. "So?"

She took a sharp breath and let it out. "Look, nobody asked you to lie. Just not to tell a civilian next coast over everything you know in the entire world!"

"What? I told him the news was not good."

"Right. He's not a fool, I assume. He's a nice old man who knows that the only kind of bad news you can't mention is when people are dead. You told him his nephew was dead. I heard you!"

Lowell shook his head. "I don't think that would hold up in court, Bedrosian."

"Oh, go stuff it. You'd probably feel perfectly comfortable lying to the law on behalf of your friends."

"That's different." He sat opposite her on the footrest. He cupped his chin and set his beer bottle aside unfinished. "So what's the bottom line? This mean I'm on police payroll? Like, maybe a consultant, something like that? How much you think you could squeeze out of that budget of yours, for freelance—"

"I'll submit a request."

In other words, he thought, I'm working for free. Again. "Great." He sighed, and stood once more. "Okay," he said. "Give me what you got. I'll bill the department. Like I said, Ernie's a friend. Also like family. This kid was my daughter's age. She could have known him."

"Yeah." She leaned back, away from him, aware of the

sweat on his pectorals. "Sorry about your daughter. Tough break, losin' her to the damn Yankees."

"Lost her to Syracuse, actually."

"She's gone north, right? Same state, same difference." She shook her head. "Never did like basketball. My husband likes basketball."

"Now, that is a surprise." He went over to the darkroom, reached in through the door, and produced a shirt, which he put on, his tacit acknowledgment of her discomfort. "So now what?" he asked.

"He mentioned a name. Are you sure it was Cecily?"

"He wasn't sure about the name. He thought it might be a possible girlfriend."

Bedrosian pondered a moment, then wrote something down on a small notepad, tore out the sheet, and put it on the coffee table in front of her. She then reached into her jacket pocket, took out another piece of paper, and laid it next to the other one. Lowell went over to look. She'd written the name "Cecily" on one, and "Cecilia" next to it. The other paper was a photo image of what looked like an anagram. Or a bunch of chicken scratches.

"What's this?" He asked, tapping the anagram.

"We found this scribbled on the lower front edge of the driver's seat, on Cross's car," she said. "I thought it might be a name."

Lowell looked. "I thought you said there was nothing else in the car." She shrugged. "Looks like gibberish," he said. "Which way was it facing?"

She frowned. "What do you mean?"

"Was the seat in the car, or out, when you found this?"

"Out. Like I told you, it's being gone over by forensics."

"So this was what it looked like, with the seat up on a lab bench?"

She looked annoyed. "Of course."

24

"Facing front?"

She looked even more annoyed. "What are you getting at, Lowell?"

Lowell twisted the paper around. "Then it's upside down. No one could write on the front edge of the driver's seat, except from above, by sitting in it." He demonstrated on the footrest. "That means he had to reach down, maybe while he was driving. Like this. So he'd be writing from left to right, which would appear upside down if the seat is sitting upright on a lab bench and you are looking at it from the front."

She scowled, realizing he was right. She looked at the paper from the new perspective. "It still looks like gibberish," she said.

He studied it a while. "Looks a little like 'Sushi,' " he said. "But it kind of trails off at the end." They both contemplated the meaning of that in silence. He tapped the other sheet of paper with the two names. "So you have a make on this name?"

"Maybe." She pulled out the envelope containing Cross's little notebook, opened it, and removed the book, ignoring the whiff of foul air that wafted forth. She flipped through several pages. "Here," she announced, tapping an entry. "Cecilia Potter. It's the only local name, other than yours, for your information." She gave Lowell a significant look. "Fifteen Sycamore Place, in East Manatee. We sent a car over this afternoon, but there was no one home. The owner is in Chicago, and we're still checking on the tenants. But it's a pretty transient area, and there's some rough trade."

Lowell sighed. East Manatee was the black section of Manatee City, hardly more than a shantytown, that spilled into the rural areas on the eastern edge of the county. It was a large area, and not conducive to police inquiries.

"What is it you want from me?" he inquired at last.

"You have family connections to the victim, you know your way around the black community some."

So that's it, he thought.

"Plus we're shorthanded right now," she continued. "Jeffries is on leave and Baker is sick. You check her out, maybe do some photo work, we'll pick up expenses plus seventy-five a day," she said at last.

"That's big of you," he replied. "But I'll pass."

"Okay, I'll ask Chief Sturbridge if we can swing a hundred. But you have to deliver. We don't exactly have deep pockets, with all the tax cuts and half the public on welfare."

Lowell nodded. He wasn't about to admit it to Bedrosian, but he would have helped Ernie for free, in any case. The money was a bonus. "I'll see what I can do. Right now, I want to take a look at the apartment, and the location of the body."

"Now?"

"Evidence has a way of disappearing. Or deteriorating. This morning would have been better."

Bedrosian put down her iced tea and stood up. "So what are you waiting for?" she said, heading for the door. "Let's get moving."

4

Night had fallen. The roads were empty as they drove. They passed a state trooper heading the other way on State Road 676, and didn't see another car until just before Mango. Then almost total blackness, other than the occasional house, or rural business with a floodlit parking lot or security area. They reached the outskirts of Orange Blossom in forty-five minutes, but Lowell couldn't recognize any of it. Just a few signs were visible, the barely lit empty shapes of a few frame or stucco houses and stores, a motel that appeared to be sound asleep throughout. What little he could see he didn't remember at all. Bedrosian turned her unmarked prowl car left onto a side street and pulled up almost immediately in front of a two-story territorial-style building. An apartment house of modest means.

"In case you're wondering," said Bedrosian suddenly, "this is not the colored section."

"You mean, we still have 'colored sections'? In *Florida?*"

"Come off it Lowell, you haven't been out of it for that long. I take it back. You have been out of it your entire life. Never mind." She opened the door and got out. Lowell followed, feeling slightly piqued. She pointed at the second story. It had the prerequisite yellow tape across the porch railings and the door. There was a number five on it.

A sheriff's patrol car drove past slowly. It stopped. Bedrosian walked over to it a moment and engaged the lone trooper in a brief conversation. The trooper nodded and moved on. Lowell was envious. No way he could ever wave a sheriff's deputy on like that.

"He says nobody's been inside yet, but it's open."

Lowell was incredulous. "Open?"

"It's how they found it. Open. I told them to leave it untouched, so I guess they took me at my word."

"Good for you. Or them. Shall we?" At her request, he'd brought his camera, some high-speed infrared film, and a nonglare flash unit for some higher-resolution Tri-X shots, for possible blowups. He felt official. Almost.

"Where the hell's the police photographer? Or am I pulling double duty here?" he'd asked her back at the house.

"He went fishing. I figured you wouldn't mind."

Lowell was speechless with his lack of surprise. "You can damn well cover the raw stock and lab costs," was all he'd had to say. He'd do his own lab work, of course. But he meant paper, and chemicals, that sort of thing.

He attached the flash to his battered but trusty Nikon, loaded the Tri-X, and started to shoot.

Bedrosian looked around the apartment at her own pace, sans camera, but with two very sharp brown eyes. "What's this?" she wanted to know, pointing at something on the floor. "Is this some kind of male sensitivity training thing?"

Lowell looked. It was a stack of magazines, mostly on parenting, or motherhood: *Mother Earth, Mothering, Working Mother, Parents,* even a *Cosmopolitan* issue dealing with the growing phenomenon of single motherhood.

"Whatever he was into, which looks pretty weird to me," she commented, "it looks like he took it pretty seriously. Some kind of fetish thing, you think?"

"Maybe he had a kid somewhere. Maybe he was a single parent himself. I'll have to check with Ernie on that one."

She grunted, and continued her search of the apartment.

Lowell took a few more shots. Nothing appeared out of order. The furniture was sparse, and rented. There was nothing personal, other than the magazines, and a few newspapers on the counter. Nothing to indicate a specific, unique human being had once dwelled within.

"No sign of any documents, letters, anything related to his relationships, what he was doing here, where he worked?"

"Over here."

Bedrosian was bent over a white plastic table in the middle of the living room. The top lifted up. Inside was an old pay stub from the State of Florida. There was also a copy of a letter to the Department of Environmental Protection of the Florida Department of Natural Resources. It was addressed to Mr. Timothy Cross, dated February sixth. It said: "Dear Sir, we respectfully deny your request for unlimited access to our subsidiary plant and mining facilities, due to insurance restrictions and liability concerns. However, you are welcome to schedule an accompanied tour to any location of our operations, per your regulations, for full inspection. Under those circumstances, we request advance notice of twenty four hours, to arrange for proper transportation and security. Sincerely, Jack Largent, Vice President for Public Relations." The heading read: "International Phosphates Corporation, Plant City, Florida 33566."

"Plant City," pondered Lowell. "You said you thought he was heading up there the night he was killed?"

"It was circled on his map."

There were no further clues, however, as to what he intended to do there. "Ready to take a look at where they found the body?" asked Bedrosian.

Lowell merely nodded, and started for the door.

"It's been cordoned off, should still be a trooper around out there."

He looked at her. "You've been up here already, haven't you? Today?"

"I'd be negligent in my duty otherwise, Lowell. Been here twice, actually. We got an anonymous tip this morning. But I wanted you to take a look, if you didn't mind. And also get some photos."

They drove in silence back out of the town and north on State Road 39. After about five miles they came to a wide open area, almost totally black, on the left side. Bedrosian slowed. Lowell rolled down the window as the cruiser slid to a stop. There was no one around. The night air literally screamed with noise: of frogs, of crickets, of cicadas, of night birds, and small creatures dying out alone in the darkness.

A young man died out here, probably in the darkness, thought Lowell. He couldn't help wondering how it had gone down, what young Timothy Cross's last thoughts were. His last feelings. Whether he'd still been alive when the gators got to him. He pulled his jacket closer around him. Goose bumps prickled his flesh.

Bedrosian looked at the sky brilliant with stars, but also some night clouds scudding by. Like celestial barges or ships, she thought. It wasn't a comforting thought. Her father had drowned on a fishing boat. Shaped a lot like some of those clouds. She walked to the edge of the road and the embankment, which dropped off sharply into the reeds, a black expanse of what had to be a fairly sizable pond beyond.

"Careful." Lowell cautioned her. "They hunt at night.

And contrary to popular myth, they're fast. They can run thirty-five miles an hour. Some even faster."

She picked her way carefully along the water's edge, shining her flashlight along the ground. "Who hunts at night?"

"Gators. You said he'd been 'chewed.' "

She froze in place. "Now you tell me," she grumbled. A native Floridian, she realized suddenly that she knew damn little about the state's most famous inhabitants. A shiver ran down her spine as she remembered the condition of Tim Cross's body. She peered into the darkness, but could see nothing. The pond was still, as though waiting for something to happen. She felt as if she was being watched.

"Don't worry," he added. "They don't usually go after humans, unless they're spooked. Or pissed. 'Course, they do tend to spook easier in the dark."

"Yeah, well, so do I," she snapped. She shrugged the feeling off and located the stakes and tape marking the position of the body.

"There." She pointed at an area about ten by twelve at the water's edge.

"Any tire marks or footprints?" he asked, unsnapping his camera cover.

"No. They had to've parked on the pavement and only stepped on the grass."

Lowell had already loaded his high-speed film in the car. He took a series of shots covering the area. He noted where the reeds had been crushed or broken, the patch of mud in the young spring grass where the body had been dragged ashore. It had been floating there in the water, unnoticed perhaps for days, perhaps only attracting attention (as torpid Florida's accelerated rate of decay kicked in) by the smell. He could still smell it in the wet, still night air. The smell of death. Something else smelled it, too. Something watching, eyes just above the surface of the water. They gleamed a moment, caught in the flash, then sank into the darkness.

Bedrosian smelled it as well. "Place gives me the creeps." She searched the area carefully with her six-battery flashlight. Something shiny glinted, just below the lip of earth, that dropped to the water.

Lowell saw it first. "What's that?" he asked.

Bedrosian got there first, mostly because she was younger and quicker. "Don't touch it!" she ordered. "Prints!"

"I know that," he grumbled.

Taking a tissue from her pocket, she parted the reeds, reached down and picked the object up very carefully and held it under the light. It was a thin piece of glass, with diamond-shaped beveled edges.

"Looks like a piece of crystal of some kind," observed Lowell. He took a few shots of it with his flash and telephoto, then Bedrosian sealed it in a plastic bag, which she locked in her briefcase in the back seat of the cruiser.

Neither of them found anything else, to Bedrosian's considerable disappointment.

"You saw the body, then?" Lowell asked her, as they returned to the cruiser.

"Of course I saw the body."

"And it was really chewed?"

"That's what I told you."

"And it had a bullet hole in the head?"

"Yes. A nice big one. He was totally dead. For several days, at least. Which fits with your friend's report as to when he disappeared."

Lowell nodded. "Mind if I take a look?" he asked.

She looked at her watch. It was ten o'clock. "I knew you'd say that," she grumbled.

*　*　*

32

Returning to Orange Blossom, they rousted out a very disgruntled coroner, Dr. Michaelson, who let them in only under duress from Bedrosian. Lowell looked at the body, still in the cooler awaiting completion of the autopsy. The boy looked peaceful, Lowell thought. His life had been short, but at least he'd done something with it. Maybe Tim Cross knew that, on his way out.

"You pinpoint the time of death yet?" asked Bedrosian.

Dr. Michaelson shook his head. "I haven't finished my examination," he protested. "It's only been a day. Maybe tomorrow." That concluded the conversation. The coroner was a gaunt, humorless man who also served as a local physician. A family physician, he'd told them.

Not my family, Lowell was thinking. If I'd had one. Which reminded him of Ariel once more, and made him sad.

"Let's go," said Bedrosian, and they left.

She drove back to Manatee City through the silent darkness. Lowell had fallen asleep by the time she reached his little bayou hideaway on Manatee Bay.

He got out slowly, careful with his camera and gear.

"I'll get the lab work done soon's I've had some sleep," he promised her.

"Take your time. Say, seven o'clock?"

It was past midnight now. "Yeah, right," he growled. "In your dreams."

"Good, then," she said, sounding almost cheerful. "See you in the morning."

He swore something inaudible, and started down the path to his bungalow. She called after him. "I appreciate it, Lowell. You have my number?"

"Etched in my left brain. Right between good times and big bucks," he called back.

She grinned. "Have a nice night."

Bedrosian knew her way out of there.

Lowell went in, dropped to the floor and did twenty push-ups, then went upstairs to shower. Mostly just to cool off—the sweat would return in minutes, in the night heat. He put on a blank white T-shirt (he refused to do free advertising for any rock band, beverage, amusement park, or other commercial enterprise), yanked on his running shorts, and turned on the radio, for the late-night news out of Tampa. As Bedrosian had predicted, there was no mention of any killings around Plant City. Just the usual couple of traffic fatalities, courtesy of the liquor trade.

Bedrosian had thought Tim Cross might have been heading for Plant City. Some twenty miles inland from Tampa, it was mostly known for phosphate mining and production, a strawberry festival that had only recently ended, and also was host city during spring training for the Cincinnati Reds, a team owned by a famous admirer of "Negroes." It was also, apparently, the headquarters for a major phosphates producer that hadn't wanted Tim Cross on its property.

And then there was Orange Blossom. Not counting tonight's midnight run, he'd been there once or twice. Tiny and hot, like a fire ant. No oranges in sight. Just phosphate heaps. Helluva place, all in all, for a black kid from Philadelphia to be starting out in life. Or ending it.

First, however, there was this matter of the girlfriend in East Manatee. A lot of bad things happened involving girlfriends. A lot of bad things happened in places where poor people, desperate and angry people, gathered, or were forced to gather. Including murder. He decided not to wait until morning to check it out. The predawn hours were a good time to look things over and not get hassled. Except maybe by the cops, even though they were presumably on his side.

Switching off the TV, Lowell picked up the paper Bedrosian had left on the table and sauntered out through the kitchen door to the back. The night air was warm and fecund, smelling of magnolia and the sea. He crossed the wet St. Augustine grass he'd started to mow (at his daughter's request) only this year, to the barn that served as a toolshed and garage. The old Chevy still ran. Barely. Lowell kept promising himself to replace it with something more PC, more ecologically correct. The problem was, the damn thing was like a Timex. It just kept on ticking. True, it slurped a lot of gas and oil, and while it usually managed to pass the emissions test, it was a major source of air pollution. He felt bad about that part, since he was conscientious about such things as recycling, and supporting the World Wildlife Fund. But like most Americans, Tony Lowell hadn't found a way to get around his dependency on the internal combustion engine yet. Not until the schooner was finished, anyway. Besides, he was chronically broke, and his old Impala was infinitely cheaper than, say, the three hundred a month in payments, plus a megahike in insurance, plus gas and maintenance, plus the anxiety factor that a newer vehicle would cost him. The anxiety factor, as he'd explained to Perry one time (who loved fast sixties muscle cars and coveted the Impala) was what one got when one had a shiny, spiffy car out on the road, surrounded by giant hostile trucks, careless tourists in rental cars, elderly drivers with hardly any sight, hearing, or motor control to speak of, testosterone-charged teenagers, and other innumerable threats to one's fit and finish. Also, while not exactly a devotee of high finance, Tony Lowell understood the economic wisdom of not fixing what wasn't broke.

Lowell headed east along the river, through Gulfbridge and along Bay Drive to Manatee City, past the mall-choked fringes, and on through the dying inner core (he still loved what remained of the Queen Anne, territorial, Spanish, and art deco architecture of the old cities, the mix of which to his mind was one of Florida's greatest, and least preserved attributes). About two dozen utterly nonsynchronized traffic lights later, he was into the black section. A surprising presence (for the hour) of dark, suspicious eyes watched his every move—some with envy at the Chevy's badly muffled rumble—as he pulled into an all-night restaurant he knew called Tiny Donny's. He'd stopped there more than once, sometimes just for the food: real authentic backwoods southern cooking: grits, pork pies, chicken, chitlins, and the best pecan pie west of Savannah. The coffee was always rank, but then no place was perfect.

Lowell entered, shrugged off the usual inquiring, sometimes hostile, mostly curious stares from the night people. Here, like in much of the South, integration had come in name only, other than in terms of federally enforced busing plans and the like. But in terms of housing, in terms of culture, in terms of economics, or education, the Old South still prevailed in East Manatee. Whites rarely ventured into this turf, he knew, except for cops and salesmen. Neither of which would show his face at this hour, close to two in the morning, hence the unusual degree of curiosity.

"What'll ya have?" the young waitress asked him, her tired drawl as distinct from that of the crackers as his own from that of the Kennedys.

"I'll take a draft, and a slice of pie, with a little ice cream if you have it."

"We got whip cream," she said.

"Good enough."

She left, rolling her eyes at a friend behind the counter, who seemed amused by the entire transaction. Lowell looked casually around the room. Most of the half dozen insomniacs present looked away. A few didn't, particularly a group of three young males, posturing grandly over their

Cokes and burgers—mostly for his benefit, he guessed—across the room. They were nudging each other, presumably for a spokesperson. Finally the biggest one of the lot, who resembled a promising candidate for defensive tackle at Florida State with a sweatshirt to prove it, came over.

"Yo, man," he said, with a glance back at his friends as though for approval. "What you doin' this part of town? You lose your way or some shit?"

His friends found this uproarious. Lowell grinned.

"You mean this isn't Longboat Key?"

The young man stared. "Longboat Key? You crazy, man?" Lowell had named one of the most exclusive white-bread resorts on the Gulf Coast.

His buddies got it, though, and snickered. "Real funny, man." said another one, coming over. "Come on, what brings a white dude with a attitude into East Manatee, middle of the night?"

"I'm looking for someone," replied Lowell.

"No shit," said the second youth. "Why else you come here? You a connection?"

"No, nothing like that." Lowell decided to get straight to the point. "I'm looking for an address." He got out the paper, and squinted at it. "Sycamore Road. You know it?"

"Plenty of people know it. Who you looking for?"

"A woman, name of Cecilia Potter, on Sycamore Place. I forgot my map, but I figure it's around here somewhere."

"He forgot his brain, too," laughed another homeboy, joining his friends. Lowell gave him a benign look.

"Why you want her fo'?" the second youth wanted to know.

"A friend of hers turned up dead, today. I'd like to let her know."

"You a cop?" This from the first one. The big one. The atmosphere chilled perceptibly.

"Private investigator." Lowell flashed his card. "The guy who died was around your age. From out of state."

"Black?" the second youth, probably the brains of the group, asked bluntly.

"Yes."

"What was the dude's name?"

"Timothy Cross."

"Sheeeeit," muttered the first youth. "That bo' who been hangin' out with her, Lenny talkin' 'bout."

"Lenny?" Tony repeated.

"You don't want to mess with her, man. She trouble."

"Can you give me directions?"

The young man looked at him, wide eyed. "Now?" Lowell nodded.

The youths drew aside in group consultation. Finally one of them spoke to the waitress, who came back over. She leaned toward Lowell. "They say you be careful, she keeps bad company," she warned him. "You better wait and see her the daytime."

"When and where, can you tell me?"

"She goes to the Publix store a lot. You might find her there. But don't go to her place."

"Why not?"

She glanced around. The young men were watching her. "Her boyfriend don't like it." She hurried away. Lowell sipped his house beer (Meister Brau) and considered. He finished his pie, got up, picked up his glass, and walked over to the young men.

"There some kind of problem about a boyfriend?"

The smart one looked at him, then looked at the ceiling. "Lenny," he said, as a deacon might say "Satan." "He own her, mister. An' you go near her, he own you, too."

"I doubt that, but I'll keep it in mind," said Lowell. So, he thought. She has another boyfriend, named Lenny. An unfriendly one. He wondered how unfriendly. At this hour he just wanted to see the house. But it might be interesting to see if they were as sleepless as he was. He paid the three seventy-five bill, left a dollar tip, nodded to the young men, and left.

He had a map in his car somewhere of Manatee County. He'd find Sycamore Place in the street directory. It had to be within a half mile radius, probably less.

Lowell crossed the parking lot. A cat screeched somewhere behind the dumpster. A homeless man was pissing in the alley. It was now nearly three o'clock. No one followed him. Once in the car, he ransacked the glove compartment (it still had a working interior light) and found the map. Spreading it out over the seats, he looked up the street, and traced the numbers. He wanted G-7. The restaurant was in G-6. It was only a couple of blocks away.

He backed the Chevy out of the lot, and headed east to the next street, East Central, and turned right. Sycamore Place was the second left. He checked the number. Fifteen. Odds were on the left. Counting down: 35, 31, 27, every fourth number. The houses were predictably shabby, of paper-thin frame construction: two stories, tar paper on the outside, about twenty feet in width, and overgrown, narrow yards in between.

He pulled up in front of what could arguably be the shabbiest house on the whole dismal street. A broken-down motorcycle lay in pieces in the front, next to part of a fifties pickup truck of uncertain manufacture. There were filthy once-white torn curtains in the front windows, and a center hall visible through the square pane in the paneled hollow front door. The hall light was on, and another upstairs. A battered faded red Nissan sedan was parked half in the driveway, half on the overgrown lawn. A white 1980s Pontiac Firebird was at the curb, directly in front.

Lowell parked behind the Firebird, got out of his car, and gazed up at the house. It looked forlorn and haunted in the darkness. A face appeared in an unlit window on the second floor. It only appeared a second, then withdrew. It was a man, light skinned. More than that Lowell couldn't tell. Could have been black or white. He heard a sharp voice, and a slapping sound. A woman cried out. Then silence.

It was three-fifteen. Strange time for so much activity in an allegedly residential household. He began to circle the house slowly, eyes on the windows. He stopped below a small window on the side alley, also on the second floor. There was the sound of crying, brief, then low voices, angry.

"I'm telling Dicky how you're treatin' me," wailed a female voice from somewhere upstairs.

A man's voice responded: sharp, curt, and strong. "I don't give a fuck what you do, I ain't worried about that asshole, Cahill. What you better worry about is me."

Lowell thought he heard another voice—a whimper, like that of a small child, having a bad dream. Living here would be a bad dream, all right, he thought. The night was silent once more. Lowell turned toward the back of the house and saw the dog. It was a wolf-malamute hybrid, the ultimate canine nightmare—an animal not of nature, a blend of the worst characteristics of two strong, intelligent, and utterly ruthless genetic strains. Wolves might be beneficial, maybe even potential dance partners, in the wild. And malamutes were loyal sled dogs. But putting them together and trying to domesticate the result had proven a bad, bad idea. Lowell had a friend in New Mexico who knew of three children from a single residential neighborhood south of Santa Fe who had been killed, in separate "incidents" by these increasingly popular animals. He guessed it happened a lot elsewhere, too, but those reports had been either minimized or suppressed by powerful interests: breeders, sportsmen's organizations, and other attack-dog enthusiasts who had mounted a strong, well-financed, and therefore usually successful campaign to legitimize these hundred-and-twenty-pound animate missiles with teeth.

After his war experience, Lowell didn't believe in lethal weapons, and refused to carry one. His hands and feet would have to do in a survival-based emergency. Such as now. The beast was almost upon him before he'd even seen it, only the overeager clicking of its teeth giving him warning. Lowell fell back on his long-ago and rarely used martial aikido training, and waited for the animal to spring, prepared to sidestep the movement, once committed, and stun the animal with a blow under its chin as it flew past him—if he was lucky. If he wasn't lucky, it would keep coming at him until he missed, or slipped, or fell. Then it would have him. Probably by the throat.

Just then there was a whistling sound. The animal stopped cold in its tracks, turned, and slunk away, tail as far between its legs as tails can go. There was something—or someone—back there a lot scarier, and more ruthless, than the dog.

Lowell decided not to press his luck. He turned, quietly walked back to his car, started it with minimum roar, and drove away. Dawn was nipping at his heels by the time he reached the bayou, scarcely able to stay awake. He stumbled into the house and fell asleep on the sofa.

5

Three hours later, Lowell awoke with a pounding headache, a ringing in his ears, and a deep feeling of depression: partly a post-parting regret for his daughter, partly due to the stress of his escapade in East Manatee, and partly in empathy for his friend Ernie Larson. The ringing sound continued as he groped his way back into a state of semiconsciousness. It was the phone, relentless and persistent. Cursing, he fought his way awake, then through the jumble of books, papers, and archaic electronic equipment that occupied most of his king-sized bed, fumbling for the receiver.

"Yeah?"

It was Lena. "Lowell? You get those pictures yet?"

Christ, he thought. She was serious. She's probably gone jogging and had breakfast and read the paper. He looked at the clock, which swam into focus. Nine-thirty. "Sorry to wake you before noon," she said sarcastically. "I've been in touch with his employers."

"Who?"

"Tim Cross. The murder victim!" She sounded exasperated. "Your friend's nephew."

"Oh, yeah. That one. What about him?" Lowell remembered last night, and the wolf hybrid. His headache got worse.

"He worked for the state. Department of Natural Resources, in the Department of Environmental Protection, out of Tampa. Maybe you could go up there and talk to his boss. Name of Anthony Solano." She gave him the address and phone number. "I took the liberty of making an appointment for you, for this afternoon, if you're not busy."

"Oh, no, after doing all your free lab work I was just going to spend the afternoon gazing into the eyes of Christie Brinkley, but no problem, of course I'd be happy to give it all up for you, and a dollar ninety-eight."

"Cut the sarcasm, Lowell. We appreciate your help. You're doing it for your friend, remember?"

Lowell remembered all too well.

"Don't forget those photos," she added. "You never know what they might reveal."

"Yeah, yeah." He was doubly annoyed, he realized, for allowing her to seize the high ground. It would be just like her to lecture him regarding the wonders of his own trade, his own profession. His former profession, rather. Hell, she liked to needle him about both his professions, come to think of it. He decided to be less tolerant of cops from now on. Especially female ones.

Aching from head to toe, he got up, did some stretches, swallowed some aspirins, and shuffled on down to the kitchen. He was starving, he realized. He looked in the fridge and found some reasonably fresh milk, part of a loaf of bread, some stale cheese, and half an avocado that was only slightly brown. It was enough to make a sandwich and gulp down some protein. This done, he unloaded his camera, took the film into the darkroom, poured the chemicals, and went to work.

An hour later, he had hung up a series of ten blowups to dry, selected from the three rolls: one of each crime scene, and one of the body. One photo had sent chills up his spine.

His flash unit had picked up something in the water, not ten feet from where Bedrosian could be seen, at the water's edge. It was something few people would ever see, especially at night. Lowell made a quick blowup, then another, to make sure. It gleamed at him in pure malice: the eye of a submerged alligator, lurking just above the surface. He wondered if he should show it to Lena, and decided not to. He'd include all the negatives, of course. But not this particular blowup. Chances are, she wouldn't notice anything, which was just as well. She'd probably quit her job and move to Albuquerque. Still, he couldn't help but wonder if Tim Cross had seen this same thing in the final moments of his life. It was a thought that was almost unbearable, and he banished it at once.

Other than that, he had seen nothing of particular interest besides that odd piece of glass, but he knew the police would want to go over the photos. Then another of the blow-ups caught his eye as he turned to go while they dried. He took it down, laid it on the countertop, and picked up his magnifier. It was a shot of the apartment. There was an old newspaper on the counter. He could see it was a copy of the *Orange Blossom Express*, its ornate banner sharp in focus. He leaned closer, studying the detail. The main headline was about a local cop under indictment for running a string of call girls. Lowell shook his head, and was about to hang the photo up once more, when he noticed a smaller story, near the bottom, that had been circled in pencil. The story was about a sinkhole. Lowell got out his magnifying glass and looked more closely. "Another sinkhole," said the headline, barely visible. "Rumors of a large sinkhole at a local phosphate plant site causes consternation among area residents," the story began. He couldn't read the rest. Sinkhole? As a native Floridian, Lowell knew about sinkholes. They were a natural part of the Florida landscape. Sinkholes were to Florida what mudslides were to California. But more than that, he realized, he didn't know. Why would a sinkhole be of particular interest to an EPA fieldworker? He checked his watch. Ten-forty-five. The library would be open now.

Grabbing his jacket and notebook, he hurried out to the garage, got the car out, and headed for town.

The local library at Gulfbridge, actually a branch of the county library, was situated in an old church off Mango Road. It was strictly up to date, though, technologically. It had gotten a new computer linkup to the county system, including access to all the area newspaper files for the past ten years.

Lowell smiled his hello at Mildred Hannigan, the librarian. She had been there ever since he could remember, and hadn't aged a bit. She'd always been spry and gray, as far back as he could remember. And cheerful. She beamed at him, put her finger to her lips, and waved. He went directly to the computer terminal, and settled uncomfortably into the hard wooden chair that seemed to be endemic to all libraries.

Entering the current year, Lowell punched up "subject" from the main menu, then typed in "sinkhole." The "searching" indicator began flashing. After a minute or so, the screen announced its findings: ninety-five files, or articles. Lowell then added two additional fields, "Florida," and "recent." That narrowed him down to eleven files. He typed in "pull down" and began to scan them.

The first series of articles were about a sinkhole in Citrus County that had ruined someone's lakeside property. The lake, it seems, had suddenly emptied out, leaving a large muddy hole in its place where the bottom had suddenly dropped into the nether worlds. The owners were displeased, and were looking for someone to sue. Swiftmud

(Southwest Florida Water Management District) was the most popular villain in central Florida. Always nagging people to conserve, pumping local ground water to cities far away like Tampa and St. Pete, and shutting down wells when they ran dry, causing much inconvenience. And dry wells were becoming as common as sinkholes of late, Lowell learned as he read on.

A more scientific piece in the *St. Petersburg Times* provided a reasonably coherent definition. Sinkholes, he learned, happened when the water level in the Floridan Aquifer (Florida's water supply) suddenly (or gradually) dropped, causing limestone rock formations that house the aquifer, and of which most of central Florida consisted, to collapse. The holes could be a few feet deep, or "bottomless." Another side effect was that whatever was in or on the lake, or, all too often, the ground above, would drop straight into the aquifer. Sometimes it was a whole house. Most often, it was simply polluted surface water.

He went over to the pay phone by the door and called Bedrosian.

"It's Lowell," he informed her.

She had her mouth full and couldn't respond for several quick chews and a swallow. "I know that," she finally managed.

Lunch on the job, thought Lowell. Probably Wheat Thins and Cup-A-Soup as usual.

"You got those photos yet, or what?"

"Yeah. No pictures of lurking escaped convicts in striped suits we didn't happen to notice hiding in the bushes. No smoking guns."

She masked her disappointment. "I thought you were the best in the business, Lowell. That's all you have to tell me?"

He considered leaving her in the dark a while longer for that remark. Luckily professionalism reasserted itself. "No, there was one thing," he went on grudgingly. "There was something on the counter we both overlooked. An old newspaper."

"Hold everything, I'll call the chief," she snapped sarcastically. "You called me up about an old newspaper. Was it soaked in blood?"

"No, but there was an interesting article."

"You called me up to tell me about an interesting article in an old newspaper?"

"I think Tim Cross may have found it interesting."

That stopped her. "What do you mean?"

"It was about a sinkhole."

"A sinkhole. Whoopee. Sinkholes happen only about once a week. What was he, a hole counter?"

"I don't know. But there may have been something about this particular one. I haven't found that issue yet, the date is obscured."

"Is there anything else, or can I finish my lunch now?"

"What about you? Any report from the medical examiner yet?"

"Not yet. I'll let you know."

Lowell agreed to drop the photos off on his way to Tampa, and hung up. His stomach didn't feel very good. Probably the aspirin, he figured. He drank some water from the water fountain, and noticed an odd color to it. He looked at it more closely. It was just ever so slightly brown. Shit, he thought, and spat the water back out. He went back to the computer and shut it down. He'd have to continue his search later.

The Florida Department of Environmental Protection field office was off Martin Luther King Boulevard, in Tampa: a neighborhood of poor housing, discount car lots and fast-food stands. An ironic reflection on America's generic blended urban-suburban environment at its worst, a somewhat restored Lowell reflected as he pulled into the lot. He'd grabbed a quick nap after finishing the lab work. He hadn't really expected any great breakthroughs, anyway. It was plain as day that both crime sites had been cleaned out thoroughly already. By professionals. Bedrosian hadn't even noticed. They'd only missed a couple of minor items. He wished he had them: the letter, the pay stub, and the little piece of crystal. At least he had kept copies of the key photos.

A man of medium height and Latino descent, neatly dressed but harried looking, came out to meet him in the sparse reception area. "Mr. Lowell?" he offered. "I'm Tony Solano, from DEP."

"They call me Tony also," smiled Lowell, shaking the man's hand. Solano had a strong grip, and smelled of cooking oil—the curse of the overworked and underpaid, who live on fast-food. Solano led him down a narrow hallway lined with stacks of computer boxes, printouts, and paperwork.

"We're under incredible pressure here," explained Solano, gesturing at the mess. "You wouldn't believe how many directions they come at us from. EPA in Washington wants us to stop stack emissions and soil runoff. The Greens want us to stop all industry and further development cold. And the developers and state Chambers of Commerce want us to drop dead, of course. We're constantly in danger of losing our funding. So what else is new? You're here about Tim Cross." He gestured Lowell into a tiny, windowless cubicle with a poster of a pristine scene of central Florida on the wall, and more boxes stacked everywhere. There were charts, graphs, and a framed letter from someone in Tallahassee. Lowell looked closer. It was a death threat. "Jesus will kill you," it declared.

Solano smiled wanly with a shrug. "That was for our taking a position against a landfill, up in Panama City. Right next to one of the last and finest sections of unspoiled wetlands remaining in Florida. This stuff comes with the territory, I'm afraid. Sit down, sit down. Can I get you some coffee? Won't be Cuban coffee, mind you, which is the best. You're not Cuban, are you?" Cubans come in all races, shapes, and colors, so it wasn't an unreasonable question.

"No," replied Lowell, with a smile. "A basic Euro-'merican mongrel, more likely. But I'll take the coffee. Cream and sugar, or whatever facsimile thereof you have." He knew better than to ask for his preferred additives of real milk and honey in a state office. He had a better chance of getting caviar and blini. Solano rushed off and came back a minute later with two paper coffee cups. He had a small carton of milk, and a little honey bear, which he set down with a grin.

"Lieutenant Bedrosian tipped me off," he said.

Lowell gave him a look of surprise, mixed with grateful reappraisal. "Thanks," he said, and meant it. He stirred up his favorite blend and took a sip. Just what he needed to reclaim the day.

"Tim was a good worker," said Solano, removing some files from his own worn office chair and sitting down. "Energetic, idealistic, maybe just a bit too eager at times."

"You have any idea who might have killed him, or why?"

Solano shrugged and gestured at the wall. "You see the kind of mail we get. Everybody loves clean air and water, long as they don't have to pay for it, and they still get to dump used motor oil or burn trash in their yard, and throw garbage in the nearest ditch or river, or trash the beaches for

49

somebody else to clean up. But it's a funny thing about where he was working. Phosphates are among the most highly regulated of all the chemical and mining industries in the country. They recycle ninety percent of the water they use, and upwards of ninety-five percent of all the materials they produce are beneficial in one way or another."

"What about the other five percent?"

"Well, it gets tricky. The raw materials themselves are full of heavy metals, including uranium, and toxic gases such as fluorine and radon. These come naturally in the rock and soil. They have to be removed, and most of it is done fairly successfully. We've been working with them since the 1975 Land Reclamation Act was passed, and they've done a helluva job in a lot of ways, which I'm sure they'll be more than happy to tell you about."

"What, exactly, was he working on?"

"Tim had a degree in environmental engineering, which is a rare and valuable asset, in this line of work. He was as-signed to the team that oversees and ultimately approves each and every land- or water-reclamation plan that comes to us—by law, incidentally—from the industry planners and designers. Every time they finish a mining operation, basically exhaust an ore deposit, they have to restore the land. Either to its original habitat, or—and here's where a lot of the other lobbies have been brought to bear—for so-called improvements: industrial parks, golf courses, hous-ing developments, even recreational areas. Since much of the waste material is in the area of hydrology, there are a lot of man-made lakes out there. We have to make sure the soil and water are safe, that the ecosystems are working, that the natural habitats are sufficient, and so forth. For the most part, it's been a very successful program."

"For the most part?"

Solano sighed. "There are always going to be problems," he said. "We still haven't worked out, for example, what's going to be done with all that phosphogypsum out there. You've seen it, if you've been out there. It's the number-one waste product, basically phosphoric slag heaps. Huge stacks, like mountains, of the stuff. They used to just dump it in the rivers or the ocean. But it's toxic. Contains uranium, for one thing, which tends to make people nervous. They can't just go dump the stuff anymore, so they just sit on it."

"I remember. Looks like hell out there, on Route Sixty."

"Well, you won't see it on any tourist postcards, I'll tell you that much," agreed Solano.

"What about a sinkhole? Would that have anything to do with his work?"

Solano frowned. "We do try to keep track of them. Some of them are in Superfund areas, and need careful monitoring, or even pumping or sealing, which can be a bitch. But there wasn't anything specific in that regard that I can recall."

Lowell thought about that. "He had an article in his apartment about one. In one of the phosphate fields. But it was on company property or something, and no one from the general public had actually seen it. Is that possible?"

"Sure. Florida is a big state. People forget, it isn't all just Miami and Orlando and beaches. There are millions of acres out there, most of it forest or wetlands. Those big mining companies own or lease huge tracts of wilderness that nobody gets into, nobody sees. A sinkhole could happen out there easy, that nobody gets to, maybe just some security patrol or ranger comes across. Ninety-nine percent of the time it's no big deal. They're usually natural phenomena and can't hurt anything."

51

"Wouldn't you have to inspect them, to make sure? I mean, they act like funnels, don't they? Directly into the aquifer?"

"That's true. But we don't have enough inspectors to investigate every report like that. I wish we did. But we don't. And now we got even one less. We're running on attrition right now," he added. "We probably won't be able to replace Tim Cross as it is."

Lowell contemplated that revelation. He stood up, went over to the hate letter on the wall, and looked at it again. "So Cross was an inspector himself?"

"You might say that. But, as I said, his job had to do with approving reclamation proposals. He wouldn't have anything to do with sinkholes."

"So. You have no idea of anything in particular that Cross was doing, that might have gotten him killed? Or who might have done it?"

Solano shook his head. "Not that I know of."

Lowell reached into his jacket pocket and took out a copy of the letter he and Bedrosian had found in Cross's apartment. "Is it possible he ran afoul of something like an overzealous production manager trying to get around a regulation, something like that?"

Again Solano frowned. "I doubt it. But let's face it. People kill people for the damnedest reasons. Y'know?"

Lowell knew. But a more mundane motive seemed far more likely in this case. Tim Cross simply hadn't been around long enough to make personal enemies, he figured. Unless he'd seriously offended someone, say, in East Manatee. Someone associated, perhaps, with a woman named Cecilia Potter. Like a boyfriend?

He showed Solano the letter. The DEP man shook his head, perplexed. "I didn't know anything about this. Tim is—was a young man of considerable initiative. But this—

International Phosphates is a large and reputable company, and one of the biggest employers in the heartland. They've always cooperated with us, and I don't know why they'd want to give him a hard time. Let alone exterminate him. It doesn't make sense."

Lowell was thinking the same thing.

"He had a report due on their latest reclamation project, in fact. And last I heard, everything was fine."

"You have a copy of that report?"

"He hadn't filed it yet, last I checked." Solano grimaced. "Look, I have to level with you. On that particular day, the day he . . . disappeared, Tim was on his way to a meeting pertaining to that same reclamation project, up at Plant City."

Lowell's eyebrows flew up. "At International Phosphates?"

Solano flushed, just slightly, and nodded. "International Phosphates. But look, I can't see any connection between—"

"Do you have a copy of *that* report?"

Solano shook his head. "That's just it. He was supposed to file copies of all reports with us. But he didn't. Maybe he was going to in the morning, just didn't get around to it. Maybe he got distracted by that woman he's been seeing."

"Or maybe," Lowell was thinking out loud, "he still needed one more piece of information, or wanted a response of some kind, before finishing it."

"Well." Solano shrugged. "He kind of had a tendency to bite off more than he could chew, at times."

"I see," said Lowell, trying not to think of alligators. He made a couple of mental notes. "So you don't have copies of any reports."

"Oh, sure, of every investigation upon conclusion, and usually preliminary and progress reports as well. It's just the current situation." Solano leaned forward, put his elbows on the only available clear space on his desk, and laced his fingers together thoughtfully. "One thing you should be aware of, the fertilizer business is actually on the decline, despite what they may tell you. They could hardly afford to do anything as crazy or risky as bumping off a DEP inspector, no matter how unpopular we are." He stood suddenly, went over to a world map that hung in tatters behind the door, and gestured at it broadly. "The Green Revolution peaked back in '91, worldwide. Food production can no longer keep up with population growth, which should be our number-one global concern, if we had half a brain. Phosphate exports are decreasing because fertilizers are getting less and less effective."

"Like pesticides?"

"Not exactly. It has more to do with diminishing returns. You can only squeeze so much nutrition out of the soil, no matter how many chemicals you dump in there. The agribusiness has gone about as far as it can go to improve crop yields and productivity. It's on a downhill curve. They may continue to export, even increase exports, but the less yield is produced, the less chemical fertilizing is going to work. We're going to have to move towards hydroponics and other methods to directly synthesize food if we can't get a grip on the population explosion."

Lowell read the newspapers. He wasn't unaware of the problem. There were already twice as many mouths to feed on planet Earth as there were when he was born. But he hadn't given it a lot of thought, either. He could still pull in a thirty-inch grouper from the Gulf if he felt like it. And he was hardly running around spreading his own seed with abandon. Still, he lived on the planet along with everyone else. It was going to affect him sooner or later.

"Maybe that fact alone could make them desperate. Profits must be down. Maybe one negative report could be all it would take to push them over the edge."

"What? To bankruptcy? Like I said, there were no—"

"Or murder. People sometimes die when there's money at stake. Even if it's just fertilizer money. It's a tradition as old as Cain and Abel."

Solano shook his head. "I'm no detective, Mr. Lowell, but all industries have ebbs and flows. They just reorganize, retrench, find new products, or downsize. It seems pretty farfetched that this would be grounds for murder."

Lowell had to admit he was right. "So as far as you know, all Cross was working on was routine reviews of reclamation permits for the phosphate industry?"

"Yes, sir. That and routine soil and water reports. I wish I could be of more help, I really do, but we're just swamped here, and those goons who came in last week didn't help either."

Lowell frowned. "What goons?"

"Those guys from Florida Fertilizers. They wanted access to our field reports on one of their reclamation deals. I was on my way to a meeting, so I told them no way, they should have their own records anyway, for crying out loud."

"You get their names?"

"No, I was on my way out. Two guys in suits. You white guys all look the same." He smiled.

Lowell smiled back. "Well, thanks for your help, Mr. Solano. And for the coffee." He got up to go.

He was almost at the door when Solano snapped his fingers. "Wait. I'm sorry, we really are so swamped here it's hard to keep track of anything, let alone everything. But thinking of those guys reminded me. I do remember one sinkhole there were some questions about a couple months ago."

Lowell waited. "You remember where it was?"

Solano looked embarrassed. "Yeah. It was on land owned by Florida Fertilizers. Out east of Orange Blossom."

Lowell sat down again, all ears. "And you don't find anything suspicious about that? Them coming here afterwards, looking for reports?"

"I thought about that. So we checked it out," insisted Solano. "We sent a hydrologist out there, and like I predicted, all the fuss and bother was about nothing, everything was fine."

"Thank you." Lowell had one more question. "Do you recall who the hydrologist was who went out there?"

"Of course. There's only one in the whole district. Harry Baumgarten. He's one of the best in the business, and believe me, if there was anything *no bueno* going on, he'd know it."

"Can you give me his number?"

"Sure, I got it right here somewhere." He fished around on his desk a few moments, and finally found a Rolodex. "Baumgarten, Baumgarten. Here he is. Out in Brandon, Alicia Lane. You want me to write down the number?"

Lowell glanced at the card and shook his head. "I'll remember it." A limited photo recall was one of his peculiar abilities, along with reading upside down. It was something he'd taught himself over time. "You have a copy of Baumgarten's report, by any chance?"

Solano looked relieved. "Sure, that one I got right here somewhere." He opened the top file drawer, almost toppling a stack of manila folders above, and rummaged around in what looked to Lowell like a hopeless task. "Ah, here we go," he announced a moment later, fishing out a thin, dog-eared document, which he handed over. "If you read it through, you'll see it's clean."

Lowell scanned it. "Can I have a copy?"

"Sure." Solano led the way down the hall, picking his

way through the stacks of boxes and documents like a half-back up the middle, to a rickety-looking copy machine, where he managed to crank out a faded but legible copy. Lowell thanked him, and turned to go. He was halfway to the door when Solano spoke up.

"I know what you're thinking," Solano called after him. "You think we're totally disorganized around here. Maybe so. You can thank the legislature and the people who keep us on such a short leash for that. But I will tell you this. Any time something comes to our attention, we deal with it. We don't go sweeping things under the rug, shorthanded or no. It's just the paperwork we can't keep up with. But you can thank the legislature for that, too. If they can't get rid of us altogether, they'll keep us bogged down doing reports, rather than out in the field."

Lowell hesitated once more. "Except for Tim. He was out in the field, right?"

"That's right. Which is why he was behind in his reports."

"And you can't come up with any reason, any reason at all, to think he might have found something seriously wrong? Something he felt he had to deal with, knowing how things are over here, maybe not even bringing it up until he had the whole puzzle put together?"

"That does sound like him," admitted Solano. "Only thing I can say is, he was spending a lot of time out there in Orange Blossom and Plant City, and he did seem kind of preoccupied about something. But he was involved with those civil rights people, too. And you'd be surprised how down they've been, at times, on us."

"Why is that?"

"The same old thing. Jobs. People of color are the last hired, and first fired. I can attest to that myself. It's possible they might have considered him a turncoat of sorts. Coming in from outside, perceived as trying to stop or at least impede projects that might be jobs for those people. Some of them could overreact. You never know."

Lowell wondered about that. "Yeah," he said. "You never know. Well, thanks again, Mr. Solano."

"It's Tony," insisted Solano, shaking his hand. "Same's you." Solano followed Lowell down the hall, seeming reluctant to end the conversation. "It's a damn shame," he added. "He was a good man. And we needed him down here."

Lowell found a pay phone in the lobby of the DEP building, got out the number Solano had given him, and dialed. It rang several times, and a machine answered. Lowell left his home number and hung up. Digging another quarter out of his pocket, he flipped through the yellow pages and found another number. He dialed, spoke with one person, waited a few moments, then spoke with another. He made an appointment with a Mrs. Jessup and hung up. Then he headed for the parking lot and his Impala.

It was time to pay another visit to Orange Blossom, and the phosphate mining region of central Florida. Also known, in local lore, as Bone Valley.

6

As Lowell drove east into the midlands, he watched a distant thunderstorm (rare this time of year) as it steamed across the land, visible for miles across the fields. While he preferred the coast, he loved the smallness and shabby charm of the tiny inland hamlets: little frame bungalows, stores of stucco and faded red tile, and a cluster of palm trees in the center, if there was a center. The land was dotted with traditional rural Americana: co-ops for farm supplies, small railroad depots and side yards, towering silos, intermittent pine and oak forests, and the wide watery flatlands that ran east as far as Wauchula.

Lowell chose to turn off 301 at Parrish and go through Duette, on Route 62, a two-lane highway that cut east from north of Bradenton, straight into Florida's inland agricultural region. He slowed only at railroad crossings and for a stop sign or two in sun-blasted drowsy hamlets with optimistic names like Mango.

That was the difference and giveaway, of course, that ended any further similarities with the upper Midwest, or American heartland. Florida was hot. Hot and humid. This region was actually a lot more like parts of Louisiana, including a preponderance of names of Arcadian descent. True, days or even weeks when the dew point went through the roof often occurred in July and August in the Midwest. But never this early. And not week after week, month after month, until the locals were rendered either indolent or crazed.

By the time Lowell reached Duette, the sun was already high enough that the road was shimmering, and the mirages of water appeared and disappeared on the flatlands ahead. Just beyond the first sign, Orange Blossom, Fifteen Miles, a barbed-wire fence began running along the roadside, on the right. It continued for a couple of miles, before Lowell passed a sign at a barred red metal gate: Florida Fertilizers. Keep Off. A few miles farther, even before he could see them, he could smell the sulfur gases from the tall reactor stacks, chemical processors and phosphate silos of the processing plant.

He reached the main gate, a military-style white guardhouse, with another red metal gate with an automatic lift. He pulled in behind a double-tank trailer rig and stopped at the guardhouse. The guard was standard-fare cracker: lined red face, thin gray hair, perpetual squint, and skeptical eyes.

"Kin ah hep you?" he inquired.

"Yes, I'm here to see someone in personnel. About a job."

"Y'all hafta come in before eight in the mornin'. That's when we do our hirin'."

"I have an appointment. A Mrs. Jessup."

The guard looked Lowell over—the deep tan, the ponytail, the denims—and shrugged. If the man had an appointment, he decided, that was no skin off his neck. They'd run this fella off soon enough, anyways. Didn't look like the kind of good Christians Florida Fertilizers preferred to hire, when those equal-opportunity assholes weren't pokin' their noses in, that is: forcin' the company to hire all them damn niggers.

"Main intrance to the left, check with the guard in the lobby." The gate was up, and Lowell was in.

The drive to the administration building—little more than an oversized corrugated shed painted white, but one of a seemingly endless row—was on a neatly paved two-lane blacktop service road, lined with more barbed wire on either side. A lot of security for a bunch of fertilizer, thought Lowell.

The main entrance consisted of a single fire door, with the words Main Office above, and a smaller, simple painted sign, Personnel, at the side.

Lowell entered, briefcase in one hand, Nikon over his shoulder. He'd worn a nice navy blazer he'd picked up at the Salvation Army store in Manatee City just for such an occasion, to make up for his jeans, and for the sake of a certain modicum of decorum. A quick nod at the security guard, and he walked straight to the personnel office, across the simple, very pragmatic soundproof tile-and-linoleum lobby. Photo blowups of old farms and tractors covered the walls. They weren't bad, actually, some done from the air. Lowell wondered who the photographer had been, and whether firms like this hired outside, or just sent some ol' boy out with a camera now and then. The work looked too good for that though. Whoever had done it had a sense of what light and shadow, perspective, and angle were all about.

Mrs. Jessup proved to be a perfectly engaging, bleached-blond middle-aged woman with small brown eyeglasses that actually enhanced her warm smile. Lowell returned her greeting in surprise, having expected someone far more severe and unlikable.

"Nice to meet you, Mr. Lowell, do come in," she offered,

gesturing him into a large, air-conditioned office with healthy plants and even some reasonable prints on the walls. "I gather this isn't about a job."

Lowell presented his (he suddenly realized) nearly expired PI license. He'd meant to get around to getting his license renewed, and kept procrastinating, due to basic inertia. He'd better deal with it. Not that he cared that much, one way or the other. His clients would find him regardless. The license's main benefit was permission to carry a concealed weapon, which Lowell didn't carry anyway. Also, there was Bedrosian. Although Bedrosian had become more tolerant in the last couple of years of his lack of conformity than he would have ever believed possible, she wouldn't stand for anything illegal. And while he certainly didn't share her fervor for the righteousness of every single letter of the law, he needed this job. For Ernie. For justice. Also for Florida Power, which was threatening to shut off his electricity unless he gave them lots of money.

"You're right." He smiled. "I'm a detective, on an investigation. You can check with Lieutenant Bedrosian at Manatee for a reference." He hoped.

Mrs. Jessup glanced at the license and handed it back, her eyebrows arched slightly. "So what can we do for you?"

"Actually," he lied, "I'm just doing a background check on a couple of people, for security reasons. You know how it is, negative references aren't gonna show up on the résumés, and lots of times a criminal record, or even personnel records, can be expunged."

He'd struck the right chord. Her eyes lit up. "I know what you mean, honey," she effused. "We had an employee one time, perfectly nice-looking young girl, had stolen all the receipts from the last company, and when they told us about it, she sued them under the privacy act, and can you believe it? She won. They had to pay—I can't tell you because it's company records and confidential, you understand, but they had to pay that lying little snippet a huge sum of money, when she's the one who's the thief!"

Lowell nodded understandingly. American criminal and civil justice never ceased to amaze him. The girl was probably hard at work getting ready to rip off the next client, after which she'd just move on. Nobody would press charges—too costly and time-consuming, and without an actual conviction, she couldn't be implicated in any way.

"So now, then, Mr. Lowell." Mrs. Jessup smiled, a true gem of a woman. "Who were the employees in question?"

"Well, there's a Mr. Cahill, Richard or Dick—"

Her eyebrows arched up, ever so slightly. "Dicky Cahill? He's one of our foremen. He's still employed here, though. He plannin' on leaving us in the near future?"

He tried to read her expression. Her voice had risen, just slightly, and he thought he detected a considerable cooling around the edges of her smile. Mrs. Jessup, he thought to himself, does not like Dicky Cahill very much. Whoever he is. Either that or she's upset at the thought of his leaving. He guessed the former.

"I couldn't say," he replied. "But I was wondering if it would be possible to ask him a few questions?"

Mrs. Jessup frowned but kept on smiling at the same time. "Well, I don't see why not, long as you don't take up too much company time."

"I could do it after-hours, if there's an address or number where I can reach him."

Her smile widened, as though hopeful there was a chance her Dicky Cahill might be in trouble. "Well, I can't give out personnel records. But I do happen to know what kind of car he drives, and if you just happen to find him in the lot before he takes off at five, well that's between you and him."

"Thanks," said Lowell, and meant it. "What's he driving?"

"A brand-spanking-new fire-engine red T-bird convertible, and, honey, between you and me, I would sure love to drive a car like that myself, but I know how much I make, which is almost as much as he does, and I sure couldn't afford that nice of a car. Between you, me, and the bedpost, Mr. Lowell, I hardly see how a man with a family and all that responsibility like Mr. Cahill can manage a car like that!"

"I know what you mean." Lowell nodded. "My daughter wants a car like that. She'll have to find a richer old man than me, though. Which she probably will." He sighed.

"Now, who was the other employee you were inquiring about, hon'?" She was back to business, ever efficient.

"A Cecilia Potter? I think she's an employee here, maybe you could confirm that."

This time she frowned at him, just slightly. "If it's who I think it is, I believe you're referring to one of our equal-opportunity employees. We keep them in a separate file," she explained, walking across the room. "I'm sure you understand." Lowell wondered about that, but said nothing. "Miss Potter didn't show up for work again today. Not for the first time. She has a very poor attendance record, and frankly, Mr. Lowell, I can't offer her much of a recommendation. Off the record, of course. She's welcome to leave here any time she wishes." She sniffed. "If that's what she has in mind."

"Not necessarily," he replied, breezily. "In her case, it has to do with a credit application."

"Well." Mrs. Jessup sighed. "Honey, all I can say about that is if they're giving MasterCards to the likes of her, small wonder those interest rates are so dang high!"

He laughed, to put her at ease. She found the file and opened it up. "She works in the property management division. An office clerk, at our base salary of twelve thousand five hundred."

"Twelve thousand five hundred? Per year?" In other words, he thought, she was getting minimum wage. He wondered what she was expected to do for it. Small wonder she stayed out of the office a lot. Probably in order to recover from whatever else she had to do to eke out a living moonlighting. Plus, she had a child. He thought about that for a moment. He wondered if there was anyone else in the house in East Manatee besides her, the child, and the alleged boyfriend. He wondered who would or could take care of a child after school or day care, when his or her mother had to work. The boyfriend? That was a scary thought.

"Can you give me any information regarding the nature of Ms. Potter's absences from work?"

She looked at the file, frowned, then sniffed. "No, I'm afraid not. I'm sorry." But the smile looked more forced than ever now. "Was there anything else?"

"Well . . ." He hesitated. "Can you tell me anything about a man named Timothy Cross, who may have been here on occasion as a state inspector?"

She frowned. "I know no one by that name."

Lowell smiled. "That's all right. Thanks for the help." He turned to go, deciding not to press it, then turned back. "By the way. Does your company provide maternity leave?"

That caught her off guard. "Maternity? Good heavens, I should say not. This is a fertilizer factory, honey!"

"Right. Sorry." Lowell headed for the door. "I guess I'll go hang around the parking lot, if that's all right with you, and wait for Mr. Cahill."

"You can't miss him," she assured him. "Bein' a southern boy, he'd hardly leave without his car."

"Good point." He was a southern boy, too. But given half a chance, he'd probably leave his car in a minute.

65

Her smile was genuine once again. "Just be . . . careful. He's a little—temperamental."

Lowell tilted his head ever so slightly. He knew the type. Macho redneck. Full of heat and rage, always ready for a fight, constantly defensive, ready to prove something, desperate to find someone—anyone—over whom to feel superior: the most dangerous type of all. They were all over the place, especially in the small inland mining and farming towns.

He was almost out the door when she suddenly called after him. "Mr. Lowell?"

He turned back. She came out of her office after him. "It occurs to me that while you're waiting for the whistle, which isn't for more than an hour and a half, you might like a tour of the plant."

Lowell had thought of that, had thought of asking for one, but hadn't held up much hope of being accommodated. He smiled his gratitude. "That would be outstanding," he said, and meant it.

She picked up a wall phone and dialed a number. "Hello, Tom?" She said. "I have a young man out here, name of Mr. Lowell, who would like to take a brief tour of the facility. Would you have the time, honey? I know this is short notice." In Florida, women called everybody "honey," Lowell knew.

As Lowell exited through the reception area, Mrs. Jessup watched him go, an expression of veiled anxiety flickering across her face for the briefest of moments as he headed down a long hallway toward a set of double doors at the far end.

As Lowell approached, a tall, slender man—late fifties to early sixties, tufts of gray hair around a red, balding pate that showed the ill effects of excessive exposure to the Florida sun—came out through the double doors to meet him. He had wire-rim glasses and numerous frown lines around his eyes, and looked like a professor. The man wore a short-sleeved white Arrow shirt with a starched collar and a spotted brown necktie, and blue-gray Haggar slacks. He offered his hand.

"Mr. Lowell? I'm Tom Freeman, Director of Operations. I understand you're interested in a plant tour?"

"If you wouldn't mind," said Lowell, accepting the handshake.

Freeman eyed him inquisitively as he led the way through the double doors. "We usually just run tours for school groups, that sort of thing. It's sort of unusual for one individual like yourself to come through."

"I know," said Lowell. "I appreciate your taking the time, Mr. Freeman. I'm doing some research on Florida's key industries, and a firsthand look helps a lot."

"Exactly," said Freeman. "And indeed we are one of Florida's key industries. People forget there's a lot more to our state than beaches and shuffleboard. As you may or may not know, our little corner of Florida produces eighty percent of the phosphates used in North America, and thirty percent of the world's supply."

Lowell whistled appreciatively. "By phosphates, you're talking about the basic ingredient in fertilizer?"

"Exactly." Freeman led Lowell into a small conference room with a large round oak table, high-backed vinyl chairs, and a large video screen. "If you like, I can show you a video explaining the process before we go into the plant proper."

Lowell nodded. He only had the vaguest knowledge, he realized, of what phosphates were all about. Bone Valley, he'd heard it called. The very name gave him the creeps. And the huge heaps of gray slag that lined local roadways such as State Road 60 for miles were hardly reassuring. He remembered what Solano had told him about the stuff.

Freeman turned down the lights, slid a videocassette into the player, and turned on the video projector. The screen was lit up with colorful scenery of Florida's interior environment: xeric scrublands, the vast saw-grass prairies he'd driven through, wide expanses of freshwater wetlands, and pine flatwoods, with sparkling blue lakes and ponds everywhere. "What you are looking at," interjected Freeman, "was once a phosphate surface mine near Homewood. It is now a county park where you can play golf, go fishing, or have a family picnic. Thanks to our multimillion-dollar land restoration and recovery projects, we lead the world in percapita expenditures for proenvironmental action," he proclaimed.

"Welcome to the other Florida," the video boomed. "A land of unspoiled beauty, as varied and differing as any ecosystem to be found in North America. It is also the source of the world's largest supply of phosphatic rock, which is the basic ingredient in the fertilizer that, literally, feeds the world." The video panned to a large strip-mining operation, adjacent to one especially pristine-looking pond the camera had been lingering on a moment before. "Without phosphatic rock, or phosphate ore, there can be no phosphorous, and without phosphorous, life itself cannot exist, because together with nitrogen and potassium it is one of the three basic nutrients for all plant life."

Lowell yawned. "What about all that gray stuff heaped up out along the highway?" he inquired.

Freeman flinched slightly. "That," he said, "is phosphogypsum, basically what's left over after the phosphates and other viable byproducts are removed from the rock and soil. We'll get to that in a few moments, if you'll allow me.

68

There are actually some very exciting developments in that area."

Lowell nodded indifferently, and the video proceeded with a glowing report on how effective phosphate fertilizers were in increasing worldwide agricultural output. Lowell thought about what Solano had told him.

"How about population control?" Lowell wanted to know. Freeman stopped the video machine again. "How about needing less, instead of trying to always produce more of everything?"

"Excuse me?" Freeman blinked, not comprehending.

"Never mind," said Lowell. "Go on."

"Rather than take you out into the hard-hat mining area, or recovery areas, which cover many hundreds of acres and would take quite a while, the rest of the video will provide a visual explanation of the ore-mining process, after which I'll show you through the processing plant itself. Would that be all right with you?" intoned Freeman.

"Sure," said Lowell, disappointed. He'd wanted a look at the mining operation, particularly the holding ponds. He wondered if the sinkhole Tim Cross had been interested in had been a holding pond. He was tempted to ask if he could see it, but decided not to. If it was off limits, Freeman wouldn't be likely to take him out there anyway. Besides, if it was way out in the sticks, there wouldn't be time. He'd have to bide his time and get there on his own. Somehow.

The tape resumed, showing a cross-section chart of a Florida landscape. "Phosphatic rock," the detached robotic voice informed him, "lies beneath a layer of sandy soil, usually around six feet thick, called the overburden." The video now showed a gigantic dredge that resembled an old-fashioned steam shovel, except much larger. "These huge digging machines," the voice continued, "called draglines, dig out the top layer and set it aside for later recovery. They then dig out the phosphate matrix, a layer of phosphate rock mixed with clay and soil. This is deposited into a pit car, where it is mixed with water under high pressure to produce a slurry. This is then piped to a washer plant, where the rock is crushed and shaken on vibrating screens. This separates rock out from the particles of phosphates mixed with sand, called feed, which are then transported by conveyor belt to a flotation machine, which further separates the phosphate rock from the clay and sand. The phosphate ore is now ready for processing."

Freeman turned off the video. "Now, if you'll follow me, I'll take you through the processing plant, which is here on these premises."

He led the way through another set of doors, down another long corridor, and out of the back of the building. The factory loomed in the background beyond the office complex, large and menacing. They passed a number of workers in hard hats who eyed Lowell with a mixture of curiosity and suspicion as they approached the plant. At the door, Freeman reached into a wooden closet next to the wall and took out two large rubber fireman's jackets and two hard hats. "Better wear these," he advised. "Oh, and I'll have to ask you to leave the camera."

"Sorry." Lowell smiled agreeably and handed him the Nikon, which was carefully stored and locked in the same closet.

"You can pick that up on your way out." Which was fine with Lowell. Especially since he just happened to have, concealed and built into his briefcase by his nefarious pal, Perry, a miniature Hi-8-mm video surveillance camera, with a wide-angle lens and enough speed for available-light interior taping.

Inside, Lowell's senses were assaulted on all sides: by a

continuous, thunderous roar, and the almost overwhelming odors of sulfur and ammonia. Pointing at a row of huge metal tanks off to the left, Freeman shouted, "Those are the reactors! We mix phosphatic rock with sulfuric acid to produce merchant grade phosphoric acid. That's the main ingredient in all chemical fertilizers." He pointed to a second, smaller, row of vats on the far wall. "Over there we react the acid with ammonium to produce two types of phosphates: monoammonium phosphate, and diammonium phosphate."

The chemical smell was almost overpowering. As they were crossing a narrow catwalk, Lowell looked down into the steaming vats on either side of him below and fought back a sudden dizziness. As he angled to tape a few quick seconds, his foot slipped. It was a bad moment, and he gripped the rail more tightly.

"What about byproducts?" he shouted to Freeman, just ahead of him.

"Good question!" Freeman gestured with enthusiasm at various tanks and pipelines. "Our byproducts turn up in a lot of useful places, believe it or not."

"Like what?"

"Like toothpaste. And soda pop. Most preservatives."

"Soda pop?"

"Sodium phosphate. Gives it that fizz."

"Amazing." Lowell wondered what they put in beer. Probably whatever was handy.

"What goes in toothpaste?" he asked.

"Fluoride, of course. It's a derivative of fluorine gas, which occurs naturally in phosphatic rock. Very toxic, actually, in its pure form."

Freeman led the way between what seemed like miles of hot, steaming pipes, to another set of reactor domes. "Here are the recovery chambers. This one recovers heavy metals, and the waste products are carried away over there, to holding ponds."

"Where are the holding ponds?" Lowell asked.

"Out in the mining areas," shouted Freeman. "Once an ore deposit is exhausted, we are required by law to fill it in, level and replant it. It's called land reclamation."

"Could we take a look at some of those areas?" Tim Cross had been responsible for approval of land-reclamation plans, he remembered.

"No can do. It's off limits on account of the mining machinery, and insurance regulations. Anyway, it's too far out there, it would take too much time. That's why we have the video."

"Right. What about the gypsum?"

Freeman pointed to a huge conveyor belt carrying tons of gray waste material to trucks waiting outside. "It goes out over there. That's what I wanted to tell you about!" He looked actually eager. "One of the properties of phosphogypsum is that it desalinates soil. We are well along the way to developing a process whereby phosphogypsum will be used to reclaim coastal areas that have become salinated from overpumping of water. What this means is that areas that are of necessity being closed down to further development today will be able to be reopened in the future!"

Lowell thought about the implications of that. More developments. More highways. More fossil-fuel consumption. More congestion. More pollution. More water use and overpumping. It was an endless cycle. "Great!" he managed to say. "Just what we need, more people."

"Right," enthused Freeman. "Growth is the wheel that drives the nation's economy. Florida can't afford to fall behind!"

Lowell had seen enough. But he wondered, as they headed toward the exit, why Freeman had been so anxious to steer him clear of several processes that were taking place in what he'd vaguely referred to as the "recovery zone." He'd find out later, he decided. He wished he had a map of the area. He should have gotten one from Solano. The library should have some. Also, he still had that article to track down first. He checked his watch. It was time to go and look for Mr. Cahill.

Thanking Freeman at the exit door, he returned the jacket and hat, picked up his 35-mm camera, and headed for the parking area, glad to be out of the heat and stench of the fertilizer plant. It smelled like death to him.

7

The sun was already low in the sky. The parking lot was mostly dirt and sand, and glowed in the softening orange light. But the sidewalk still felt like a griddle as Lowell stepped out into the late-afternoon sun. The company clock said four-fifty. Ten minutes to go. The shift would end at five sharp, thereby causing the twice daily traffic jam on State Highway 574, which was otherwise empty for most of the day. Some bright local politician would probably eventually lobby for a widening of the road to four lanes in order to ease the rush-hour problem. And also provide employment and a fat contract for his or her brother or nephew in the road-building or asphalt business. No one would, in all likelihood, think of changing the work pattern at the plant. A working man or woman worked eight to five, with an hour for lunch. Not seven to four, or six to three, or nine to six. That's how it always was, and always would be. At least in rural Orange Blossom, Florida.

He found the car with no trouble. As with blue-collar working men in most parts of the country, here a man's car was everything. It was how status was determined. It was the best measure of whether, and how well, and how often a man got laid. It demonstrated whether or not he was employed, or employable. Lowell drove a piece of shit because he didn't care. He wasn't a working man. Except on his boat, which no one else ever saw. His car, in its current condition, impressed nobody, and that's the way he liked it. Fixed up, it could probably be a show car. As long as Tony Lowell owned it, however, it wouldn't be. The red T-bird, looked right off the assembly line. Cahill probably spent two hours on the car for every two minutes with his kids. He probably spent more money on his car in a month than on his wife in a year. He probably loved his car. It had tinted windows and black trim and glowed, as sizzling hot as it looked. Cahill had put one of those cardboard sun visors in the windshield, but that wouldn't help much. He'd have to open it up, at least a moment, and air it out before taking off. It was probably a hundred and thirty degrees inside. If he stopped to put down the top, that would give Lowell even more time. He wouldn't need much time, he knew, and the man probably wouldn't give it to him even if he did.

The whistle blew, exactly on time. As the plant facility emptied out—a sudden burst of humanity with lunch pails like a dam floodgate opening—Lowell watched the workers with interest. Most were familiar types: the southern descendants of poor Irish, Italian, Spanish, Portuguese, Cajun, and English immigrants.

Cahill's complexion was a deep brownish red, his crewcut almost the same color. He was short, lean and mean, about a hundred sixty pounds of water moccasin with legs. He did have laugh lines around his eyes, though. Lowell wondered what he would consider funny.

Cahill wasn't amused, it seemed, to find the man reclining against the fender of his bitchin' new T-bird.

"Yer leanin' on my car," he stated, sizing Lowell up. He lit a Marlboro and inhaled, waiting for a response.

"Sorry," said Lowell, stepping away from the car and toward Cahill, which seemed to throw him off. "You Richard Cahill?"

"Nobody's called me Richard since the doctor slapped my little ass," said Cahill. "Which, I might add, nobody's done since. My friends, which you ain't one of, call me Dicky."

"Why's that, Dicky?" asked a large man in company overalls, getting into an adjacent Ford pickup. He had a tone of mockery in his voice, and wasn't afraid of the foreman. Lowell wondered who he was. He looked to be classic cracker, and more. There was a certain wisdom, perhaps even melancholy in his eyes.

Lowell watched as Cahill turned his attention to the big man. Corcoran. He made a mental note of the name on the uniform, wondering if he could get another crack at Mrs. Jessup in Personnel. He doubted it. But it might be worth a try. "On account of I got the biggest, fastest, wettest, stiffest dick of any white man south of Bang Her Maine, as any woman in town shoulda told you by now!" Cahill was boasting.

"That ain't the way I hear it. Way I hear it, you cain't even get yours up no more," drawled the big man. "And that's a sad thing. That saddens me to hear." He even looked sad, thought Lowell.

Cahill bristled. "Yeah? Who'd you hear that from? If it was your wife she was lyin'." He glanced around the parking lot, where an audience of workers had gathered, expecting homage for his version of wit. Cahill had status, apparently, among these men. None of them could compete with him vehiclewise. Several of them, mostly owners of modest pickups, snickered uncomfortably.

Corcoran's sorrowful look intensified, and he shrugged, almost tolerantly, as he started his engine. "Hey. If Candy was gonna fool around, which she don't on account of she likes livin'—she'd probably wanna do it with a *man*. Nah, where I heard it from was *your* wife!"

Cahill seethed. "Fuck you, Corcoran!"

Typical male bonding, Lowell was thinking. These guys must be close.

"Keep dreamin', you sorry asshole," said Corcoran, throwing his pickup into reverse. Cahill flashed Corcoran the finger. Corcoran responded with a blast of smoke from his ancient exhaust pipe and drove off, calm as the eye of a hurricane, leaving Cahill fuming.

Cahill looked around the parking lot where his audience was slinking away as fast as their wheels could carry them. It was obvious his grip on their loyalty was tenuous. Lowell guessed that they didn't like him a whole helluva lot.

Cahill turned his venom back on Lowell. "You still here?"

"You're a funny man," said Lowell.

"So what the hell you want?"

Cahill's name had been mentioned during Cecilia Potter's wee-hours argument with her presumed boyfriend, the night before. He had some kind of leverage over the boyfriend, it sounded like. But what did that have to do with property management, where she apparently worked? Cahill was a labor foreman.

"I want to ask you about a woman named Cecilia Potter, I understand works for you," said Lowell.

"She ain't working today. Why, you wanna fuck her? You into black pussy?"

Lowell winced. "That's very impolite, not to mention demeaning to African-American women," he commented.

Cahill stared. He looked at the blazer, the briefcase, the camera, and his eyes narrowed even further. They narrowed any more, he'd be cross-eyed. "What the fuck is this?"

"Actually, I'm wondering what exactly she does for you."

Cahill's blue-eyed stare wavered a bit. "You from child welfare or some shit?"

Lowell made a mental note of that. "Why, should I be?"

Cahill pushed past him. "Excuse me, but I'm outta here." He stopped, when Lowell didn't step aside, and drew up, almost in Lowell's face. "You got a problem with that?"

Lowell didn't move, and met his look squarely but mildly. The man had bad breath. He reached for his shirt pocket, and watched Cahill's eyes following his hand. The man is quick, he thought. And stupid. Lowell could have broken his nose during that instant, if he were into violence. Which he wasn't. "No problem. Just curious. The other thing I was wondering was whether you might happen to know about a friend of hers, name of Timothy Cross." He showed Cahill his license.

Cahill glanced at it, and glared at him. "You're a cop," he accused. "What do you want, anyway? I don't know nothin' about it."

"About what?" asked Lowell. Official word of the murder discovery had not yet been released to the media. The county sheriff was sitting on it, for some reason. Or Lena was.

"Nothin'." Cahill pushed on past and unlocked the car door. "So if you'll excuse me, bud, I got a hot date, and a hot cock, so step aside, unless you got some kinda legal grounds for buggin' my ass."

Lowell winced again, but managed a benign smile. From his experience, men who felt compelled to boast about their sexual prowess usually didn't have much. Far be it for him to rub it in. "Not really. Have a fun night."

"I always do," said Cahill, and started his engine with a fury, revving it to a defiant 5,000 RPMs. Lowell stepped back from the cloud of blue smoke. This car already shows signs of serious abuse, he thought, wondering what else Cahill liked to abuse. Probably his family, for starters. He was a bully.

Cahill opened the window and tossed out his cigarette as he backed out of his parking space. "Look," he said, a touch of whine entering his voice. "You want to know about Tim Cross, talk to that nigger organization he hung around with, or those environment assholes. He never caused nobody around here nothin' but trouble, anyways."

Cahill sped away, ignoring the posted 5-MPH speed limit as he tore out through the exit gate, turned right toward Orange Blossom, and headed for town.

Lowell watched him go, considered following him. The red T-bird wouldn't be hard to spot in a town that size. He turned to leave when his eye caught a second wave of workers leaving the plant. They were all wearing coveralls indicative of the lowest job categories, and stayed together in a tight group. They were all black. At which moment Lowell realized that no black faces had appeared among the departing workers prior to that moment. Cross had been involved with civil rights, Lena had informed him during a breakfast briefing over the phone. Several black women followed the men out. Again Lowell realized that no women had been among the first main group of plant workers who had left the plant building. The white women, Lowell decided, must all be kept in clerical. They had a smaller lot in the next building, where he'd parked. That's where he'd find Mrs. Jessup.

The black women were leaving with the black men. Interesting, he thought. The men kept their heads low, eyes watchful and wary as they walked to their cars, which were almost all old and shabby. One woman, however, seemed unbowed. She strode fiercely across the parking lot, head high. She was wearing a neat women's suit and blouse of good quality. She looked like an executive type. A doubtful likelihood, he thought, at a place like this.

The woman approached him, pausing to light a cigarette. A recent-model black Toyota Corolla was parked opposite Cahill's now-vacated space. The woman ignored the stares of the few remaining white workers, most of whom, he noted, were making a genuine attempt to put on an appearance of camaraderie. "How's it goin', Carla?" asked one young white worker from a car two spaces over.

"Hangin' in there," she responded with a cool, professional smile.

Lowell approached her. "Excuse me. Um, Carla?"

"Miss Brewer, if you don't mind." She looked him over. "Who are you?"

"My name's Tony Lowell. I'm a private investigator."

"No shit," she said.

"I have some questions regarding a man named Timothy Cross. Did you know him?"

She seemed startled by the question. "Why? Something happen to him?"

"I can't say just now. How well did you know him?"

"Oh, my God." Carla leaned against her car. A couple of the black male workers noticed her distress and hurried to her. One of them, one of the biggest and oldest, had a white Afro, and clothes more faded than the others'.

"You okay, Carla? What he doin' to you?"

"Nothing. It's all right, Ben, thank you." Carla stood firmly, pulled herself together, and looked at Lowell. "I'm sorry," she said. "But I can't talk to you. Not here, anyway." She got into her car, started it hastily, and drove off. The older man looked at Lowell accusingly.

"I asked her if she knew anything about Tim Cross," explained Lowell, offering the man his card. "Do you?"

"Me? I don't know nothin'."

"Sorry to bother you, then," said Lowell, turning to go.

"Wait!" the big man called. "Why don't you come to the AME Church tomorrow night. There's a supper meetin'. Maybe you talk to some of the people there. Maybe some of them might talk to you then. But not here, mister. Not now."

"What's your name?" Lowell asked, quickly.

"Name is Ben Tompkins. Everybody knows me." With that, Tompkins got into his pickup truck and left, followed quickly by the remaining black workers. Lowell felt very much alone. A few of the more belligerent white stragglers had been watching him. They'd obviously disliked him from the start. He didn't look or dress cracker, for one thing. And although plenty of rednecks and country singers wore ponytails these days, they sensed he wasn't one of them. They didn't like anyone who wasn't one of them. Especially strangers who talked to black people before they talked to them.

No one made an overt move in his direction. Lowell beamed at everyone and left the parking lot, hurrying along the periphery sidewalk that wound around the plant building and over to the headquarters building. He reached the staff parking lot just in time to spot Mrs. Jessup backing out of a space near the door in a blue '89 Subaru Legacy wagon. It was in reasonably nice condition, but as she'd observed to him, it hardly compared to a spanking-new Thunderbird.

"Mrs. Jessup," he shouted, sprinting over to her and catching up to her driver's side window just as she began to move forward. She looked up, almost fearfully for a moment, until she recognized him. Reluctantly she ran the power window down. "Any luck?" she asked.

"Well, I had the pleasure of meeting your Mr. Cahill."

She scowled, then managed a brief little laugh. "He's somethin', isn't he? He try to push you around?"

"Sort of. Listen, there was one more person I was wondering about. A man by the name of Corcoran?"

"We got twenty Corcorans in this town." She laughed. "But you probably mean Buster. I wouldn't cross him, I were you."

"He didn't seem too intimidated by Cahill," agreed Lowell.

"Wouldn't be. I'll tell you one thing, then I really have to go. Mr. Corcoran is one of the best workers we have at this plant. Honest as the day is long, and doesn't cut corners, like some people." At that, she started to leave.

"Wait!" shouted Lowell. "Where's he work?"

"Wastewater Disposal," came the reply, and she was gone.

Lowell wondered why she'd sounded so nervous.

On his way home Lowell decided to detour through Manatee City and stop by East Manatee once again. It was just past sundown, dinnertime for all but the elderly, who always seemed to eat early. Maybe Cecilia Potter would be home this time. Or at least be receiving visitors. Maybe the dog would be chained, or inside. Maybe the voice he heard, that deep, chilling male voice, belonged to some perfectly reasonable, normal human being who lived downstairs, or out back, or next door. Maybe the moon was blue cheese.

He parked in front and went straight to the door, deciding on the direct approach since it was still daylight. He'd decided to leave the cameras. Both the video cam and the Nikon were too obvious, and would draw an instant hostile response. He'd have to get the boyfriend on film later and run him through Lena's new computer program. Which, he realized, ought to be her job. Suppressing his annoyance, he climbed the three porch stairs and knocked. Rap music boomed from a second-story window, open to the early-evening breeze. He rang the bell. A dog barked. *The* dog. He heard voices, uncertain, and a sharp command. The male voice. Footsteps approached in the hall, and Lowell stood back as a woman peered out at him apprehensively. She was visibly bruised, her hair a tangled mess, still in a nightgown.

"Mommy?" called a child's voice in the background. *The* child's voice from the night before.

"Shut up," he heard, from the male, and a slap, followed by a whimper. He wanted to push on in, but the woman blocked his way. She looked barely twenty. She was beautiful, despite her appearance and condition.

"Yes?" she asked, opening the door barely a crack.

"Sorry to bother you, ma'am. Are you Cecilia Potter?"

"Who wants to know?" she asked. Her eyes were sharp, and bright. Her complexion was medium. She resembled Whitney Houston.

"A friend of Tim Cross," he lied. It was half true, anyway. He was Tim's uncle's friend.

Her eyes widened. She glanced over her shoulder. "Where is he?" she asked, her voice a hush.

"You mean you don't know?" he asked, incredulous.

"Who the hell is it?" growled the male voice, closer now. Lowell's skin crawled.

"Sorry, I gotta go," she whispered, and began to close the door. The girl looks terrified, he thought. She knows something.

"When and where can we talk?" he asked, quickly inserting his foot. He could hear heavy footsteps approaching. She looked panicked, but hesitated the briefest moment. "Women's Health Center, we go there for medicine mornings." She turned away. "It's nobody, baby," she called out. "Just a salesman. He's leaving." She slammed the door to prove it. Lowell barely got his foot out in time.

Lowell left without looking back. The place, the whole situation, gave him a bad feeling in his gut. The woman was a prisoner, he knew. A prisoner of love, probably. Or what passed for love among desperate people. And she wanted out, and was too afraid to go, he guessed. He didn't blame her.

As Lowell got into the Chevy and drove away, a curtain parted, just slightly, in the dining room. The man inside the house grunted to himself. "Bitch," he muttered, and turned away. Whoever the white dude was, he hadn't stuck around long enough to find out much. Probably scared off by the dog. He wondered if there was any connection between this and the thing last night. Somebody'd been around the 'hood who didn't belong. He turned as the dog, Cyrus, padded into the room and whined obediently at his feet. He could tell the animal was itching for action. He was himself. But he didn't want to draw any more attention to himself, to his house, to his woman, than necessary. He switched on the safety of the TEC DC9 automatic pistol he always had ready, and set it on the table reluctantly. Going back to the window, he could see the car going off, just as he'd seen it arrive. Cecilia said it was a salesman, but she always lied. Could have been anybody, people were always coming and going at all hours in this shithole neighborhood. One of these days, he'd have him a decent place, maybe in St. Pete or Tampa. Meanwhile, he'd protect what was his.

Leonard Smith was ever watchful, had to be. And not just for burglars, or the random marauders that plagued neighborhoods like this. There were always the cops to worry about. Or worse. He'd learned of necessity long ago that pre-caution pays—on the South Side of Chicago, then elsewhere in his travels, including a stint in Salvador, then later Panama, as an unofficial government mercenary. He'd loved those times. A basic blank check just to kill a few asshole wetbacks.

He hefted the pistol again thoughtfully. It was one of many weapons he owned. Assault guns, automatic pistols, shotguns, high-powered rifles. In fact, he owned an entire arsenal, courtesy in large part to the intense lobbying efforts of the good ol' National Rifle Association, of which he was a proud member. He chuckled to himself at the thought. He'd lied on the part of the form that so subtly, so casually inquired as to the applicant's race. Little did those assholes know who he really was. He knew who they were, of course. White racists, all of them, whose smoke screens about "sportsmen" and "law-abiding citizens" and "rights" were nothing but that: smoke screens. What they really wanted, what they really were all about, as was revealed again and again in their literature, was to arm the white populace for a race war. Well, what they'd gone and done was arm the inner cities. And the angry, impoverished black enclaves in the smaller cities. The Crips and Bloods in L.A., for example, or the Tonton Macoutes in Miami (and he had worked with them all more than once) had more and heavier arms per man than the average police department. He himself could probably outgun most of Manatee City. And it might come to that, the way things were. Because he was one nigger who took no shit from nobody. He could pass, with his light skin, he knew. But a nigger was what he'd been dubbed as a child, what had defined who he was his whole life, and he was proud of it. Nobody fucked with him and lived, it was that simple.

"Lenny?" her voice whined at him from the kitchen. She

had her little girl in her arms who looked down at him fearfully with wide eyes.

Damn woman, he thought bitterly. Couldn't do a damn thing right.

"You comin' to eat, honey?"

"Shut the fuck up, I'll be there in a minute," he growled, putting his pistol back in the metal case where he kept his weapons. "And get that kid the fuck to bed. What she doin' up?"

"It's only seven, baby. She ain't even eaten yet."

"Well, get her fed and the hell out of here. Don't want no cripple kids in my fuckin' face when I eat, got that?"

He knew she'd obey. She'd crossed him a couple of times already, and paid dearly for it. He started up the stairs, feeling weary all of a sudden. It had been a long, hot day. He hoped he wouldn't have to beat her this time. He was just too damn tired. On the other hand, if she was askin' for it, like she was half the time, he'd just have to oblige her. One thing Leonard Smith could not stand was an uppity woman.

She sure had a lot goin' on behind his back, though, it seemed. Too damn much. He was gonna have to deal with it, like he always did.

8

The next morning, Lowell called Cecilia's number and got no answer. With a sinking feeling, he went to the Women's Health Center in Manatee City and waited until noon. It was a waste of time. She never showed, and he finally left. Swinging by the house in East Manatee, he noted that there were no cars. Only the dog on a chain, frothing with malevolence. He drove on.

He hadn't been able to dig much further, except to confirm that Tim Cross had been spending a lot of time in the vicinity of Florida Fertilizers. He'd called Bedrosian and told her about his meeting with Solano at DEP, his tour of Florida Fertilizers, and subsequent encounters with Dicky Cahill and Carla Brewer.

"Any idea what was so special about Florida Fertilizers?" she'd asked.

"Not yet. He was supposed to inspect and oversee some of their environmental operations, make sure they got the right permits, did everything by the book, that sort of thing. Nothing unusual. Except for the sinkhole I mentioned."

She hesitated a moment, thinking. "There was something in the news about a sinkhole, out around Orange Blossom a while back. Was that the one you were talking about before?"

He reminded her of the photo and newspaper clipping he'd sent over. The one she'd scoffed at. "Nice of you to remember that. That's the one, all right. It's on private property, industrial land. And Florida Fertilizers, which just happens to own the thirty thousand or so acres around it, won't let me out there."

"Nobody's allowed out in those areas. But I did hear some of the environmental groups were screaming bloody murder for a time. I don't know what about."

"Yeah, well, no one listens to them anymore, anyway."

"That's because people are fed up with government regulation of property rights," she barked.

"Sure. Especially property rights of big chemical companies."

"So?" she said, stiffly. "What did the DEP guy say about it?"

"He didn't think it amounted to anything. But I'm trying to get hold of the hydrologist who went out there. What were the environmentalists so upset about?"

"I don't know, the usual crap. Something about the water. The Floridan Aquifer, or some damn thing."

"You think you could get a search warrant, so we could check it out?"

"I doubt it, it's not my jurisdiction. But I guess I could try."

"You do that." He hung up, wondering.

Returning to the bayou, he packed a cooler—a thermos of sun tea, two tuna sandwiches on seven-grain with alfalfa sprouts, and a small bag of Cape Cod potato chips, his new far-and-away favorite. No beer, this was a workday. He set out for Orange Blossom, hoping the Chevy wouldn't overheat. He always kept a spare five-gallon jug of water in the trunk, with coolant and an extra radiator hose, just in case. He stopped by the Alafia River for a quick late lunch, and then drove on.

But for the clumps of lush laurel oaks and saw palmettos, and the persistent greenness of the grasses (despite this being the dry season) from its approaches, the town of Orange Blossom, Florida, might be mistaken for many a small mining or farming town in Minnesota, or southern New Jersey. It hadn't caught on with the tourists, despite its flowery name. At least in Florida, it seemed, at the time of its settlement, the snowbirds had preferred the coast, and Orlando had not yet been invented. The town of Orange Blossom had been built on flat, low wetlands and marsh grasses giving way to woods and higher prairie terrain. It had hardly grown at all since the first phosphate miners had rolled in, a century before. It featured low scrub brush, pampas grass nibbled at its edges. There were thick groves of pine and oak, sycamore and magnolia, with an occasional farm tractor, or single-track freight train crisscrossing the periphery. In March it held a strawberry festival: faint competition for the much bigger one up in Plant City. The rest of the year, it slept.

Lowell's Chevy was making noises of protest by the time he reached the outskirts of the town. A short distance further a small bungalow proclaimed itself to be the Orange Blossom Tourist Bureau. An optimistic declaration that the ravages of time on the building itself had failed to obliterate. Lowell parked on the tarmac in front, squeezed past a couple of overgrown poinsettias, and went inside. At least the place was air-conditioned. Tourist brochures lined the walls advertising strawberry picking and a water slide somewhere else. A puzzlingly busy woman sat behind a desk as he entered. The air-conditioner blasted away, probably consuming the tourist office's entire monthly budget.

"Good morning," said the woman, surprised by his appearance. Apparently she wasn't expecting visitors. Or at least, not visitors that looked like Tony Lowell.

"Morning," he replied. "I was wondering if you could direct me to the AME Church."

She looked puzzled. "Is that Methodist? We do have a Methodist church, and of course the Baptists, but—"

"AME," repeated Lowell. "African Methodist Episcopal."

She blinked in astonishment. "You mean the Negro church?"

"Bingo!" beamed Lowell. "The very one. Which way is it?"

"Are you one of those Bible salesmen or something?" she queried in wonder.

"Nope. Just visiting. Heard they had a first-rate church supper going, and thought I'd try me some soul food for a change."

She looked at him more closely, and concluded that he was a crackpot. "Make a left at the light, go through town across the tracks. It'll be on the left," she stated, dismissing him.

"Thanks a bunch. Have a nice day."

"You sure you aren't looking for the Methodists?" she called after him, as though trying hard to give him the benefit of the doubt. He went out the door, stopping only long enough to sniff the air. There was a blend of aromas wafting on the breeze: of citrus, and sulphur, and something else he couldn't quite place. Then he recognized what it was—that time-honored southern tradition of searing flesh: a barbecue!

The joint was jumping when Lowell got to the church, which he found with no trouble whatsoever. Inside, a gospel choir was rehearsing for a later performance, but the music resounded throughout the neighborhood. Most of which was black, and impoverished. Some of the houses were in good condition, wooden porches freshly painted, showing a pride of ownership. Others looked ready to blow away in the next hurricane.

Lowell parked around the corner in front of one especially neat bungalow and walked to the church across the wide, scorched meadow that had once been a lawn. A long row of tables had been set up on the walkway in front, laden with all manner of foods: from black-eyed peas to potato salad to corn bread to fudge brownies. Two large barbecues were loaded with ribs and chicken. Lowell took one sniff, and wondered how the whole town could possibly resist descending on the place in droves. Instead, his was the only white face visible.

"Welcome," beamed a stout woman with a large white collar. "Are you here for the festivitives?"

"Indeed I am," said Lowell with a smile. "Where do I buy tickets?"

She looked at him in astonishment. "Tickets? You just make yourself at home, honey. We don't charge to share our bounty."

Lowell thanked her, and helped himself to a paper plate. Two teenage boys smiled at him, and got in line behind him. He was spotted by a large, athletic-looking white-haired man. Ben, he remembered from yesterday at the plant. The man who'd invited him. They shook hands.

"Ben Tompkins. Glad you could make it."

"Tony Lowell." Lowell was in his usual jeans and T-shirt, a far more familiar and comfortable attire for him. There were lots of younger people here, he observed, who were dressed the same way. Others wore more citylike clothes, long baggy shorts, tank tops. But he felt no hostility coming from them.

"Welcome, brother," another man said, a touch of West Indies in his voice. With a dazzling smile he handed Lowell a lemonade. "Make yourself at home." The new man was even larger than Tompkins, and a decade or two younger. Around Lowell's age.

Lowell took the food to one of a row of picnic tables that had been set up on the field that served as a parking lot, aware that he was being observed. Glancing around, he noticed several of the workers from the fertilizer plant watching him. Carla Brewer, the young woman he'd encountered the day before, spotted him, and marched directly over. It seemed to be her style.

"What are you doing here?" she demanded. "This is a church supper, and you got no right harassing these people when—"

"It's all right, Carla," said a soft voice behind him. Lowell turned, and recognized the man he'd just met. "I apologize for not introducing myself before, mon," he said, offering his hand. "I'm Yasha Dromes. I'm one of the people. I gather you met Miss Brewer and Benjy."

Carla frowned and grudgingly extended her hand. "I wish I knew this really was a social call, but white folks don't pay black folks too many social calls, I ever knew of."

"You're right," nodded Lowell. "She's right," he confirmed, to Yasha. "This isn't a social call, although I'm grateful for your hospitality, and these ribs, by the way, are outstanding."

"Thank you," beamed Dromes. "I created the recipe myself. And you can't have it," he added with a glint in his eye.

"I'd know better than to ask, but thanks." Lowell turned back to Carla Brewer, who was waiting expectantly. "All right. I need to find out what Tim Cross's association was with Florida Fertilizers, and with this community. And what was so important about this meeting he was headed for at Plant City."

"You came to a church supper to learn all that?" She was almost amused.

"That plus the food and music. I love gospel music. In my next life, I want to be a gospel singer. Also, I've been trying to locate a woman he knew, by the name of Cecilia—" It was at that very moment that he saw her coming across the parking lot, a young girl skipping along in front of her. The girl was light skinned, he noticed.

"Speak of the devil in a blue dress!" breathed Carla, following his gaze. Cecilia was indeed wearing a short blue dress. She looked as though she should be at a dance club, not a church supper. The little girl looked cute. She seemed inhibited somehow, though. Her movements were slow for a child. Almost cautious. Her mother seemed to hover over her. There was a man with them. Black, with light skin. Big, athletic, head shaved, and looking for trouble. Lenny, the boyfriend, figured Lowell.

"Uh-oh," said Carla Brewer. "Here comes trouble with a capital *T*."

Lowell looked again at Cecilia and back at Carla. There was something between them, he felt. Carla wasn't just talking about the boyfriend when she'd said that. The two women wouldn't look at each other. The man, now holding Cecilia's arm tightly enough to hurt her, bristled with power, and was cock-sure of himself. What he was, which Lowell instantly recognized, was dangerous. A strange pair (plus child) for a church supper.

The couple seemed to sense it, too. Lowell could tell the man didn't belong. But then he'd already guessed who he was. Cecilia seemed anxious, as though here in hopes of finding salvation. The man was a fish out of water. A very foul, very poisonous, very large, and very angry fish.

"Welcome to our church," said a tall man, whom Lowell had noticed earlier, offering them each a plateful of food. The girl accepted, but the boyfriend brushed the plate aside. He had just spotted Lowell, and recognized him at once. He squeezed Cecilia's arm. "Who that?" He nodded in Lowell's direction. "He that honky come over last night. Maybe the night before. What he after?"

"I dunno."

He squeezed harder. "He after your pussy, ho'? You sellin' behind my back?"

"I'm not sellin' to nobody. 'Cept to you."

He slapped her, in plain sight of everyone, as though it were the most natural thing in the world. As though he had every God-given right. Like it was spelled out in the Bible, not to mention the Koran. "I don't pay you, ho'."

She blinked back tears and met his gaze. Lowell came over. Dromes joined him.

"Excuse me. But that's no way to treat a lady, young man," said the tall man, joining them before Dromes or Lowell could say or do anything. Bless his naive soul, Lowell thought grimly. Maybe he even knows what he's doing. That was when, for the first time, Lowell noticed the collar. The man's a cleric, he realized in sudden embarrassment.

The other man, the boyfriend, however, was accustomed to confrontation. "Step aside, old man," he snapped into the clergyman's face, "and mind your own business." At which point in time Lowell stepped forward.

"Excuse me," he said. "We haven't met, but my name is Lowell. Tony Lowell. I'm a private investigator, and I've been asked to come here, on behalf of a brother on the East Coast. Maybe we could talk."

"What about?" demanded the boyfriend.

Lowell met the man's gaze. "A man named Tim Cross. I think your lady friend here knows him. Or rather, knew him."

Smith took this as a gauntlet. He reached out and seized Lowell by the wrist. "My name Smith. Leonard T. And I'm gonna break your arm," he said. "Followed by your face."

Lowell didn't reply. Instead, he simply twisted his forearm outward, against the man's thumbs. The thumbs, Lowell knew, happened to be just about the weakest part of the body. A little old lady could break a hold like that, without even practicing, if she knew how. Immediately, his hands were free, hanging loose.

A startled Leonard Smith looked at Lowell's hands, as though they were snakes he'd hallucinated on an acid trip. He didn't have any guns with him. He didn't think he'd need them at a lousy church barbecue. He backed off. Smith had been ready to take the dude down, in front of all these church assholes, just to show them who was really in charge. Instead, the man fuckin' flicks free of the grasp of the toughest dude this side of the Everglades, and talks to him like they were friends or business associates or something. It didn't figure.

"You dissin' me?" he demanded.

"I don't think so. Depends what that means, though, exactly," said Lowell with a thoughtful smile. Dromes, at his side, loved it, and slapped his thigh with a delighted laugh, which served to confuse Smith even more.

"I was just gonna suggest," said Dromes, "that y'all have some chicken and a lemonade, and sit down, and all of us get acquainted."

Carla had heard all this, and was even more taken aback than Smith. She gripped Lowell by the upper arm and tugged. "Could we talk a minute?" she whispered. Lowell beamed at her and gently removed her hand.

"Excuse me a sec'," he said to Smith and company, with a quick glance at Cecilia. Again, the girl looks terrified, he thought. He kept her in his peripheral vision as he turned back to Carla. He wanted his camera, but it was in the car.

"Over here." She literally dragged him away. "What are you trying to do, turn a peaceful church thing into the OK Corral?"

"Not at all, I just wanted to ask some questions."

"Some people you don't ask."

"How about you?"

The tall preacher man looked in their direction. Obviously the pastor for the church. Pretty hip for backwoods Florida, he thought. But then he'd only experienced white backwoods Florida, mostly. Or redneck cracker backwoods Florida. This might be an entirely different backwoods. Like the misty mythical isle of Avalon—maybe this was like some totally different dimension.

"Go ahead. Ask," Carla was saying to him.

"Good. Thank you." Lowell brought himself back to the moment, front and center. "What I am trying to do," he explained, "is find out what happened to Timothy Cross. My intention is to ask that dude, and more directly, Ms. Potter, the same question. They seemed to have had some involvement with him in some way."

"He won't let you near her."

"I've noticed."

She looked nervous again. "She and Tim were involved. I can't tell you more than that. She's been involved with a lot of men." She said it contemptuously. The righteous church lady side of her coming out, he decided.

"She doing street trade?"

"No. She's just popular. She's a beautiful woman, look at her. Men around here, like most places, like to have a beau-

96

tiful woman on their arm. Especially under their control, like that SOB."

She's educated, he thought. "How do you know them? They're not from Orange Blossom."

"They both work at the same place we all do."

"How'd they meet? Her and Cross?" he asked.

Again her reaction was surprising in its intensity. "How does anyone meet? On the job, probably. Same as her and Smith."

"What does Smith do?"

"Drives trucks. Works part-time for Cahill, in Water Reclamation." She glanced at Smith as she spoke. He was staring straight at them. He seemed to make a decision, and started toward them. Cecilia tried to grab his arm, and he brushed her off. "Speaking of which," Carla added, watching the big man's approach.

"You," said Smith, pointing accusingly at Lowell. "What you want with my woman?"

"Just some questions regarding her employment," said Lowell smoothly. "My present employer wanted to know how things were going there, in regards to civil rights, equal opportunity, that sort of thing."

"Civil rights?" Smith stared, incredulous.

"Have you ever been discriminated against, on the job, on the basis of race, creed, or color?"

"You got to be shittin' me, man," growled Smith.

"With your permission, I'd like to ask your lady friend the same question. I understand she wasn't given maternity leave by her employer, which is a breach of federal guidelines in regards to—"

"Jesus Christ," muttered Smith, and turned around, not noticing Carla's puzzled look. "Ceecee! Get your a—get your act over here, and talk to the man. He's from Wash'-

nin. Lookin' after your welfare or some sh—somethin'."
Back to Lowell. "What you say your name was?"

"Tony Lowell."

Smith threw up his hands and stalked away with one suspicious glance back. Lowell sighed a secret sigh of relief, and turned his best smile on Cecilia. He offered his hand.

"Ms. Potter, I'm so glad to meet you," he said. "Again," he added, lowering his voice. "Is this your daughter?"

She frowned suspiciously. "You was at the house, right?"

He nodded.

"You from child welfare?"

"Not at all." He glanced at Smith, now at the food tables, busy piling prodigious amounts of food onto a paper plate. He lowered his voice. "I'm working for a man named Ernie Larson, from 'cross state. A brother, and friend of my family for a long time. Tim Cross was his nephew."

Her eyes widened, and her soft, pink mouth opened and closed. "What happened to Tim?" she demanded immediately.

"He was killed. About a week ago. The police think you know something about it." He glanced at Smith, who was now watching them. "Or maybe he does."

She looked at him, horrified. She put her hands to her face. "So it's true? Timmy's dead?" she murmured, barely a whisper.

Lowell nodded. "I'm sorry. I knew—know the family."

She glanced furtively in Smith's direction, trying to pull herself together. "Lenny a bad man. He could hurt somebody, he wanted to." She looked at Lowell as she spoke. "They think he did it?"

"They don't know. What do you think?"

"It's possible. Lenny found out about Tim and me the day he disappeared."

"Not good timing."

"Timmy was with me at the clinic most of that day. Took off from work and everything."

"The whole day? What about the night?"

"I don't know. But Lenny didn't come home, I know that."

"When can we talk? Have coffee, meet me somewhere?" he asked, urgently. Smith was coming back. Apparently his tolerance for freedom of speech on the part of his woman had reached its limit. Smith looked as though he hadn't heard about the Constitution. Women's rights he'd probably heard about, and laughed his ass off, Lowell was thinking. A woman was a hole to him. Personal property, good for pussy, occasional domestic services, and little else. What rights?

"The medical center," she whispered. "I'll be there this time. He won't go there. It's for my daughter," she added defensively. "He thinks he's too important for that stuff. It's where I used to meet Tim. In the morning."

"You said that before," he objected as she turned to go. She just shrugged. It was as much of an answer as she could give him. She looked back as they left. There was a different look in her eye altogether. "Watch out for her," she whispered, nodding toward Carla. Then she was gone.

"I wonder what they came here for," remarked Carla, rejoining him as he watched the white Firebird drive away with a squeal of rubber. Lowell thought he knew. Cecilia was determined, somehow, to maintain a place in this community against all odds. She'd managed, at great personal risk, to come, even drag her boyfriend along, bully that he was. The woman has strength, Lowell thought in admiration. But then, she was a single mother. She had to be strong.

Carla had one bit of information to add, after Smith and Company left. "Tim was always pushing for something, he had this righteous side a lot of people found pretty irritating. Like he was always on some kind of crusade."

And you're not? he thought. "You don't know what it was about?" he probed.

She frowned. "Meaning what?"

"You ever hear any rumors, anything about a sinkhole?"

He could tell that she had. And that she didn't want to talk about it. "Sinkholes happen all the time in Florida. The soil is sandy, and there's a lot of water underneath. It ain't no big deal."

That was pretty much what Solano had said.

"What if he thought it was. This particular one?"

"We don't know nothin' about that," she said with finality, and turned away. She'd just handed him the company line.

Lowell noticed that Dromes was listening from nearby. Carefully, it appeared. He looked concerned. Edging closer, he glanced right and left. "They not supposed to discuss company business with outsiders," he said in a low voice. "That young fella, Cross, he was probin' about things weren't his business."

"Maybe it was his business," Lowell said.

Carla turned back one more time, as though determined to end the conversation. "Look, mister. These are poor people. Poor black people. They got mouths to feed, souls to save, their own skins to watch out for. Anything they ever had, you white folks managed to take away from them. Now they got a piece of this town, a livelihood, their own church, their own members on the town council, a voice in government for the first time ever. They got steady jobs, many of them for the first time ever. They getting their children fed, even educated. They got two members on the Board of Education. They hired two black teachers, just this year, at the school."

"That's good," said Lowell, and meant it. "But could we get back to Tim Cross a second? He's not resting in peace yet. He was a good kid. A promising citizen with a fine education. Somebody blew him away for a bad reason. And either it had to do with his work, or it had to do with his personal life."

"He was seeing *her*," was Carla's reply, nodding in the direction of Cecilia's departure. She walked away. A hand tapped Lowell on the shoulder. He turned. The ever-present Dromes, offering him another plate of food.

"Eat something. The music is about to begin." Indeed, the gospel choir was filing out of the church. They lined up on the portico, and even a few of the local whites began to appear on the fringes of the block. They knew what was coming.

Pastor Farnsworth joined them, just another singer. The leader was a short, middle-aged black woman who could have passed for Aretha Franklin. She raised her hands.

"Let us pray, for a moment, for our lost young shepherd, Brother Tim." There was a groundswell of murmuring and "Amens," then a moment of silence. Then they began to sing: "Go Tell It on the Mountain." It was only then, while relishing what he'd really come for, that it dawned on Lowell what this was all about. It was a wake of sorts. Despite Bedrosian's wishes, word had gotten out. This was a memorial for the strange young man who'd appeared among these good people for a few short months and become one of their own. Timothy Cross, may his soul rest in peace, thought Lowell. He still didn't know the first thing about him. But it seemed that a lot of people, fine people, had cared about him. Cecilia, for one, who'd even risked the wrath of her boyfriend to make an appearance. It was going to be interesting to hear what she had to say about Tim Cross.

9

The Manatee County Women's Health Center occupied one of the larger buildings in Manatee City—a crumbling four-story stucco edifice in the central government district, painted a faded, peeling yellow. The parking lot smelled of urine. Lowell's Chevy fit right in with the other junkers in the lot. He parked, negotiated his way around a couple of homeless men, and went inside.

The room was packed, mostly single mothers with screaming children. Most were black or brown, but there were a fair number of whites as well. Some looked angry and frustrated, others seemed resigned to having to once again put up with endless waiting, and bureaucratic harassment. The workers seemed not so much callous as numb: overburdened beyond belief trying to help people who hated having to be helped, with ever-diminishing resources at their disposal.

The din was deafening. He thought about Tim Cross, the activist. This would have been a good place to hold a conversation if one didn't want to be overheard. The noise would make a perfect cover, and there is nowhere more anonymous than a medical clinic.

Cecilia was there, just as she'd promised, her little girl,

Natasha, with her. Natasha was dressed in clean clothes of good quality: pink shorts and a white halter top. Cecilia was wearing a simple summer dress, and although her face looked ravaged, she still looked ravishing.

"Hello," said Lowell, taking an adjoining seat. She seemed genuinely surprised to see him. "Glad you could make it," he said.

"It ain't like I got any choice, my little girl needs medical."

So do you, thought Lowell, noting the dark circles under her eyes, the bruises visible around her neck and shoulders. She seemed frail and damaged. "I looked for you here yesterday morning. What happened?"

"Sorry about that," she apologized. "I had to work that day, or Mr. Cahill said he'd fire me."

"You come here regularly, though?"

"Most days I can get free. We come here for pediatrics, and stuff like that." She sounded evasive. Lowell wondered what kind of stuff. "Tim used to bring us. He was very nice to my daughter. Tasha," she said, turning to her daughter. "This is Mr.—?"

"Lowell," finished Lowell. "Tony Lowell." He smiled at the girl, who hid her face in her mother's lap. "Nice to meet you." Lowell didn't know too much about little girls, he realized. He'd missed the entire upbringing of his own daughter, now grown up.

"Are you a doctor?" asked Natasha, peeking up at him after a bit.

"Nope." He glanced right and left furtively. "I'm a detective."

"What's that?" she wanted to know.

"Somebody who does puzzles."

"Cool!" she shouted. "Mommy, he does puzzles!"

Cecilia smiled at him. There were some tables set up in the back of the room with toys, blocks, and coloring materials.

"Tasha, you go back there and color for a while, I have to talk to the man a few minutes," she instructed.

"You mean like you always did with Tim?"

"That's right, sweetie. But be careful," she added.

Tasha obeyed, and Cecilia turned her attention to Lowell. Nice-looking man, she thought. Wonder if he's married. She didn't want to mess with married men anymore; bad enough getting in this mess with Lenny. Maybe this guy could help her get out of it, though. She hoped so. That had been in the back of her mind when she'd agreed to meet with him. Which is probably why Lenny had been so furious at her this morning. Her bruises still ached some, though she was used to it by now.

"She's a great kid," observed Lowell.

"She has somethin' wrong. They don't know what," Cecilia confided, just the slightest tremble in her voice.

He knew better than to ask for specifics. She'd tell him if and when she wanted to. Which was fine by him. "She's beautiful. And smart," he said.

"I know. But her bones are weak. They break. She gets calcium and stuff. But we can't afford no tests or nothin', without insurance. The company don't pay for insurance. I have to watch her all the time."

Lowell watched the child play. Fragile bones were the last thing she needed, living with a man like Leonard Smith, he thought. "I'm sorry to hear that," he said.

"Ain't nothin' you can do. Anyways, it ain't your fault. The reverend says God just made her special, is all. More delicate, like a flower. Tim understood that. He was so nice to her." Again her lip trembled, hinting at feelings that lurked just below the surface, yearning to pour out.

"Can you tell me about Tim, and your relationship with him?"

Her guard went up again, right away. "We just acquaintances," she said. "We never went out or nothin'. But he was nice. And real good with my daughter. We would talk about stuff."

"What kind of stuff?"

"All kind of stuff. About love, and kids. Relationships, family, what he saw for the future. He wanted to make things better for us, but I don't think he had much notion how to go about it, except with his 'vironment work. He knew a lot, 'cause he went to college."

"Was he in love with you?"

She looked at him sideways. "I don't know. Maybe."

"And you. Were you in love with him?"

She looked at the floor, then directly at him. "Not the same way. I don't know what I felt. I felt a lot of things. Sometimes I felt like I was in love. Other times not. He was different. From anybody else. I wasn't used to men bein' like him. Gentle, like. And smart. Lenny called him my girlfriend."

Lowell was getting to dislike Leonard Smith more and more each passing moment. There wasn't much to like. So what did this lovely young woman see in him? He couldn't ask her, of course. The answers would be vague, or glib: "Oh, he takes care of me good, mostly. He just gets mean sometimes." Implying: "I can take it, it's the way things are."

"Did Tim ever talk to you about his work?"

"No, he just come to the plant once and a while, but he didn't work there none. Lenny, he work there part-time. As a driver."

"Did Tim ever have any run-ins with a man named Cahill?"

Her eyes widened. "Dicky Cahill? Why? What'd he say?"

"Didn't say anything. I was just wondering."

"Cahill is Lenny's boss. Lenny my boyfriend," she added, lowering her eyes. "I don't think either of them was too crazy about Timmy. Lenny's jealous of anybody even looks at me; as for Mr. Cahill—" She shuddered visibly. "He a bad man." She glanced at Natasha, busy scribbling in the back of the room, as she spoke. Which made Lowell wonder. About how many children had to live like this. And how many women. And why they did, and how come they couldn't, or wouldn't, get out.

"Bad how?"

"Just—bad." She didn't want to talk about Cahill anymore.

"Can you tell me if Tim was doing anything that might have gotten him in trouble with Cahill? I know he was with the state DEP. But do you know of any specifics? Any particular problems, anything that might have caused a stir at the plant? Problems about a sinkhole, anything like that?"

She thought for a while. "He did mention that sinkhole. But he been kind of sick, lately. It was botherin' him."

"What was?"

"I don't know. But he was feelin' bad. I think he was goin' to that meetin', up at Plant City, to complain about somethin'," she said. "Somethin' about toothpaste."

"Toothpaste?"

"Somethin' like that. I don't know nothin' about it, he didn't talk to me much about that."

Tom Freeman at Florida Fertilizers had mentioned toothpaste. The active ingredient of which was fluoride, a by-product of phosphate processing. Lowell wondered how that could tie in with a remote sinkhole. Or did it? Clearly something going on at Florida Fertilizers had troubled Tim Cross. Maybe enough to cost him his life. But toothpaste?

"If you don't mind my asking, why did he spend so much time with you? I mean, you got a boyfriend and everything, so—"

She looked nervous, and slightly secretive. "What you say your name was again, mister? I'm sorry, I'm bad with names."

"No problem. It's Lowell. Tony Lowell."

"Well, Tony Lowell. All right. So he was sweet on me. Ain't you never been sweet on a woman who had mixed feelin's?"

He had. Yes, indeed, alas, hallelujah, heaven help him, he had. But he chose not to interrupt.

"It was kinda nice," she went on. "A good-lookin', educated boy like that takin' so much interest in a po' girl like me. I guess he hoped he could one day get me away from Lenny, some way."

"How did you feel about that?"

She looked down. "I thought about it plenty. Lenny'd never let me go, though."

"You have no say in the matter?"

She looked at him through half-closed eyes that revealed a sorrow and wisdom far beyond her years, perhaps some kind of shared knowledge that all women have, passed on genetically or by some more profound means, from one generation to the next, since the beginning of time.

"It don't work like that," she said.

Lowell grabbed a quick lunch of a grouper sandwich and Molson's at the Red Top Café in Manatee City. He'd practically given up on getting Kirin in restaurants anymore. All there was now was Budweiser, Miller's, and Molson's. Maybe a Heineken now and then. No more obscure product brands, no more quaint downtowns or one-of-a-kind shops, no place to get centered, no more hometowns because they'd all be basically identical: the same old big-name corporate franchises in every town.

Lowell called Bedrosian from the pay phone in the parking lot.

"I heard you've been out slumming," she said.

"Not at all. I've been going to church, escorting mothers and children, and doing some consciousness raising. It's all very enlightening. I'd recommend it."

"Yeah. I heard the music was good, too."

"Okay. That, too." He wondered who her sources were. She seemed to be getting around some, herself.

"One thing I'm curious about. Did you get a copy of the coroner's report yet?" he asked.

"Only the preliminary report," she snapped. "Why?"

"Do you know if they ever ran any toxicology tests, that sort of thing?"

"Why should they? The man had a bullet in his head, Lowell. You don't need to be a rocket scientist to figure out the cause of death."

"They've established time of death?"

"Approximately. Some time around March tenth. You have to remember, the body was already beginning to decompose when they found it. Talk to forensics, you want details. What's this about toxicology?"

"Just an idea. I'll tell you later. I want to have a talk with somebody I met at Florida Fertilizers, first. And I'm still trying to get a hold of that hydrologist Solano mentioned."

"Maybe it's time you run up to Plant City, while you're at it, and pay a visit to Mr. Largent, at International Phosphates."

Lowell had been intending to do that. But he hated being reminded.

"And do what? Ask him if by any chance he killed Tim Cross?"

"Well, I have a bit of news for you. For your information, International Phosphates is the parent company of Florida Fertilizers."

Lowell wasn't surprised. "I figured as much. There had to be a connection."

"Oh, really?" she said. She sounded miffed. "I only found out because Sergeant Baker owns some stock."

"But don't you see? That's where the meeting was being held that night, that Tim Cross was going to."

"I'm aware of that. That's why I'd like you to go talk to them."

Suddenly he was filled with resentment. How come he was the one running all the errands? What was she doing, for Chrissake? Well, she'd just have to wait, he had his own agenda.

"I think I'd like to take another run up to Orange Blossom before hitting Plant City, if that's all right with you," he told her. "And by the way, I expect reimbursement for all this gas and mileage."

"Yeah, fine. But don't hit Plant City too hard just yet, all right?"

"Meaning what?" he demanded, his annoyance growing.

"Just don't stir up any hornets' nests. The Reds play up there, and they hate public controversies."

He couldn't believe it. "Let me get this straight. You want me to help you investigate this murder, but only so long as I don't upset the Cincinnati Reds?"

"Let's put it this way. The chief is a closet Reds fan. He has a season ticket for all the games up there. Matter of fact, he went up there today. So more to the point is, don't do anything to get the chief upset."

"God forbid. So why don't you have *him* check this out, while he's up there?"

"Lowell, you really can be amusing sometimes."

"Anyway, Sturbridge is from Atlanta! Why isn't he backing the Braves?"

"He hates that Turner guy, ever since he married that peacenik person."

"The chief married a peacenik person?"

"Very funny. Just take my advice, Lowell."

He decided to change the subject. "So what angle are you working on?"

"Not that it's any of your business. But for the moment, we're interested in that colored woman—"

"You mean African-American."

"Whatever. The one who works for Florida Fertilizers."

"You talking about Carla Brewer?" asked Lowell. It was an interesting angle. She had taken a rather overly righteous attitude with him during their two encounters.

"Apparently she and this Cross fella had a blowup or two over his meddling at the plant. Something about undercutting equal opportunity, or threatening jobs, or something. I'm not saying any names, and you let me handle her," insisted Bedrosian. "You have a way of pissing people off."

Lowell hung up, annoyed, choosing not to tell her about his meeting with Cecilia Potter, or the boyfriend. He checked his Timex: two o'clock. Plenty of time to get to Plant City. He intended to stop at Orange Blossom first, though, and have another conversation with Dicky Cahill. He dialed directory assistance for Orange Blossom, and asked if there was a listing for a Richard or Dick Cahill. There was, on Poinsettia Road. He wrote down the information alongside the number for Florida Fertilizers in his tattered notebook. He dialed the plant offices.

"Mrs. Jessup, please, in Personnel—no, wait. Could you connect me to one of your foremen?"

"Which department, sir?"

"Wastewater Disposal."

"Which foreman, sir?"

"That would be Dicky Cahill."

"He has a mobile phone. Let me check for you."

There was a series of rings, and the switchboard operator came back on. "Sorry, sir. Mr. Cahill is not in today. Would you care to leave a message?"

"No, that's all right. Do you know if he's home?"

"I don't think so. I think I heard something about a meeting in Plant City."

Plant City again. It was getting to be high time to visit this popular place, Lowell decided. First, Tim Cross, who never made it. Then Chief Sturbridge of the Manatee City Police, and now Dicky Cahill of Florida Fertilizers. Next thing, Newt Gingrich would be dropping by. He'd better get there and look around while he could still find a parking space.

On a whim, he hung up and walked over to a newspaper box by the restaurant entrance. Putting in a quarter, he got out the last copy of the *Manatee Record* and yanked out the sports section. Sure enough, Reds versus Marlins, at the Plant City Stadium. Lowell hadn't been to a baseball game since the Senators still played in Washington. Maybe it was high time to go, he decided. Should be a fun one. The locals would be out in droves to root against the Marlins, ever since their owners were implicated in the prevention of a local franchise for Tampa-St. Pete.

Gassing up the Chevy, he headed north on 301, and sped east onto Route 62, not even slowing down this time for Parrish. Hopefully, if he got ticketed, Bedrosian would handle it. Maybe. Maybe Michelle Pfeiffer would drop in on him one night, to fuck his brains out. Maybe he'd better slow down, he decided. The roads being good, and traffic nonexistent, however, he got to Orange Blossom by midafternoon, not even slowing as he passed the plant. He stopped by the Tourist Bureau once more. The woman behind the desk remembered him, and feared the worst. He smiled at her, picked up a map of the town showing all the high spots, like where the Burger King was located, and walked out.

Poinsettia Road was on the far side of the town, a typical Florida suburban tract of carbon-copy ranch houses in pastel colors, each on a little half acre despite virtually miles of vacant land all around, each with an attached two-car garage with more square footage than the entire living space, each with three small bedrooms and two baths with linoleum tiling, and a thoroughly up-to-date all-electric kitchen courtesy of a major 1950s TV marketing campaign by Ronald Reagan on behalf of the General Electric Company. The resulting utility bills were typically astronomical. The Cahill residence had a collection of children's toys and bicycles scattered on the lawn, and a battered maroon station wagon of dubious manufacture: its emblems long since torn, ripped, or bashed off. Lowell turned into the drive, set the brake, and got out.

The woman who answered the door, given a makeover and fresh start in life, might be very attractive. In her midthirties, she had long sandy blond hair tied back in a bun, a ruddy complexion from too much sun (probably from outdoor housework or child care, rather than sunbathing) and a worn-out look about her.

"Can I help you?" she asked, a small boy clinging to her knee.

"Afternoon, ma'am. I'm from Swiftmud. We're doing a survey on water quality, and wonder if you would mind answering a few questions." Swiftmud was the government agency which supposedly governed and protected the water supplies for the entire region.

She looked him over, and opened the door a little wider.

"Sure," she said, "C'mon in. Don't mind the mess, I got kids all over the place, can't hardly keep up with 'em these days."

"I know what you mean," said Lowell, who didn't.

"Can I get you some coffee?"

"Wouldn't mind, if it's no trouble," said Lowell. He could use a shot of caffeine, all the driving he was doing lately. He wished he could be out on his boat with a tall cold Kirin waiting for him when he landed. But work was work. Even as-of-yet unpaid work.

He followed her into the house, noting the shabbiness, the tawdry Kmart furniture, the mass-produced art, and total lack of any printed matter whatsoever—not even children's books. There were several children about, all small, all with faces so smudged they were (to him) indistinguishable. He suspected Dicky Cahill spent as little time here as possible. And put as little investment into the place—and its inhabitants (presumably his family)—as he could get away with.

"Your husband at work?" he asked casually.

"You gotta be kiddin' me. He ditches out every chance he gets. He's up at Plant City now with the boys watchin' the Reds. After that he'll probably go for about ten six-packs, and roll in here 'round midnight to complain about how come dinner's cold." She grinned at her predicament, and Lowell liked her at once. He also felt bad for her. He felt the beginnings of an attraction to her, based on a deep-seated preference for women who were (like himself) flawed. Against his better instincts, he decided to play along, do the dance, and see what happened.

"I really don't want to be a bother," he said. "It's just a couple of questions. I know you're busy with the kids and all."

"Nah, they pretty much look after themselves. Susie, she's eight, watches after Katie, and she keeps Danny in tow. It's no problem." She led him into the kitchen, which was large enough to accommodate a beige Formica table, and four beige vinyl-backed chairs, plus a wooden high chair. Presumably for Danny, who appeared to be around three. Lowell thought of Bedrosian. Also a mother. Hard to figure. This one, he decided, deserved a break today. It had to be hard, living with someone like Dicky Cahill. He didn't notice any bruises, at least. Which probably made her a rarity on the rural southern domestic frontier. He gave her his best smile, the one he saved up for when he really needed it.

She glanced up, caught the look, and blushed. Turning quickly to the cupboards, she reached up and got down her two best cups and saucers: it was drugstore china. But it was *old* drugstore china.

"I got Folgers crystals, or I could make some fresh, I got some Maxwell House in the cupboard." She nodded toward one of the corners: a perilous path strewn with various imitation lethal weapons. Danny ran through, brandishing one.

"Pow, pow! Yak yak yak yak!" he went, and ran off. Hit and run.

"Daniel, you stop that, no shooting at people!"

"Daddy lets me!" shouted the boy from the next room, still blasting an endless wave of villains assaulting his imaginary fortress.

"Folgers will be fine," said Lowell, watching the boy. In training for life as a future redneck, he reckoned. Of course, a man like Dicky Cahill probably couldn't wait to arm his son to the teeth, if not his daughters, with the real McCoy.

Protection against the "nigger invasion," or something. Start another civil war, against "uppities" or "yuppies" or Yankees. Somebody, anybody. Anybody who was different.

Lowell felt her looking at him. He saw her eyes, and could tell she was wondering at his thoughts, what he was thinking. He smiled again. "Actually, I like honey and milk. But not a lot of people are into honey, so if it's just sugar that's fine. As for the milk, anything that comes from cows, goats, or sheep will do."

"I got honey," she said. She had to reach for a high shelf for it, and her lumpy work shirt rose up, revealing a slim waist and firm hips. Somehow, she had managed to keep in shape, despite the drudgery of her life, despite having brought three children into the world. Cecilia, he realized, was another mother who still looked great. Why was it that most men had two entirely different images of women, before and after marriage? Single, they were supposed to be babes, svelte, narrow waist, long luscious legs, no cellulite, and huge firm tits. Married, they immediately became busy, tired, sexless, and sagging. Which perception served in husbands' minds to justify their perfidious ways.

"Great," he said.

"Got milk, too. Two percent all right?"

"Perfect."

Now she smiled for him. Her teeth were perfect.

"Microwave all right? I usually use it when I'm in a rush, which I always am," she said. He felt a swelling in his groin.

She sensed it as she brought him the cup. One of the girls looked in. The older one.

"Mommy, Katie kicked me," she whined.

"You hush up and deal with it yourself. You tell her not to do that!" scolded the mother.

"My name's Tony Lowell, by the way," said Tony, extending his hand. He always felt awkward about that, shaking hands with women. But it seemed right nowadays, so he didn't hesitate.

She shook his hand and smiled again.

"Briana. Briana Cook Cahill," she said.

He got that. She was giving him her original name along with her married name on purpose. A declaration, of sorts.

"So what were those questions you had, Mr. Lowell?"

"Tony." He took a sip, and she watched him.

"Tony," she repeated, trying it out. "You Italian or somethin'?"

The question surprised him. Her tone had an edge of prejudice to it. He cooled down some. "Look, Mrs. Cahill—"

"Briana." She smiled.

"Briana. Truth is, I don't work for Swiftmud. I'm a private investigator. I am interested in the ground water, though. And your husband's work."

She, too, cooled considerably, and drew away slightly. "He don't talk much about his work," she said. "And I don't appreciate your lyin' to me, mister. I got children in here, you could be anybody."

"I'm sorry," he said, and offered her his card, with Detective Lena Bedrosian's along with it. "I am on a case that required some discretion, and I apologize for trying to mislead you. But please understand, your husband is under investigation right now—he's not a suspect just yet, mind you, I'm not trying to implicate him—"

"Implicate all you want, he's a son of a bitch!" she exclaimed, startling him. "It'd serve him right, he done anything wrong. Has he?" She looked at him, wanting to trust him, wanting to get back where they had been.

"I don't know. I want to find out more about his connec-

116

tion to a young black man who may have had some interaction with him."

"You mean, like a run-in?"

"Right."

"Tony, there isn't hardly a man—or a woman, for that matter, black, white, or what have you—who hasn't had at least one run-in with Dicky Cahill. He's an asshole—you get out of here, honey!" she shouted suddenly to the same little girl who'd been peeking in. "And I'm sorry that I was ever such an airhead to marry the man, let alone even get involved with him."

"I guess people see things differently, when they're in love," said Lowell gently.

"I guess. Or maybe some of us country girls, the way we're raised, are in such a hurry to wear that ring, we don't look too close at who's puttin' it on our finger. We're all afraid to be old maids, worse than anything. Like this"—she gestured vaguely at her home environs—"is supposed to be better. I'm teachin' my daughters to be independent, not in such a rush, and never, never marry a man who drinks more than one beer before dinner."

That leaves me out, thought Lowell.

"Coffee all right?" she asked.

"Fine. Anyway, I'm sorry to have bothered you, I should probably go on up to Plant City and talk to the people up there—" He started to rise from his seat.

She quickly refilled his cup. "Dicky never talks too much at home, hell, he hardly ever comes home at all, but I have heard him on the phone a few times, talkin' to his bosses—"

"You know who that would be?"

"The Division Manager, I guess. But there was somebody up at Plant City—I'm tryin' to remember who—anyways, he was gettin' all worked up about somethin'—"

117

"You can't remember a name?"

She thought a moment. "No, it's just that every time he goes up to Plant City, he comes home drunk, and flush with cash—none of which me and the kids ever see again, mind you."

Lowell thought about that. "Did you ever hear him mention a young black guy, name of Timothy Cross, in any way?"

She gazed past him, out the window, listening as a car passed by. "I did hear him mentioned, I think. He was the one who was botherin' them, about the reclamation plans or something."

"You think there was anything to it?"

"Yeah. I think Dicky and this guy, whoever he is, were tryin' to do something illegal. Or wrong somehow, with the pond water. He seemed real edgy about it. Maybe the company is pressurin' him, I don't know, it ain't like he's got any virtue or nothin'. Then this sinkhole thing happened, and all hell broke loose."

Lowell sat up and paid attention. "What can you tell me about that?"

"I don't know too much. They were all pretty hush-hush about it. I asked him a couple of times and he blew up. But I think it messed up these big plans they had." She almost spat. "Big plans. Like as not didn't include me, anyway, the asshole."

She sounded like her husband was the grand champion all-time loser, which he probably was. That didn't mean she wouldn't forgive him his trespasses come tomorrow. She probably would. He had to be careful.

"You think he could be taking money? From this mystery guy, or even the company, on the side, maybe?"

He was thinking about the car. The shiny new T-bird,

118

that even Mrs. Jessup couldn't afford. She was thinking about it, too, he could tell.

"It's possible," she admitted. "Of course he's always complainin' he's broke, so he can't even feed and clothe his own children properly, but he can buy himself a brand-new car now, can't he?" She sounded bitter. She has a right, he thought.

"Plus," she added after a moment, "there's all that child support money goin' out. I mean, look, everybody's got a past and I can understand that, but this happened since our marriage, and that money is half mine. It isn't like she's ever even going to make it in our society, she's just a—"

Lowell looked up. "What?" he asked.

"Nothin'." She looked away. "I shouldn't say that. It isn't her fault."

There was something about her tone that made Lowell want to probe, but he decided against it. It wasn't pertinent to the subject at hand, and basically was none of his business.

"So, he pays child support, plus car payments, plus presumably he does provide you and the little ones with something—?"

"Precious damn little," she snorted.

"I'm not trying to defend the man, believe me. I'm just trying to get a sense of how much is coming in, going out."

"All right, he makes twenty-eight thousand, more or less, at the plant. So he tells me. Not bad, not great. I get the household account, about six hundred a month, plus an allowance, a hundred a week, so that adds up. He pays the mortgage, about a thousand. The other little girl he pays out for is another four hundred. A lot for a—never mind. He keeps another fifteen hundred for taxes or somethin', beer money, car payments, I guess. Anyways, that's about two thousand five hundred a month. It ain't like he's rich."

"You didn't have to tell me your financial history," said Lowell. "But it does leave the question open. Conceivably he could do it on his income, especially if he doesn't pay the full withholding. He might be declaring twelve dependents or something, it's done all the time. So he spends his full income, every dollar in, every dollar out. Or maybe he's got a little private account somewhere. Like Barbados."

"He ain't that smart." She was smiling again. He wasn't sure if it was his imagination, but he could swear now that one of the buttons on her blouse had come undone. He could see a curve of breast underneath for just a moment as she turned.

Lowell had a deep yearning to stick around and see what was going to happen next. The Reds could wait. Her eyes, her mouth, even her ass as she bent over a moment, were inviting him. Begging him, almost, to stay. He wanted to stay. He wanted to a whole helluva lot. But he had a job to do, and it didn't feel quite right. It wasn't a moral thing. It was more like an ethical thing—fucking a woman while her husband was out and the kids were around. It wasn't the kind of thing Tony Lowell wanted a reputation for doing. It could backfire on him, sooner or later. Much as he wanted her.

He left, full of regrets. She watched him go, possibly also full of regrets.

Shit, he was thinking. What a stinking lousy job this is. Why didn't I stick to photography?

10

It was close to three o'clock by the time Lowell headed for Plant City. He had to make a decision: go to the International Phosphates offices and pick up an annual report (they tended to reveal all sorts of hidden sins, if you knew how to read one), or go to the ball game and find Dicky Cahill. After his encounter with Briana Cahill, he wasn't quite ready for baseball, he decided. He picked up the game on the local radio station. It was the sixth inning, and a pitcher's duel, so it was going slowly. He still had time.

He got to Plant City in less than thirty minutes. It was a beautiful little town, one of the last vestiges of old Florida. Built by the nineteenth-century railroad magnate Henry Plant, who was the first major developer of west Florida, it was virtually dripping with charm—huge magnolias and oaks hung with Spanish moss, Victorian and Queen Anne cottages and houses, streets lined with queen's palms, lush groves of citrus, and green, green, everywhere.

The International Phosphates building was in an industrial park just outside the city—a long, low glass-and-steel structure such as might be found anywhere from Los Angeles to Wilmington. He decided on a frontal attack, requesting copies of all available documents in the public record: permits, applications for Environmental Impact

Reports, and any development, expansion, or reclamation proposals currently under consideration. Entering the glass lobby—all succulent plants and metal furniture—he asked for Jack Largent, from Public Relations, and gave his name. After what seemed like an inordinate delay, he was ushered into the courteous, if not exactly welcoming, custody of Mr. Largent's executive assistant, a Miss Bell. He gave Miss Bell his card and asked if he'd be able to meet with Mr. Largent himself. She was apologetic, and explained how busy he was. She was corporate from head to toe, but agreed, when Lowell insisted, to go ask.

A few minutes later, Largent appeared. He looked the perfect executive—a short razor haircut, gray gabardine suit, pinstriped Van Heusen shirt, and a narrow blue necktie. He showed no emotion as he pocketed the card. He didn't even look at it, noted Lowell.

"How may we help you, Mr. Lowell?" Largent wanted to know.

Lowell decided to stick with the credit investigation routine that had worked so well with Mrs. Jessup. He decided, for spice, to add Carla Brewer to his list of inquiries, however.

"You'd probably want to talk to Personnel about that," said Largent. "We don't deal with employee matters, except at the corporate level. Sorry I can't help you."

"There is one other thing," said Lowell quickly. "My client is a stockholder in your company, and asked me—just as a favor, really—if I could pick up an annual report, and copies of any permit applications and so forth that are in the public sector, mind you. He's thinking of a making a major investment, and would like to know what the prognosis is for the phosphate markets, if you know what I mean."

Largent looked at him thoughtfully. "Can I ask the name of your client?" he said.

"Sorry, that would be a breach of professional confidentiality. I'm sure you can understand that. He could request those documents through channels, it's just that he's in a bit of a rush, he's just rolled over some major notes, and you know how long the mails and what-all take."

Largent laughed. "You're right about that. Let me see what I can scrounge up." He ushered Lowell to a luxurious leather-and-steel sofa in front of a rack of magazines with such titles as the *International Mining Gazette,* and left him to browse. He was back in a few minutes with a dauntingly large stack of glossy booklets and brochures, as well as a thick document that Lowell guessed had to be the annual report. He was going to be in for some dull reading, he figured. He thanked Largent, and departed from the building.

He left the corporate offices just after four o'clock. A quick inquiry at a gas station while he filled up the Impala revealed that the Reds and Marlins were still locked in a tight game, one to one, top of eighth. Getting directions, he hurried over to the Plant City Stadium less than a mile across town. There were a lot of red cars in the lot, and he didn't take the time to search out Dicky Cahill's T-bird.

Hurrying to the ticket window, he finagled a four-dollar bleacher seat for half price, since the game was mostly over, and hurried in. There was a crowd of around six thousand, noisy and enthusiastic. There were at least as many people out from Tampa-St. Pete, or up from Manatee County, as locals here for the game. Virtually every town from Sarasota to Tarpon Springs had a major-league team of its own during spring training, but a lot of people had come simply to root against the Florida Marlins. The Marlins had stirred up huge amounts of resentment in St. Petersburg, particularly, but on the Gulf Coast in general, because a video entrepreneur on the other coast had stolen away Florida's first major-league baseball franchise, even though St. Pete had built a brand-new domed stadium and everything. Perry had explained it best to an apathetic Lowell one night over beers.

"Shit, took fifteen years to get the Devil Rays, and us a major metropolitan area now. Four mil and growing, we shoulda had a baseball team years ago. California got five teams, and they're *losing* population. Tampa Bay is already comparable in size and scope to the San Francisco Bay Area: we got two cities, a major Gulf seaport, we got symphony orchestras, opera houses, art museums, performance centers, libraries, beaches, industry, you name it. We got culture. But they kept us from baseball! That was wrong, man. Wrong, wrong, wrong."

"Maybe it was because everyone thought we were all either dead or dying," suggested Lowell. "Anyway, we got the Rays."

"Fuck that," declared Perry, working up a head of steam. "Look at San Francisco: They get two teams before we ever got one. And they still don't have a decent ball field out there!"

The Thunderdome was a sore point with a lot of locals around St. Pete, including Lowell. It had been paid for by the ever-suffering taxpayers, mostly on blind, long-unrequited faith. Small wonder they still hated the Marlins.

Lowell found a seat in the bleachers, a Bob Uecker special, and checked out the action, as well as the crowd. Dicky Cahill was here somewhere, but his chances of finding him in one inning were slim (although extra innings were a distinct possibility). The Marlins had just gotten a hit, and were threatening to break the tie, in the top of the ninth. Lowell decided, for the hell of it, to stroll the aisles. Maybe Cahill would spot him, and want to do something about it. Lowell had a couple of questions for him, although he didn't really expect any answers. It was just in the nature of his job that he had to try. He also wanted to find out with whom Cahill was associating. Maybe he'd get lucky: spot Cahill, and invite him for a beer. Loosen him up, maybe meet some of his buddies, pump them for info, as well. Yeah, right. Maybe the heavens will open up and the *Challenger* will make a miraculous safe landing, reemerging from a time warp in the ionosphere, and everyone on board is safe and sound. Lowell was willing to give it a shot, whatever happened. One thing about Tony Lowell. He wasn't armed, but he wasn't afraid either. No fool, he knew how to avoid or deter violence. He would resort to it only if all else failed. Which, despite the world that all those action movies glorifying violence depicted—especially in Florida—was rarely the case.

People like Dicky Cahill, when firmly confronted, usually backed down. So the outcome often ultimately depended on who stood behind them. In the parking lot at Florida Fertilizers it had been men under his domination. Here it would be his baseball buddies. Who would be his drinking buddies—always a prime opportunity for violence. But also maybe his business buddies. Dicky Cahill, according to his wife, was making extra money. Enough to get a sizzling new car. What about a sizzling new girlfriend? Briana's ardor, he had a feeling, would be downright explosive. She had the look, to him, of a woman who had suffered long years of being ignored, not to mention abused. What *had* Cahill been doing, he wondered, with that prodigious sex organ he kept boasting about?

Lowell bought a hot dog and strolled the length of the grandstand without being hailed or accosted. He heard the crowd roar, and turned to watch a slick double play as the Reds and their rookie pitcher prevailed on defense. Still no sign of Cahill. He climbed to the top of the bleachers, and looked out over the other side into the parking lot. It would be easier to find the car out there, he'd decided, than the man in here. Brighter color, and smaller numbers. There were at most a hundred red cars out there. Probably no more than a dozen T-birds. There were several thousand men in here.

He had brought his Nikon with him, just in case. He snapped in the 28-125-mm telephoto zoom lens he'd finally broken down and acquired (in his salad days with the *Times* he'd always carried two or three cameras, each with a different lens, and had later resorted to changing lenses on a single camera body). This was a radical change for this old dog, he'd thought, when he'd finally shelled out the four hundred eighty dollars for a Nikon zoom lens. No point using anything less, he'd felt. He scanned the crowd a few times before turning away to scan the lot. It was empty, even the few vendors were at the fence, looking in, caught up in the rising tension of the game. The Reds had gotten the pitcher out. It was a tie score, bottom of the ninth, the local favorites were coming up to bat.

He lowered the camera to search the area with his naked eyes first, because the human eye was still the most effective optical instrument for wide-angle viewing. If he could spot a likely subject first with a quick overview, then he could zoom in with his telephoto lens. He quickly eliminated the sports cars and pickups, of which there were quite a few. That left the midsized coupes, which unfortunately were in great demand these days among working-class Floridians. Especially the American-made ones, although it was really hard to tell anymore, the multinationals having taken over the world economy (in Lowell's opinon) some time earlier.

He soon spotted the car in a prime location, and his pulse

quickened. It was a cinch to recognize: Cahill had been unable to resist a vanity license plate proclaiming "DICKY." It sat right by the exit, in a handicapped zone. It had been there eight and a half innings, and had not been ticketed. Interesting, he thought. He could see at least one cop at this moment, watching the game from the gate not thirty feet away from the offending vehicle.

The crowd roared again, and Lowell had to turn and look. The Reds had opened the bottom of the ninth with a characteristic bang, and their all-star second baseman had just slid into second for a double. The crowd was on its feet, presumably Dicky Cahill among them. Feeling a tinge of regret and just a slight bit of resentment at being the only person aside from the players out of the entire six thousand or more in the vicinity who, at that precise moment, was actually working (even the ushers and vendors had stopped to watch), he jogged down the stairs and out the side exit. As he circled quickly around toward the entrance behind home plate, he heard the distant crack of a bat. The crowd roared again, even louder, followed by an equally loud groan, and a few cheers of relief from the minority Marlins rooters. Tourists too ignorant, presumably, to be aware of Florida politics. Lowell stopped by the fence and took a quick look. The Reds had hit into a double play: line drive to third, a quick pick-off at second. No one showed any signs of leaving. He hurried along the bottom of the grandstand to where the red car stood waiting. There was a small crack in the windshield. Lowell wondered if it was new. A couple of teenagers, one white, one black, were cruising the lot, possibly looking for a radio or other valuables to steal. The thieves, at least, were integrating, he thought. Some progress, anyway. He reached the car and assumed the identical pose he'd assumed in the parking lot at the plant, his last encounter with Dicky Cahill.

He never saw whoever came up behind him at all, and felt the blow to the back of his head for only a searing split second. Then everything went black.

11

Perry Garwood was on a roll. "When probability slit the underbelly of oblivion, the universe is what spilled out," he expounded. "It's hard physics, man. And there's a debt for the gift of that ultimate colossal birth. It's called solitude. Someday it's all gotta be squeezed back in there, and then we'll be together again in the womb of existence. Meanwhile, we're all fuckin' on our own."

"That's hard physics?" Lowell spoke through a dense fog, that was pressing painfully outward from the inside of his skull.

"Either that or metaphysics. I took a lot of both. I get them confused."

"Small wonder."

Perry handed Lowell a beer and stared at the sky. They were sitting on Perry's veranda, in the backwoods near Terra Ceia. Perry had brought Lowell back to his place after the call from Lena. Lowell had his head wrapped in a white handkerchief, and looked more like an Indian than Perry did.

"Just what I need," groaned Lowell. "A hangover, on top of my headache."

"You're lucky it was only a concussion. You lost a lot of blood, bro'."

"That probably explains why I see red."

"Nah, that's more like due to atrophy. The brain don't use much blood anyways, it's all circuitry, which in your case was obviously not functioning at the time anyway, going up there expecting to take on every fuckin' redneck—"

"Cracker—" corrected Lowell.

"—in the phosphates industry, which happens to be a major industry in central Florida—"

"Number five," said Lowell. "After tourism, agriculture, drugs, and dancing girls."

"Right," effused Perry. "It's big bucks, man."

Lowell was recovered enough to slap mosquitoes. Perry seemed immune. Lowell studied him, his vision almost back to normal now. Huge, like most Creek Indians, Perry seemed like a larger-than-life figure, at times, able to wade through life like Paul Bunyan through a Minnesota lake. Perry had driven out to the Plant City Hospital where the cops had brought his friend. Lowell had been found within minutes, as the first groups of disgruntled fans left the stands, heading for home, or the nearest bar. Rush hour, Plant City style. They'd taken him to the emergency room in the ambulance that was in routine attendance at the game, where he was treated for a concussion and contusion, and charged about a thousand dollars. He was still unconscious by the time the Manatee City Police were called (per Bedrosian's card in his wallet).

She got there in an hour, just as he was coming to. There had been no witnesses, but the cop on the beat did report that Cahill's car had left early. How early, he wasn't sure. The game had ended in the tenth, a home run by the Marlin's pitcher. The local cops were used to muggings in stadium parking lots. It was part of the new life in the small city. The fact that Lowell hadn't been robbed was unimportant. A mugging was a mugging. They would blame Tampa, or New York City, or Los Angeles, for their growing level of local crime and violence.

Lowell had come to, seen where he was, and demanded to be permitted to leave immediately. Bedrosian, who didn't have time to baby-sit just now, had asked him if he had any friends who could pick him up. That was the other thing, she informed him. Lowell's car had been impounded. Something about suspicion of drugs, she explained with a shrug.

"What!?" He couldn't believe it.

"Easy," she said. "I'll see what I can do."

The hospital let him go after getting him to sign a routine form or two. Lowell had self-pay health insurance, a hundred and twenty a month. Which meant that if he got hit on the head maybe two more times this fiscal year, they might start helping pay some of the bills. Meanwhile, he had to pay his own way as the bills came in. To their credit, Plant City Hospital was willing to bill him later, the nurse assured them as Perry had wheeled him out. Perry had balked, quite rightfully, at the notion of signing the forms himself.

That had been this morning, the day after the Reds-versus-Marlins game. Now Perry gazed morosely out at the thick woods that surrounded his house, and the lowering sun. The sky was brilliant, all hues of blue, pink, and orange. The air smelled of pine. Lowell stayed inside, nursing his blues, and avoiding the mosquitos. He preferred to be near the water, if he was going to risk his skin. At least with water there was something to look at. Always shimmering, sparkling, dancing, always different, unpredictable, never still. Even if the surface was like glass, something would stir it from below. However, as Perry had explained to Lowell long ago, "That's all well and fine. But who the fuck can afford to live by the water anymore, bro'?"

"Me. Barely."

"You. Sheeit, you bought that dump twenty years ago. Could you buy it today?"

"Guess not."

"There you go. Anyway, I hate fuckin' water. All it does is breed mosquitoes. This here is dry ground. Less bugs. I'll take this any day."

"I'd just like a place to launch my schooner one day. That requires water."

"By the time you finish that thing, the polar ice cap will have melted, this'll all be part of the second Atlantis, and the nearest coastline will be somewhere up in Georgia. You'll have plenty of water."

"I have a hedge of citronella around the house. It keeps the bugs at bay." Which was true. They hoisted their beers and drank.

"Here's to the planet Earth," shouted Perry into the listening forest. "God creates it, and man destroys it!" He took a swig and looked at Lowell. "You know what that makes man, don't you?"

"Shortsighted?"

"It makes man greater than God! That's what it makes man. But not greater," he added, "than the Great Spirit."

"How about the Great White Father?"

"Fuck him and all his girlfriends." Perry took another swig. "Hey, what's up with this gig out in Bone Valley?" Before Lowell could answer, he launched into one of his enthusiasms, which was old-time rock and roll. An enthusiasm which Lowell, of course, shared, while preferring the blues. "Hey, you wouldn't believe what I heard on the radio today. This dude from Sarasota, Mitch something, right out of the armpit of Wolfman Jack. Not an original note on his cranial keyboard. Anyway, he gets this brilliant idea, his first ever!—to do a call-in, a popular vote, mind you, to determine what was the Beethoven's Ninth of rock and roll. Dig it, man. Beethoven's Ninth!"

"You have a point," said Lowell. "It's like comparing simple arithmetic with quantum physics. It's a ridiculous concept."

"Yeah, maybe. Or maybe not. I got a couple of entries, anyway, just in case history and posterity decide that rock and roll was actually a superior art form."

"There's an interesting thought. Got any specifics?"

"Sure, lots. The Doors had no less than three: 'Light My Fire,' 'The End,' and my favorite, 'When the Music's Over.' "

"What's that from?"

"The second album, *Strange Days*, with the photo of this place called Sniffen Court in New York, a place which I actually got drunk and threw up in once."

"Good for you. All right, I'll play. The Stones. 'Goin' Home.' "

"Fair. But that's blues. It's not rock and roll. What we need is an epic piece, a lot of instrumental, a lot of quality workmanship."

"That means somebody had to take a couple of music lessons, which eliminates a lot of people. Like Elvis Presley, a musical illiterate, who couldn't read or write or play and never wrote a note or a lyric—the father of rock and roll—is supposed to be compared to Ludwig van Beethoven."

"Hey bro'," warned Perry. "I happen to like Elvis. He was the King. He knew how to shake that thing."

"Yeah. Ludwig and Elvis. Food for thought. Can we eat now? I'm having a serious case of protein deprivation."

"Oh, hey, sorry. Where's my head at?" Perry got up, went inside, and rummaged around in the kitchen. He had on stock, as it happened, he informed his friend, a huge fillet of fresh swordfish courtesy of a sports-fisherman pal, plus a case of cold Kirins, Lowell's favorite. He'd found them at a liquor store in Sarasota.

"What say we put on some blues while I get things rolling," suggested Perry as he fiddled with his ancient, arcane "hibachi thing," as he called it. As in "I'll fire up my hibachi thang." With a Florida-southern accent, Creek Indian style.

"Good idea," called Lowell, getting to his feet too fast, and sinking back as what was left of his blood supply rushed out of his head.

"There's tapes all over the place. Some are even in boxes. Good luck. Just no jazz, please. I'm not in the mood for jazz."

"Not even Miles?"

"There I might make an exception. You like pickles?"

Lowell did. And they both liked rehearing a long-forgotten *Something Blue*, which had been crouching in a dusty corner all these years.

"So. What it really comes down to is self-defense. You need a refresher course, pal," Perry finally offered, licking his fingers after a feast of sodium. "I'd be happy to run you through some moves, if you want."

"Why, you interested in some freelance work?" inquired Lowell. "I'm not looking for revenge and retribution here. Anyway, when I'm into something that gets somebody this panicked, I'm on the right track, and that's good. Don't worry, I can take care of myself."

"Yeah, right. Like you did yesterday. You owe me one blood-soaked handkerchief, bud," said Perry.

"Hey," protested Lowell, "they hit me from behind, there was a crowd yelling, I couldn't have heard 'em if they'd been wearing an elephant."

" 'Wearing an elephant?' "

Lowell frowned. His thinking was still a little fuzzy. "Walking on elephants. Whatever."

Perry put his hand on Lowell's forehead. "Tony, hey, man, you must still be delirious. You don't make sense."

"Fuck off. I don't need a bodyguard, is what I'm saying."

Perry's background in special forces, they both knew, made him a good candidate for a support team—should Lowell ever admit to needing one. Right now, though, the only thing Lowell would admit to was that he owed his buddy for bailing him out of Plant City. Not to mention dinner and beer.

"Hey," he said suddenly, sitting up in his chair. "What happened to my camera?" He'd forgotten all about that, and most other sundry details of his life, until this very moment.

"Welcome back to Earth, brother," said Perry. "I got it right over here." He fetched the camera, case and all. "Your lady friend the lieutenant had it."

Lowell said a silent blessing for Lena and gingerly picked up the case. Opening it up, he examined the camera. There was a new ding on the case and lens holder. But the optical integrity, after a quick check, was intact. The film, however, was missing.

"Thanks, Perry," he said. "I owe you one." This, of course, reminded him of Ernie Larson. He needed to give Ernie a call. And let aunt Marsetta know what happened, as well. He was always permanently in debt to Ernie for one favor or another, and this was one hell of a lousy way to pay him back. He gave Perry the basis of the case. Perry showed no signs of bigotry when he described Ernie and his nephew as being black. You never knew, even with Native Americans, when somebody was prejudiced until it got laid on the table. Perry wasn't prejudiced. Except, as he might put it himself, against crackers and rednecks. Although even some of those could be damn good folks, he had to admit.

"Mind if I use your phone?" Lowell asked. Perry shrugged, and nodded in the direction of a cordless plugged against the baseboard. Not even on a table.

"Help yourself."

Lowell used his calling card, and dialed Ernie's number from memory. Prior to his concussion, he realized, he'd had to look it up. Funny thing, that.

"Hello, Ernie?"

"Tony, how ya doin'? We've been worried about you, boy."

"No sweat, Ernie. But this situation has gotten kind of complicated. I can't honestly tell you the whole story yet because I don't know. But Tim was a good kid, you can tell that to Aunt Marsetta. He fell victim to some bad people while trying to make this world a better place. That's all I can tell you at this point."

There was silence. Finally Ernie said, "God bless you, boy. You go on out there and catch those people for what they done. I'll tell Marsetta. You take care, hear?"

"I will." Lowell hung up.

"So," said Perry after a while, "let me get this straight. Your friend Ernie's nephew came down here from up north and got involved with local business. If you don't mind my saying so, in other words, he was kind of like an industrial freedom rider. Here to liberate the environment, rescue us poor Floridians from our own folly. He ran afoul of some good ol' boys who wanted to be doin' business as usual, somehow, and considered him a pain in the ass. Sounds like grounds for some butt kickin', some threats, even some Klan shit, maybe, since the black-white thing got brought into it. But it don't necessarily sound like cause for murder."

"The freedom riders got murdered, since you mention them."

"Maybe I shoulda made the comparison more to the carpetbaggers. A black carpetbagger."

"You think that?" Lowell was offended.

"Easy, bro, I believe he was a good kid, tryin' to do right. I'm just sayin' that's how he might be seen down here."

"And so that justifies somebody killing him?"

"C'mon, not at all, I don't mean that. I'm just sayin' I can see how it might happen. 'Course it could be some totally different thing, right? Maybe a woman thing, from what you told me. This Cecilia, her boyfriend sounds like a scary cat, bro'."

"Or a civil rights conflict, some kind of in-fighting. An outsider, competing with a local organization for the hearts and minds, so to speak, of the people. One issue versus another, that's led to deaths and killings over the abortion issue, right here in Florida. It might be something like that."

"Like the ANC versus the Zulus, a tribal thing?"

"No, not a tribal thing. A political struggle. In a lot of places in this world, political disagreement is a killing offense."

"You think that could happen here?"

"I think it has happened here. Oklahoma City. The Kennedys, among other instances."

Perry turned the fish steaks, pondering. "I still think you should let me go over your self-defense methodology." He reached into a cabinet by the window and pulled out a metal footlocker. Inside was a selection of weapons that would intimidate a terrorist. Lowell knew Perry had a murky background. He'd no idea it was this murky, though. Perry picked up one particularly innocuous-looking weapon. "This is a Glock nine-millimeter police special from Austria. Holds seventeen rounds, plus one in the chamber.

It's light enough you could wear it in your jock. Or I got a—"

"No guns," said Lowell, glad he didn't wear jocks.

Perry looked at him. "Oh, yeah, I forgot. The pacifist peace-freak detective dude. Sorry, man. I really salute that attitude. If everybody felt that way we'd have no need for these. But everybody don't." He put them back. "The world ain't like that. There are really bad people out there, and a lot of them would just as soon blow you away as wipe their nose."

"I know all that," said Lowell. "I just don't carry weapons anymore. We have to stop somewhere."

Perry checked the coals, then snapped his fingers. "Look, I know a couple of startle-reaction techniques, if somebody comes up behind you they are dead in their tracks before you even turn around."

"That's my point. I do not care to leave a trail of dead bodies everywhere I go, every time somebody sneezes. And remind me to stay away from you come hay fever season, pal."

"I don't mean 'dead' dead. I mean you stop them. Cold. Of course, you want them 'dead' dead, I got a follow-up reaction blow to the—"

"Enough!" said Lowell. "I don't want to hear it. I might just do it sometime and wind up having a very bad day. I hate it when I kill somebody, even if they deserve it."

Perry got serious. "You actually killed people?"

"Not in the line of work, no. But in war, yes. In the war."

"Ah, shit, we all killed people in the war, one way or another. That's not what I meant."

"The answer is almost, many times, but no."

"Well, I have."

Lowell chose not to pursue it. His friend liked to boast at times. Maybe this was just an odd boast of his. He hoped it was meaningless, yet felt, in his marrow, that it wasn't. Perry served up the swordfish, and it was wonderful.

"I've been thinking, actually," said Perry after a while, his mouth full.

"Clear the decks," responded Lowell, opening another beer.

"Seriously. I've thought about it. Going into your line of work," said Perry. "Beats the shit work I've been doing lately. I'd go big-time, though, advertise and shit. Like that outfit up in Pinellas. Put up a big billboard: Investigations, Inc., Suspicions Confirmed."

" 'Suspicions Confirmed?' "

"Yeah. Cuts right to the chase, wouldn't you say?"

Lowell reserved comment. He realized he didn't even know what kind of work Perry did. Maybe he didn't want to know. Perry was such a free spirit—like himself—it was hard to imagine him working at all.

"What kind of work have you been doing?" he asked.

"Fuck that," said Perry evasively. "I'm talking about a career change here. Industrial surveillance, possible security, possibly even intelligence."

"That's a rare commodity. No Special Weapons?"

"That too. By the way, did I ever show you what I could do with a soda can?"

Lowell didn't want to know. He already had too much of that kind of knowledge. But he believed now that revenge and retribution left you with nothing, ultimately. Because even the satisfaction they gave you now would be gnawed away by guilt and doubt and time, leading to new resentments, possibly a cycle of new retaliation, endlessly repeating, leaving you poisoned and bitter, a cancerous legacy which, if left untended, will surely kill you. His friend, though, was such an amiable character that when he spoke of death and mayhem, it was hard to take him seriously.

They finished dinner, and darkness closed in, almost total. The night insects screamed at them. The trees loomed, threatening against the night sky. They were surrounded. Lowell stood on the veranda looking out, and felt a chill. Unfinished business waited for him out there.

Perry got an idea. "Let me help you, bro'. Just a practice run. Maybe like for credits, like when you teach courses."

Lowell still taught photography, off and on, at the community college. But more off than on lately. Presently off. One of the redeeming values of his work, Lowell realized, was that it allowed him to utilize, every now and then, the photographic skills that had been the high-water mark of his profession. As he'd pointed out on more than one perilous occasion, his camera was, in many ways, his real weapon. He sat forward suddenly. The sinkhole! He wanted to get a look at it as soon as possible. As soon as he could get hold of that hydrologist, that is. Baumgarten. Two times he'd called and gotten the answering machine. Maybe it was time to try again.

"Mind if I use the phone again?"

"Mi casa es su casa," Perry said, stepping out onto the porch, listening to the woods.

Lowell dialed. A man's voice answered. A real person.

"Is this Dr. Baumgarten?"

"It's Harry Baumgarten," said the voice. "I don't actually have a doctorate. I'm an engineer, with a master's. Is there something I can help you with?"

Lowell gave him his name, and told him what he was interested in. Baumgarten seemed perturbed. "I really don't think there's a problem, but if you want to meet me at my office, say tomorrow at ten, I'll take you out there."

"Great. Thanks for your time, see you then," said Lowell, and hung up.

"What've you got in mind?" Perry asked, picking hopefully at the remains on his plate. Like true bachelors, they'd gone straight for the protein and a few carbs, leaving such incidentals as B-vitamins for some other time and place. Like a pill.

"You want to check out a sinkhole with me?"

"Nah, I hate those things. Too sinister. You go ahead and get your ass drowned in a puddle of muck if you want to. I'll do something else."

"Such as?" asked Lowell, somewhat annoyed but curious.

"The boyfriend," said Perry. "Let me watch him for a while. I'm a person of color, I can go down there without drawin' attention like you would—a fuckin' wolf in a sheep pen."

"That's no sheep pen. And be careful, he's dangerous," said Lowell simply.

"So am I," said Perry. "Only more so, 'cause he's probably just a jealous bullyin' asshole. I mean business. There's a difference. Just when he loses his cool is when I nail him."

"Don't nail anybody, just follow him, then check him out, how often he's there at the girl's house, where else he goes, who else he sees, that kind of shit."

"Cool!" said Perry, actually pleased. "How soon can I start?"

"Soon's you're ready," said Lowell. "Me, I'm ready for some more swordfish."

Perry went to the railing and looked up at the sky, sniffing the air. It was pungent, with warm smells of the sea and the woods. "Funny thing. People save up their every last nickel, dime, and shekel to move down here where it's warm. Then, first thing, they go inside, turn on their air-conditioners full blast, and try to cool off."

Lowell shrugged. "Maybe they just want to be comfortable. There's a difference between cooling off on a hot day, and freezing to death."

141

"True, but I still think it's just perverse human nature, Lowell. Alter reality. Chronic hubris."

"Yeah, sure, like original sin," scoffed Lowell. "Hate our world, as ourselves. Like some innate sense of restless discontent. Nothing is ever good enough. The grass is always greener, if you load it with fertilizer. Which gets back to the issue at hand."

Perry grinned. "Kafka got it wrong," he said. "Man is not a cockroach. Man's most basic self is like that of a wood tick: plunge that poisoned proboscis into the earth, and suck it dry of all its remaining natural resources."

"That's kind of a reach. Some of us actually like Earth the way it is. Or was."

"That's just it! Point is, we keep tryin' to take out Mother Nature by presuming we have a blank check from God. We were wrong. Mother Nature *is* God! We're in for it, bro'. Hurricanes, typhoons, floods, fires, all those people bailing out of Los Angeles—"

"How about sinkholes?" Lowell picked up his Nikon, and checked the action. "Us? Or Mother Nature's retribution?"

"Who knows?" Perry lit a joint and took a long hit. "All's I can say is, if it causes trouble, man can't be far behind."

"If you think things are that bleak for us and our planet, you ever consider looking elsewhere?"

"Where have you been, bro'? I *am* looking elsewhere!"

They beat back the rest of the night with music.

12

In the morning, Lowell felt almost human again, aside from a splitting headache and severe nausea from too much beer and protein and too little fiber and common sense. He also didn't know where he was at first, until he remembered he'd slept over at Perry's, on the couch. He and Perry had agreed that Perry would begin a watch on Cecilia and her boyfriend, while Lowell checked out the sinkhole. Lowell remembered he'd made an appointment, and looked at his watch. Seven o'clock. Better get a move on.

Perry wandered in wearing an old Pendleton robe that still had some color in it, with a where's-the-coffee look on his face. "You're up bright and early," he remarked. "Feeling okay?"

"Great. Never better. Except I'm supposed to meet that guy Baumgarten at ten."

"No problem," opined Perry, filling a kettle. "You got time for some of the world's most outrageous java since the invention of espresso."

"I can't," said Lowell. "I have to get a move on, get home and change, maybe take an actual shower."

"Relax, I can loan you some stuff," said Perry. "You're about the same as me, give or take a size or two. The shower's down the hall. Live a little."

While Perry ground the beans, Lowell retreated to the bathroom, stood under the shower nozzle letting the hot water run down his face, and ran off a mental checklist. He still needed to do some background research on wastewater treatment, possible permit violations, and any related controversies such as Tim Cross might have stumbled into. He had read over the corporate papers from Plant City, but at least at first glance they'd revealed nothing. Not that he'd expected much. But there was something going on out there. There had to be. And the sinkhole would be a good place to start.

Gulping down a day-old Danish and doing proper homage to Perry's special Kenya-blend coffee, he sprinted for the door. "Sorry to eat and run," he said, "and thanks for putting me up, but I've gotta go." He stopped on the veranda, and looked around, perplexed. "Hey!" he exclaimed. "Where exactly is my car?"

"In the pen," chuckled Perry. "But no sweat, I'll run you in."

They left in Perry's four-wheel drive Cherokee with the prerequisite fat tires. Lowell checked his watch. Eight-fifteen. Time was running short. Perry agreed to drop him off at Manatee City Police Headquarters to check in with Bedrosian and see about getting a car.

She seemed glad to see him. "Good news," she announced right off. "I got your car back." She tossed him the keys. "I had to kiss some major butt at the sheriff's office, though, I have to tell you. You owe me, Lowell."

"Thanks," he said, and meant it. "It's old, it's ugly, but it's mine, and I need it."

"How's your head?" she asked.

"Still attached, I think."

"No thanks to you," she said. "Why don't you get a brain implant and apply for a gun permit? I can slide it through."

"Thanks, but no thanks." He sat down and told her about Dicky Cahill's wife, and her concerns regarding the family financial situation. Lena gave him a look, sighed, and agreed she'd check out the car purchase, find out if Cahill paid cash, and get a search warrant to run a check on his accounts.

One other thing Lowell wanted to look into was Cecilia's child—her mother's background, and whether the boyfriend was the father. For one thing, Lowell was convinced that the child was being abused, and that social services should intervene.

"That's fine, but can you hold them off until we finish our investigation? We may want to talk to the kid before we're through, and they'll wrap her up in red tape tighter than a straitjacket."

"Well, I got someone lookin' after her and her mother a little. Maybe he can keep her from getting hurt any worse than she already is. But if things deteriorate, I want to see her out of there. Investigation or no. Deal?"

"Sure, Lowell." Bedrosian's voice softened a little. "You may forget, but I'm also a mother."

"Good. Then you understand. See you later." Lowell headed for the door.

"So where you goin'?"

He stopped in the doorway. "Bone Valley. It's time I check out this sinkhole. The state hydrologist is going to take me in."

"Be careful. I can't help you there without a court order. It's on private property. You're on your own on that one."

"I'm used to that."

"Anyways, you sure you want to get back in the fray that fast?"

"You know what they say. You fall off a horse—"

"Yeah, yeah. Just be careful. Okay, Lowell?"

145

"Not to worry. I'm always careful."

"Yeah, right. And don't bring my name into it, if you intend to go sniffin' around Bone Valley without a warrant. If somebody had something to protect enough to kill Tim Cross, they won't hesitate with you."

"I appreciate your concern."

She paused a moment. "All right. I'll see what I can do about the Health Center, too. Maybe I can get a court order to get access. I have to show due cause, though."

"What, exactly, might constitute 'due cause'?"

"Why, what do you have in mind?" She sounded suspicious.

"The safety of the child, for starters," he said. "She's got some kind of medical problem that needs special attention. I doubt she's getting it in that house, although the mother is probably doing her best. Also, I think her paternity needs to be established, it could relate to the question of motive, in our case."

Now it was Bedrosian's turn to fume. He'd just told her how to do her own job. "All right, all right. You got any more evidence to offer?"

"I heard some things, when I was there."

"Anything that would hold up in court?"

"Not yet," he admitted.

She thought a moment. "Well, it's just a gut feeling, but there is something strange about this web of relationships she's got going. Or had going. She's got this walking nightmare in this guy Smith—"

"Who my friend Perry Garwood is going to keep an eye on, by the way—"

"Who?"

"Perry Garwood. Lives near Palmetto. Native American dude—"

"Jesus, Lowell, you *know* him?" It sounded like an accusation.

"Why? What's he done?" he asked defensively.

"Nothin'. I don't know. Probably plenty. He's just weird. Like you, come to think of it."

"Case closed. So he'll be watching them, as a favor. Good luck at the Health Center. She told me Cross used to meet with her there."

She was silent for a moment. "I know this is far-fetched, but I've been trying to think why a man like Tim Cross would spend so much time with a woman who's got a boyfriend, and a child, unless . . ." her voice trailed off.

"You think Cross could have been the father? How?"

"Well, I know it doesn't follow, he was new to the area, and the kid is, what, five or six? But what if they have a history that goes back, before Smith, before this job in Florida? What if they met someplace else, and she was the real reason he came back down here?"

"Like you said, far-fetched. But like you say, it is strange, him hanging with her, in spite of all the risk, and probably with no payback, that I can see."

She nodded, lost in thought.

"Anyway, if you can access the birth and medical records for the child, that might answer a lot of questions."

"Or not." She sighed. "All right, I'll talk to Judge Winfrey about all this. Easier said than done, though. I'm still trying to get an angle on this thing, Lowell. If it turns out Cross is—was—the father, then we have to look at this Smith guy as the prime suspect."

"You can look at him even if Cross isn't the father. The kid could be Smith's, for that matter. Maybe he knocked her up six, seven years ago, came back for her."

"He's shown no interest in the kid, she said. But neither do a lot of fathers."

"True." Lowell thought about that. But even if Cross's attentions were primarily focussed just on the daughter, if Smith considered himself as having a claim on the mother, he would take a very dim view toward the young interloper. . . .

Then there was the woman activist. "Anything on Carla Brewer?" he asked abruptly.

Bedrosian was caught off guard. "What about her?"

"You said she was a suspect. Is she still a suspect?"

"So far we haven't ruled out anybody," she replied noncommittally.

Lowell had thought about Brewer. She'd been pretty adamant about his laying off the phosphate business, particularly in regard to employment for blacks. Could she have considered Tim Cross a threat to the extent of going to the extreme of murder, just to protect jobs? It didn't seem likely. Unless there was some other connection. Some other motive. That was one of the problems, with murder. Motives could be pretty obscure at times. Or buried very deep. Like at the bottom of a sinkhole?

Lowell glanced at his watch. "Shit!" he muttered. "I'm late."

"You can call him from here," she said, and offered him her desk phone. Lowell got out the slip of paper Solano had given him, still in his wallet, and dialed.

"This is Baumgarten Environmental Services," the voice intoned. "Sorry we can't take your call just now . . ."

"Shit!" Lowell slammed the phone down. "I better get up there and find him. See you."

Bedrosian nodded in bemusement as he ran out the door. She checked the time. Ten-fifteen. Plenty of time before lunch. She'd try to get hold of the judge.

*   *   *

Brandon was a typical American suburb. Situated on the
east side of Tampa, it was crisscrossed by a couple of free-
ways, had a few smokestack industries, and a selection of
shopping malls. What it didn't have, or no longer had, was a
downtown area. As Lowell left I-75 at the State Route 60
exit, he found himself on a strip identical in most ways to
every other suburban strip in America: large chain stores,
smaller chain stores, franchise gas stations, franchise fast-
food, franchise "family" restaurants, even franchise singles
bars. Mom and pop were out to pasture. He found the address on the map, and hurried.

Alicia Lane was on the east side of town, just south of SR-
60, in a pleasant residential area of large lots, large trees,
and good-sized homes, mostly built in the booming fifties,
when northerners were buying into Florida with their post-
war money, sight unseen. This particular neighborhood had
declined just slightly. Just enough to allow for a few zoning
variances, opening the way for the first intrusion of busi-
nesses, especially business-residential combinations. Such
as this one. Baumgarten's place was a nondescript yellow
stucco building, square aluminum windows along the front,
phony white shutters, and a shake roof. A discreet wooden
sign on the lawn stated, in two-inch black roman letters,
Baumgarten Environmental Services. And underneath,
Investigations and Testing, with the phone number.

Lowell went up and rang the bell. He thought he could
hear Muzak from inside somewhere, and little else. No one
came to the door. He checked his watch. Ten-fifty. Nearly
an hour late. Baumgarten might have gone out on a call. He
might be down in a basement lab somewhere, wearing head-
phones. He might be out in a soundproofed garage, a closet
rocker, making loud noises with an electronic keyboard, or

blasting away in his own basement firing range. Out of range. There were a lot of possibilities. The silence was almost uncanny. Lowell glanced around the area and walked around to the back. Someone came out of a house on the adjoining property behind, looked over at him a long moment, then walked to a newly blossoming orange tree, examined a sprig, and went back inside.

There was a garage behind the house-office-lab. It was separate, also yellow stucco, with what appeared to be a small studio or guest apartment attached to the left side. There were no vehicles in sight on the driveway or visible through the glass panes in the garage door. A breeze picked up, and he heard a sound. A rattling, clicking noise, coming from behind the garage, in the direction of the guest apartment. Tensing his muscles, Lowell walked carefully around on the right side of the garage, to the back. There was a small veranda with screened vertical windows looking out across the overgrown back lawn toward the neighbor's house. The windows were covered with venetian blinds that had been lowered all the way with the slats open. One of the windows was open wide, and the breeze was rattling the blinds.

Lowell drew closer and, mostly out of curiosity, peered between the slats. The porch had a hardwood floor and white rattan furniture. A four-foot-wide round table was scattered with documents. Some had blown onto the floor in the breeze. He strained to see better, and considered going out to the car for his camera. Then he tried the screen door, and found that it was unlocked. He was about to open it when he heard a door opening from the house behind. The same door as before. He looked over, and a gray-haired man stood there, arms folded. He had a military bearing. Lowell hesitated, then turned and walked straight toward the man, who followed suit. They stopped, each about ten feet from the back fence—a Mexican standoff.

The man was midfifties, rugged, with a dark tan. He regarded Lowell with distaste.

Lowell ignored the vibe. "Hi. I had an appointment with Mr. Baumgarten, and there doesn't seem to be anyone around. Did you happen to see him this morning?"

"People come and go over there all the time. Guy runs some kind of lab operation. I've complained to the city, but they don't do jack shit. Probably makes drugs or something, for all anyone cares. You one of those drug people?"

Lowell was having trouble liking the man. Aside from the direct insult, considering his watchfulness, the guy had never even bothered to go past the house on the next street and read the sign. Not that it would have necessarily been accurate, of course, but still . . .

"No, I'm not DEA. I'm a private investigator," he said, deliberately misconstruing the man's meaning. "And this man, your neighbor, is a hydrologist. He tests water for contaminants, that sort of thing. I very much doubt he makes drugs." While the man was reacting to that double blow to his preconceptions, Lowell offered him his card. The man stepped cautiously forward and grabbed it, like a raccoon snatching at a food tidbit. He had to put on glasses to read it, which made him look more like Steve Martin than a drill sergeant. He looked back at Lowell, his expression puzzled, doubtful, but no longer sure.

He's trying to decide if I'm wearing a disguise or something, Lowell thought. He's trying to fit me into his media-packaged notion of what a private eye should look like. Lowell's once-blond hair was bound back in his usual ponytail, but then even bankers had ponytails these days. At least in some places. The blank T-shirt and jeans were what mainly threw him. Plus Lowell exuded an aura of freedom, of independence, of iconoclasm that was very threatening to businessmen and others who were accustomed to, even dependent upon, social conformity. Of course, Lowell would have been the first to tell him that he himself was a conformist, according to his own self-image. His choices of jeans over suits, long hair over crew cuts or Mohawks, no guns over guns, all were deliberate self-constructs. So he didn't mind that the man was locked into his own world view. Most people were.

"I did see him this morning," the man finally said, handing the card back. "He went out."

"Keep it," said Lowell, referring to the card. "Maybe you'll see something, drug guys sneaking around or something, and want to give me a call. Plus I'm sure he appreciates your vigilance in the neighborhood. I'll be sure to tell him when I find him."

"Don't bother," the man said. "Long as he's legal."

Lowell took a calculated chance. "Look, I am not a burglar or anything, I think you realize, and I'll be happy to show you ID to confirm that I'm the guy on the card."

"Don't bother," the man said. But this time he looked a little more relaxed.

"What I'd like to do, what I was about to do, was step in to that porch over there, in case it's like a waiting room or something. Maybe that's what it is, I mean, there's magazines and stuff. Maybe he'll be back in a while. Would that be all right with you?"

"Do what you want," said the man. "Just keep the hell off my property."

"Thanks," said Lowell, not meaning it. They both walked back, the man to his house, Lowell to the screened porch. He opened the door and stepped in. It was cool despite the fact that it was mostly closed, owing to the shade from the huge magnolia tree that loomed over it.

"Hello? Anybody here?" called Lowell, just in case. There was no answer, just the rattling of the blinds. There was a white lined pad on the table with notes scribbled on it. Lowell saw his own name and phone number on the top page. He would stop and read the rest of them in a moment, after an overview of the premises. There were several file copies of letters with "Baumgarten Environmental Services" on the header. Lowell glanced at them. They were mostly about water tests, in various parts of Hillsborough and Polk counties. There was a road map on the table, as well. It had been used as a chart of sorts, and there were numerous notations on it, and places circled in red and black magic marker. Lowell looked more closely. Then looked again. One small circle in red leaped up at him from the southeastern corner of the map, below the little town called Orange Blossom. Next to the circle was plainly written one word: "sinkhole."

Lowell went for his camera, not bothering about the paranoid neighbor still watching from the house behind. He quickly photographed all the documents he could find, and jotted down some quick notes of his own, including the location of the sinkhole. Then he left. The pad had revealed nothing further that he could construe, but he'd photographed each of the three pages on which there'd been writing, just in case. More work for Bedrosian, he thought wryly. And why not? This was her show.

The fence seemed to go for miles. He found a small unmarked road off of Route 37, north of where State Road 674 dead-ended, deep in the heart of nowhere, well east of the main road into Orange Blossom and the main entrance to the factory. Lowell had followed the barbed wire, looking for a gap. The fence was clearly marked with red signs every hundred yards or so, PRIVATE PROPERTY. KEEP OUT. And in smaller print, PROPERTY OF FLORIDA FERTIL-IZERS, and in even smaller print, A Subsidiary Company of the International Phosphates Corporation. The sinkhole was in there, somewhere, according to the notations of the missing-in-action Harry Baumgarten.

Another mile or so, and the trees grew thick along the road, in some sections heavy undergrowth serving as well as a fence. Then Lowell came to a small dirt road, unmarked, heading due east. He turned down the road on a hunch. It was a single lane, running through thick dense woods, the oaken canopy completely overhanging the road. It was nearly dark in there. Spanish moss hung down in thick drapes, sometimes dragging across his windshield like some nature-crafted deranged car wash. He glimpsed an expanse of water through the trees off to the right. It looked like a fair-sized lake. The road climbed briefly, then began a long, gradual descent.

After about half a mile, he knew he was close. There were recent ruts and markings indicating a lot of traffic, includ-ing heavy machinery. Then he saw the gated single-track dirt road going off to the south. The gate was open. Sensing he was close, he turned into the road. It wound for about about a quarter mile, where he came to a meadow area, with indications of a great deal of recent clearing and cutting. Here the ruts and tracks were everywhere for an area of about an acre. Something big had happened here not long ago. Lowell parked and got out with his camera. There was no one around. He took several frames with his zoom lens from 28- and 50-mm settings, and saw that all the activity had funneled onto a now deeply rutted, heavily tramped path through the saw grasses, and across a wide field.

He began to walk along the path. There was a familiar pungent smell in the air, growing in intensity as he went. He reached the far side of the field, where a narrow stream meandered slowly along the edge of a thick forest of cypress and scrub pine. The path turned north, following the stream. The smell intensified, and there was a new smell as well. A smell Lowell remembered only too well from southeast Asia. Death. Death came on the water: trout, perch, even some wading birds. Belly up, bellies swollen and bloated, expanding with the gasses of decay in the Florida heat, floating downstream. A recent fish kill had occurred, somewhere close by. The other smell grew stronger as well, as he walked, and he began to feel nauseous. This other smell he knew very well from much more recent experience. Sulfur. Then he saw a large swollen belly, white in the sun, floating toward him. At first he thought it was human, and his pulse raced. Then as it drew closer, he fought back a surge of nausea. It was a dead alligator. Not a small one, either. Something powerful had entered these waters, and very recently. Powerful enough to kill anything that swam.

Lowell fumbled for a bandana in his jeans pocket he often carried for just such emergencies, covered his mouth, and pressed on. There were fresh tire tracks now, from what looked like two sets of wheels. He quickened his pace. He almost passed the spot where the heavier vehicle, probably a big four-wheel drive, had made a three-point turn. Only the second set went forward. There were no return tracks. The saw grass was so thick he almost walked straight into the hole before he saw it. It had appeared just to the west of the stream, in the field. He looked down and caught his breath.

It was an almost perfect funnel cone, dropping a hundred

feet or more to a narrow pool at the bottom filled with foul yellowish liquid. It looked like something from one of Dante's worst nightmares. The sulfur smell was coming from here. He'd smelled the same odor at the fertilizer plant. Sulfur, and something more. Something acrid. He looked closer. There was something in the pool, mostly submerged. Something large and dark. He focused his lens, set on full telephoto. A pickup truck, it looked like. He could see a hand protruding from the half-open window. Just part of the door and the top of the cab, lying on its side, was visible. The lettering on the door was even legible, through the lens. A portion of Baumgarten Environmental was all that was visible. But it was enough. Lowell snapped several frames at varying exposures, and headed the quarter mile or so back along the path to the clearing where he'd left his car.

He stopped short as he came out of the underbrush into the clearing. Someone was waiting for him. Two people. One of them was armed. He recognized him right away. The big guy from the parking lot. The one he hadn't been able to find out much about, except his name. Corcoran. Buddy, or Buster, something like that. Again Lowell noted his sad eyes. Almost pensive. That, and hostile. The other man was around Lowell's age, a little older. Like an athlete gone to pot, thought Lowell. His face was familiar. He was tall, over six feet, with a deep reddish tan, graying hair, bald on top, thick arms and shoulders. Lowell wondered where he knew him from.

"Sorry to spoil your little outing," said Corcoran, sounding almost apologetic. The designated spokesperson. "But this is private property. Maybe you didn't see the signs every hundred feet out there?"

"There were signs?" asked Lowell innocently. He was watching the weapon. It wasn't at the moment deployed. A good sign. Maybe they didn't even know about the body.

The other man spoke up. "Relax, Corky. He's probably just a camper, got lost or something, am I right?"

"I wish you wouldn't call me that," sighed Corcoran.

"Hiya!" the other man came over to Lowell, hand extended. He was smiling all over the place and sounded cheerful, even jocular.

"Can I help you with somethin'?"

Lowell was sure he recognized the face, but couldn't place from where. The voice sounded familiar as well. High-pitched and earnest. From a conversation once overheard, or one of a thousand utterly inane radio interviews or TV commercials that had somehow intruded their way into his subconscious. It wasn't Rush Limbaugh. Too cheerful. Beyond that he was at a loss.

"I came to meet someone from the EPA," Lowell replied smoothly. "About the sinkhole. I assumed that he had right of access. Looks like he went ahead without me," he added, nodding in the direction of the path. "And by the way, looks like a major fish kill happening in that stream back there."

"That so?" The man's smile faded, but only for a moment. He hesitated, glancing in that direction. Corcoran looked melancholy. Lowell decided they were either both good actors or they had no idea who or what was down there in that hole. They knew about the hole, of course. They'd come in a brand-new Range Rover, which was parked in such a way as to block Lowell's exit. Thoughtful of them, he mused. He saw a stack of large rolled-up documents in the back window. They looked like they might be blueprints. Or plot plans. Or maybe reclamation plans. He hadn't gotten to see one of those yet, thanks to Solano's lack of organization. He wondered if these were the two men who had visited the EPA a couple of weeks earlier.

"I'm afraid you assumed wrong about that right of access," said the cheerful one. "You're trespassing."

"You from the EPA?" This from Corcoran. The tone seemed a little more threatening. "I saw him the other day, Virgil," he informed his companion. "At the plant. He's nosin' around about somethin'. Just like that nigger kid."

So, thought Lowell. They know about Tim Cross. He wondered what else they knew. "I think you'd better call the police, and maybe a rescue 'copter. The man I came to see is down in the hole."

They stared at him as though not knowing whether to believe him or not. The man called Virgil grinned. "Corky, why don't you entertain our friend here while I go check it out," he suggested amicably. Accustomed to giving orders, thought Lowell. The big man sighed, and shrugged grudgingly.

"If you say so."

"Be right back." Virgil beamed, gave Lowell a little chuck on the arm, turned, and disappeared along the track. Corcoran leaned back on the Rover, gloomily brushing flies and mosquitoes away from his face.

"I see you've got a radio," observed Lowell, noting the rear-mounted antennae. "While we're waiting, you might want to call the authorities. He may still be alive."

"Relax," said Corcoran. "I ain't callin' nobody till Virgil gets back."

"You could be held responsible," said Lowell. "If you take no action when action is clearly called for—"

"Save it," growled Corcoran. This time he deployed his weapon pointedly. It was a Colt AR-15 assault gun with a thirty-round magazine. More than adequate, Lowell would have thought, for guarding fences. Or sinkholes. "Don't make me do anything I'm gonna regret later, please."

Fifteen minutes passed, then twenty. Corcoran began to look restless. The other man, Virgil, came running back, winded. He looked decidedly less cheerful. "Call HQ." he ordered. "Our friend is right. Looks like we may have a problem out there."

"He may still be alive," repeated Lowell.

"Corky, I'm afraid we're gonna have to get a chopper in here," said Virgil, otherwise ignoring him.

"You gonna call the police?" asked Lowell. He should be so lucky.

"Shut up, please," ordered Corcoran, and picked up the radio phone.

"Be nice," suggested Virgil.

"You can't sweep this under the rug," Lowell told them. "The investigating police detective knows I'm out here, and I'm here by her authority." Then he remembered that he wasn't. It was too late, though. The man called his bluff without even blinking.

"That's bullshit, come on," he scoffed, while Corcoran traded noises over the radio. "You're on your own, pal."

He's some kind of a gamesman, thought Lowell. "Tell you what," he proposed. "Maybe you should show me some ID yourself. I'd really like to know what authority you have to detain me by force. Are you an employee of Florida Fertilizers?"

The man gave him a peculiar look that suggested Lowell should know more than he seemed to. "I'm afraid that ain't really relevant at this point," he said. That pretty much answered Lowell's question, but it wasn't good news, since they were out in the sticks, there was a probable homicide in the vicinity, Corcoran was armed, and he wasn't. This would take some thought. He hoped he had time to give it some.

Corcoran stepped out of the cab. "They're on their way," he said sorrowfully. "Is it that guy?" This was directed at his partner.

"There's somebody in a truck down there, is all I know."

The man named Virgil shrugged. He didn't seem that upset about it, thought Lowell. But then, he didn't seem to be perturbed about much of anything.

Virgil looked at Lowell with a half smile. "So. What did you say your name was again?"

"Lowell. Tony Lowell."

"Well, Tony—you don't mind if I call you Tony—we have a little bit of a problem here. Do you know that guy down there?"

"Only that I was supposed to meet the man this morning, and he left without me. And like I have twice tried to explain to your somewhat dim associate over there, I really think it is incumbent upon you to call the police about this, don't you think?"

"I don't know why you're in such a rush. You're the one they're gonna have all the questions for."

Lowell knew that was true. Meanwhile he still had a few of his own.

"Do you have an explanation for all those dead fish? Or that yellow stuff down in the hole back there?"

"Yellow stuff?" Virgil laughed. "I wouldn't worry about it. There's all kinds of things that can affect how something looks. Light, shadow, Florida's a colorful place." He laughed again. "Anyway, I'm sure there's nothing wrong that a couple of pumps can't take care of." His smile vanished for the first time. "Not that it's any of your business," he added.

"Maybe Mr. Baumgarten saw it differently."

Virgil gave him a blank look. "Who?"

"The guy in the pickup." Lowell had gotten only a glimpse of the liquid contents of the sinkhole. But he would be willing to bet his Impala on what it was: sulfuric acid. The same stuff that had killed Lake Apopka over at Orlando fifteen years before, the consequences of which were still being uncovered. Did these people intend to bluff their way through this?

"I'm afraid I don't know what you're talking about," said Virgil with an affable smile. He signaled for Corcoran to come over. "Corky, would you mind escorting Mr. Lowell here to the plant, and show him some proper hospitality while I figure out what to do with this situation?"

"Sure, Virgil." Corcoran looked more sorrowful than ever.

Corcoran put his gun at Lowell's back, and said, "Get in your car, and drive, please. I'll tell you where."

Lowell obeyed, thinking hard and fast. He had a bad feeling about the plant. He didn't want to go there.

13

Corcoran ordered Lowell to back around, and follow the dirt track out past the lake to the main road. He seemed apologetic.

"Turn right," he requested.

Lowell remembered from the map, that would be in the direction of a little hamlet called Baird.

"I thought we were going to the plant," he said.

"Shut up, please," ordered Corcoran. "Just drive."

The road straightened out. There was a drainage canal along the right shoulder, deep and foul looking. Almost as foul looking as the contents of that sinkhole, Lowell thought. He didn't want to end up in either place.

"You're not the one who hit me on the head yesterday, perchance?" inquired Lowell, trying to sound conversational.

"It wasn't nothin' personal," came the reply.

"Oh. That's a relief."

"There's a dirt road a quarter mile up, on the left. Turn down there," instructed Corcoran, looking gloomier by the minute.

Time was running out. "Who's your friend?" asked Lowell, trying to maintain a calm demeanor. He didn't feel calm.

"The Virgil guy. You guys play cards together or something? You and him and Cahill? Maybe you need a fourth."

"Shut up," ordered Corcoran. Not a man of many words, thought Lowell. Other than those few colorful exchanges with Cahill, a few days earlier.

Lowell glanced sideways briefly. Corcoran wasn't seat belted. He slowed for the turn, and checked to his right again. One thing about old Chevys—they tended to come apart in time. This one, for example. The doors hadn't closed right in years. You had to slam it just so, and jiggle the handle. Lowell hadn't bothered explaining that particular detail to his guest, who hadn't asked.

"I'm really sorry about all this," Corcoran was saying.

"Me too."

The turn was just ahead. Lowell braked and began to turn the wheel. Just as he entered the turn he gunned the engine. One other thing about old Chevys. They had great engines. This one responded like a young colt, and at that instant several things happened. The first thing was that Lowell slammed on the brakes in the middle of the turn, and the Impala, amid great protest and resisting tremendous inertia from its excessive weight, slid into a three-sixty spin.

"What the fu—" spluttered Corcoran.

The second thing that happened was the passenger door flew open. The third thing that happened, thanks to the wonders of Newtonian science, was that Corcoran, unrestrained by a seat belt, flew out the open door into the road, giving Lowell a fleeting reproachful look as he went.

Lowell felt only a momentary twinge of regret as he saw the big man roll and tumble across the pavement and into the drainage ditch. Then he straightened his wheel, hit the big V-8, and was out of there in a cloud of burning hydrocarbons and Firestone rubber. The gun was still in the car.

Heart pounding, Lowell slowed one more time, a quarter mile or so down, hurled it into the canal, and drove on.

Lowell made a decision. It was early afternoon, and while he was clearly a marked man in the vicinity of Orange Blossom, there was something he had to do there. He stopped by the fertilizer plant first. There was no sign of Dicky Cahill's red T-bird. He was probably out slumming again. Lowell didn't know if the Reds were at home today. It wouldn't matter. If baseball was on his mind, barring another strike, there were major-league teams playing all over the area: the White Sox in Sarasota, the Cubbies in Dunedin, the Phillies in Clearwater, the Cards in St. Pete. Cahill could be at any of the games inside an hour. Orange Blossom was centrally located when it came to spring baseball.

Lowell knew he was taking a chance when he pulled his Impala up at the curb on Poinsettia Road, set the brake, and walked the two houses back to the Cahill residence.

She was home. It looked as though she'd been doing some kind of workout. She was wearing a white leotard, and nothing else. She was sweating. Her lovely green eyes widened. She hadn't been expecting him. Then, remembering his rejection of her the day before, her eyes narrowed again.

"What do you want?" she demanded.

Lowell knew he had his work cut out for him. No woman likes to be put off. Especially for logical, cerebral, work-related reasons that have nothing to do with chemistry.

"Hey, you look great!" he exclaimed right off. Which was true.

"You didn't seem to think so yesterday."

One thing about her, he remembered. She was very direct. He liked that. But this was going to be an uphill battle, to regain her confidence. He'd better not even mention his real business. Not for a while yet. Maybe not at all, this time. It could wait. Now, if good ol' Dicky would just accommodate him long enough. He looked at her nipples, pressing hard against the spandex she was wearing. He began to feel some heat and pressure of his own in his nether regions.

"Listen, I am really truly sorry for running off like that. Putting business before a beautiful woman was a foolish, thoughtless thing to do. And I apologize."

She stared, and yielded just a little, in spite of herself. Men, she was thinking. They always get it wrong. But this one was trying. And he was still cute. Actually he hadn't gotten it wrong, he'd gotten it just right. It's just that she was still angry for the choice he'd made. "You men are all the same. Chasin' windmills all damn day. You miss a lot of life that way."

He knew she was right, and told her so. She smiled, just a tiny bit. She glanced back over her shoulder, and grudgingly nodded for him to enter. "Susie and Katie are at a girlfriend's," she said, her voice husky. "Danny's napping, but he sleeps good. You can come in, just keep your voice down."

"Thanks," said Lowell, and meant it. He followed her in. Watching her buttocks flex, the muscles in her back ripple, he knew he wanted her, and that she knew it too. It would be up to her. This was her house, and her call.

She headed for the kitchen, always the good hostess. He followed.

"Can I fix you a drink?" she asked. "Or do you want to talk about sinkholes and bank accounts some more first?" She turned, one hand on her curvaceous hip, challenging him.

He liked her a lot just now. He didn't waste energy wondering how such a fine woman could have wound up with a moron like Dicky Cahill. It happened all the time, he realized. Lovely, beautiful, sensitive women making simply dreadful choices in terms of men. Now she would choose him. Another bad choice. He, too, would ultimately be a disappointment to her. It was the way it was. But for now . . .

"No sinkholes, I promise."

She cocked her head, turned, and went to the refrigerator. "What was that you liked again? Kirin beer?" She'd remembered. Or had learned, somehow. He didn't even remember telling her that. "I asked them at the package store. Never even heard of it. All the men I know drink Budweiser, or Miller Light, that's about it. But I did get some Molson's, would that do?"

"It'll do just fine, thanks," he said, accepting one. It was more than he could have expected. She stood in front of him. Close. Her nipples stood even closer. Erect. He took one sip, set the beer down, and reached around her. Putting his hand at the small of her back, he pulled her to him. Her mouth tilted upward, open. They kissed.

Lowell knew what to do. She led him to a better place to do it, bringing his beer, and another just like it for herself. She was a brave and adventurous woman, he was thinking. She could have been thinking the same thing herself as they made love all through the hot afternoon, until the first small fist banged on the door.

"Not yet," she called as she lay in the crook of his arm, sweat and love juices intermingling, both limp and naked. "In a few minutes, honey."

The second fist that banged on the door wasn't little, and the door flew open with a crash.

"Well, well," came a furious, sarcastic, nasal-sounding snarl. "I'll be a motherfucker." Briana's husband had come home. Drunk, and madder than a bee-stung bull, brandishing a tire iron.

"Hey," said Lowell, pulling his pants on quicker than

Ricky Henderson could steal second. "If it isn't the man of the house."

"Man enough for you, you son of a bitch!" shouted Cahill, lunging for him. At that moment, two things happened. The first thing was, a small blond head popped in the door to take a look. The second thing was, as Cahill saw his little boy, his attention wavered, and he lost his momentum. Lowell simply stepped aside and let him crash into the bureau.

Lowell helped pick the dazed Cahill up off the floor. "What the—" muttered Cahill.

"Sorry about that," said Lowell, offering about as much an apology as he felt the man deserved.

Briana, meanwhile, was busy pulling on some clothes of her own.

"You wanna explain this?" moaned Cahill, stunned.

"Not in front of Danny," she said firmly.

"Fuck you!" bellowed Cahill, recovering fast.

Lowell picked up Cahill's tire iron, to keep it out of harm's way. "Easy, man," he suggested. Cahill sat down sullenly, and then, surprise of all surprises, burst into tears. Another child's head popped in through the doorway, then another. The girls, it seemed, were home. A now-clothed Briana hustled the bewildered kids out of the room without even a glance back.

Lowell turned, just as Cahill came at him again. He had no time to do anything but put his hand up, a reflex action, in self-defense. Unfortunately for the lunging Cahill, that was the hand that was holding the tire iron. There was an ugly thudding noise as Cahill ran smack into the bar and dropped to the floor with a groan, landing like a sack of Uncle Ben's white rice.

Lowell looked remorseful. "Sorry about that." Taking a couple of polyester Kmart neckties from the closet, he bound Cahill's hands with an orange spotted one, and for good measure, tied his feet with another featuring dancing cowboys.

"I'd really try not to use foul language around the kids," he suggested to the inert figure. Cahill wasn't listening. Lowell went into the kitchen and rejoined Briana. She'd hustled the children into the living room to watch cartoons. They were alone again for a brief moment.

"You okay?" he asked her.

She nodded, her jaw set. She was in for it, they both knew. She felt an odd mixture of shame and exultation just now. She wasn't exactly ashamed of what she'd done—only that she hadn't done it better. Lettin' that fool walk in on them like that. At least he hadn't come any earlier, she thought. Now an hour ago, that would have *really* ruined the day! She smiled to herself. That was the exultation part.

Lowell put his arm around her and pulled her close once more for a moment.

"I'm sorry about this," he said, and meant it. "Anything I can do to smooth things over?"

She shook her head. "It ain't never been smooth around here," she said. "Anyways, I've caught him more times than a cat gets kittens, one way or another, over the years. Deep down, he'll know he had it comin,' and he'll calm down some."

Lowell doubted that. "Why don't you get out?" he urged her. "Right now. I'll help. He's gonna be tied up for a while," he added.

She hesitated. It would be one of those little motions, little gestures, he knew, that he would remember forever afterward.

"I gotta stay," she finally said. "On account of the kids."

He knew he wouldn't be able to dissuade her. And he felt certain he wouldn't see her again. Not like this, anyway. He shook his head and turned to go. She came after him.

"Wait!" she called. "I remembered something. That guy Dicky's been hangin' out with, the big shot?"

He waited.

"I remember his name," she went on. "Doc something."

"Doc?"

"I think he used to play baseball with the Reds. Some big all-star guy. Now he's retired, and he's like a big local honcho. Doc. Or, wait, I remember now. Virgil."

The pieces fell into place. They fit perfectly. Lowell knew a few names in baseball. He'd even been known to watch a game or two, in his lifetime. "Doc Malone!" he exclaimed. "Virgil Doc Malone. Of course." He should have recognized him. Doc Malone had gotten that moniker after a sportswriter from Boston had referred to him as the "Doctor of Doubles." He had a great batting eye, with an all-star lifetime batting average to show for it. The man had really gone to seed, he realized, since his playing days.

"I got a black eye that time for not knowin' who he was when Dicky mentioned him."

So, thought Lowell. Virgil Malone had become notorious in these parts. After twenty years in the majors, he'd thanked the public by racking up six or seven indictments for racketeering, all dismissed by awe-stricken local judges. Eternally affable, he remained as popular as ever. He also had another nickname, given him by some of his less ardent followers, Lowell recalled. It was Gator.

"So Virgil Malone works for Florida Fertilizers?"

"Not exactly. I think he's got a deal of some kind with the company, like a spokesperson or something. But Dicky was braggin' about hangin' out with him."

"Business? Or do you think Virgil Malone just likes your husband for his innate charm?"

"You're funny," she said.

"Thanks," he said. He looked back toward the other

room, where sounds of stirring could be heard. "You just gonna let him loose, and jump back, or what? He's dangerous, surely you know that better than anyone."

"I know," she said. "I'll take the kids to my sister Carol's, and call my brother-in-law from there. Jerry O'Brien's a big boy. He'll come over and untie him, and make a few jokes at Dicky's expense, a few more at my expense, and that'll be that. It'll blow over."

"You really think so?" Lowell doubted it very much, and made a decision. He kissed her farewell. Knowing her hopelessness, knowing the choice she'd made, and how she was determined to stick it out, knowing what would ultimately happen, damn near broke his heart. . . .

Ninety minutes later, Dicky Cahill had managed to get himself loose, and was just undertaking a rage-filled search of his house for someone to abuse, when there was a loud rap on the door. "Bree?" he bellowed. "Where the fuck are you, girl!?"

"What the f—?" he snarled, and threw open the door.

"Richard Cahill?"

"Who the—"

"You're under arrest," announced Det. Lt. Lena Bedrosian, of the Manatee City Police, together with a sheepish-looking deputy named Davis from the county sheriff's office. "For assault, domestic battery, and suspicion of murder."

The deputy read him his rights.

14

Perry Garwood didn't smoke. Other than the occasional joint, that is. Otherwise, this would be the perfect time for it. It took patience, he realized, watching, watching, sitting in one place, not moving, having to be constantly vigilant. He was still waiting for the fun part. He'd have to give some more thought to this private investigations business. On the other hand, he had to admit to himself, he'd hardly had time to give it much of a chance. There might be some action yet.

The dog had been a minor problem, but not for long. He'd learned how to handle attack dogs as a matter of course. Just a little blow between the eyes when they came at you was all it took, combined with a kick under the chin. It usually broke their necks. It always rendered them senseless. He almost hated to do it, dogs were such beautiful, loyal animals. But what had to be, had to be. And he could tell (and had been forewarned by Lowell) that this one was unnatural. It was just as well, to send him back to the great campground in the sky, for recycling. He'd wait some more. After all, he was part Crow. Didn't Crow Indians know how to be patient? Hell, they probably invented it. Patience there, bo'. Patience.

* * *

Leonard Smith was getting more and more impatient. He knew there was someone out there. He knew, deep down, instinctively, that whoever it was, was kin of some kind. Maybe not family. Maybe not even racially. But in some way. Another "gangsta": a fellow predator, a brother hunter, a backdoor, back-alley, backwoods, back-streets man like himself. Wouldn't matter if he be friend or foe. Either way meant it was time to be watchful. Where the hell was Cyrus, the damn dog? That bothered him. Cyrus should make roadkill out of anyone out there. Something was wrong. He whistled softly. There was no response.

He loaded his latest acquisition, a brand-new Fabrique Nationale FNC assault gun with a thirty-round magazine, newly purchased at a gun show in Tampa (no questions asked), and sat by the upstairs window.

"Lenny?" It was the bitch, calling from downstairs. The child was whining again. "Chill!" he ordered. He was gonna have to do something about them pretty soon. Mama bitch and the little girl bitch were getting to be a real pain. He was supposed to tiptoe around the little kid like she was made of glass or some shit. Fuck that. He heard a sound outside. Was it up on the roof? No motherfucker better be up there, he thought to himself. Or he is about to get aerated. Evaporated. Coagulated. Harp City. Muh fuh, man!

Crouched on a tree branch not fifty feet away, Perry had finally made a move. He'd been listening with mixed fascination and repulsion as the two adults inside traded mostly barbs, occasional hostilities, and an odd, rare term of endearment, usually at the top of their lungs, plainly audible. They sleep together, he decided. She's one of those women who needs to be held. And he's big on holding. Reins, mostly. Or whips. She'll take it 'cause she's too scared to leave. He'll dish it out 'cause he's a bully and it's easy pickin's. A codependency, he decided. That's what Lowell would call it. Some shit like that. As for the girl, he couldn't decide. Her reactions to Smith seemed to fall between dread and fascination. A bad combination for any female to be falling into, he reflected as he tossed another handful of acorns onto the roof.

He saw Leonard Smith now, stepping out onto a narrow balcony from an upstairs bedroom, searching the roof above. Smith was heavily armed, he noted. He wasn't even trying to conceal the fact. Looked like one of those banned imports—a schoolyard special. He must have the whole neighborhood scared shitless, Perry thought. And he's getting more and more confident. He does this all with impunity. The cops don't care about the neighborhood, they aren't going to protect it from him. Their job, in their view, is to protect the rest of Manatee City *from* the 'hood. Long as he keeps his head down, don't do nothin' too obvious or outrageous, the turf is his.

Perry pretty much saw it that way. Now, what to do about it? What was it Lowell had wanted here? To watch over the mother and daughter, and keep an eye on the homeboy. But what could he really do to protect them, without taking him on? One on one. Except there would be no free throws in this game.

He reached into his pocket and drew out his favorite weapon: a length of heavy-duty quarter-inch nylon cord. He'd already fastened a three-ounce fishing weight to the end. Now he would await the proper moment, and toss it over that large branch of the big oak tree directly above him.

Smith heard a sound. He cocked his weapon and turned, searching the darkness. Wishing he had his damn sniper scope. The battery was dead, and he hadn't figured out where to go yet for a replacement. It wasn't exactly Radio Shack shit. He turned his attention to the roof. Maybe I can surprise the sonuvabitch, he thought. Make him squirm a little before I quietly drop his ass into the street down there. Won't even need no gun for that, I can do it with my bare hands. But I'll bring it along, he decided. Just in case.

Perry could see that the big gun was slowing his quarry, making him tantalizingly vulnerable at this moment. He could swing in three moves through this tree, and be on him while Smith was busy trying to hang on to the steeply sloped gable with one hand and aim his gun with the other. It would be a mismatch.

He glided to the next branch, swung silently around the trunk, and onto another branch that overhung the back porch. He was almost on him now, and Smith hadn't even heard him. Now for the fun part, Perry thought. It would be over in a moment. But then he remembered. What was his mission again? It wasn't search and destroy. He was supposed to watch the dude, not off him. Lowell had no idea, he supposed, of how dangerous he, Perry Garwood, actually was. How lethal. Or maybe he did.

Perry hesitated then, and in so doing made the tiniest noise as his sneakered feet dug in to the tree trunk in a braking motion. A small piece of bark fell to the ground. An inconsequential noise, to most people. But Smith heard it. And at that moment three things happened. The first thing was, Leonard Smith spun around on the roof, gun ready, in order to spray the area of darkness directly behind him. He'd been in the service too, before they'd thrown him out with a dishonorable discharge, just for fuckin' that officer bitch a couple of times without saying "Requesting permission, sir!" or some shit first. It hadn't helped, either, that she was a white chick.

The second thing that happened was that the entire area was suddenly flooded with a searchlight, just as Perry was reaching for his backup weapon—a small throwing knife—

and Smith was about to pulverize him and the rest of the neighborhood as well with his weapon of war.

"Freeze!" shouted a no-nonsense female voice through a bullhorn.

"Shit!" swore both would-be combatants simultaneously.

The third thing that happened was that Leonard Smith lost his grip, slid, nearly fell off the roof with a yell, just barely managed to grab on to the gutter, and dropped his highly illegal assault gun right at the feet of Det. Lt. Lena Bedrosian of the Manatee City Police.

She wasn't pleased. First, Lowell had disappeared. He'd badgered her into taking down Cahill—not even in her jurisdiction—which meant she owed one to Sheriff Pearson up in Hillsborough. Then he'd promised to meet her at ten, and hadn't shown. She'd waited half an hour, then something had told her to look here, in East Manatee. Lowell had mentioned his friend Perry. And now, sure enough, here he was, causing trouble. Along with this Smith character. She signaled to her backup, Peters and Baker, who were more than happy to get these two perps behind bars, even though she wasn't ready yet with any charge that would stick. Now the question was, where was Lowell?

She began to worry. What if something had happened to him? Again? He was a big boy, but still. . . . On the other hand, there wasn't much she could do at this point, except wait. He was probably just delayed or something, she decided, as she drove back to the station house, filed her report, and booked her prisoners. She'd go home now, catch a few nods, and hope Lowell showed if only to bail his friend out. Assuming he was all right, it might take him a while, she realized, before he even knew where his friend was. But if nothing else, Cecilia would tell him. She'd witnessed the arrests. He'd ask her, all right. It was the babe factor, and she was a babe, Bedrosian had to admit.

She wondered if her husband ever thought of her as a babe anymore. He had once, she knew. But now, thirty-something, three kids at home, different schedules. She still dressed nice, took care of herself. But she was no longer so sure, these days. She went to the women's rest room to wash her face and check her makeup. Her hair was a mess, but she was too tired to care. Her husband and kids would be asleep by now, anyway. It was the way it was.

$\mathbf{F}$ifty miles north and east, Tony Lowell had lost all track of time. After seeing that Cahill's wife and kids were safe out of the house, he'd placed the call to Bedrosian. She had grudgingly agreed to come get Cahill, and was shocked to hear about Baumgarten.

"That's going to have to fall to the sheriff's department, though," she told him. "It's not my jurisdiction. I'll file a report, and I'll need to take a statement from you. So will the sheriff." Pearson was becoming less and less pleased with this situation in Bone Valley, she knew. She didn't look forward to having to call him again.

"Okay, but later. I have things to do."

He had hung up, then gone underground to catch his wind, stopping off at the same small park where he'd lunched two days before, on the Alafia River—a lovely winding vestige of old Florida—to catch a few minutes of badly needed shut-eye.

Two hours later he'd found a pay phone on State Route 64 to check back with Lena. She couldn't decide if she was relieved or annoyed to hear from him. She'd been busy, first helping to arrest Cahill in cooperation with the sheriff's office, then sending a search party for Corcoran. He'd been found, wandering in a dazed condition along the road. He had a lot of cuts and bruises, and was madder than a hornet with its wings clipped.

"I think, all in all," suggested Bedrosian, "you'd better keep your nose out of Orange Blossom for a while."

"Don't worry about me," he said.

"I have no jurisdiction there," she reminded him. "The sheriff is willing to keep Cahill on suspicion of domestic battery, but only if the wife files a complaint. As for the murder of Tim Cross, I'm afraid the judge threw that one out. We don't have the evidence to make it stick yet."

"What about Corcoran? I'll give you a statement that he kidnapped and tried to kill me."

"Where's the proof? You got evidence?"

Shit, Lowell remembered. The gun. He'd tossed it, during an excessive surge of adrenalin. It was doubtful he'd be able to find it again without a team of divers and a backhoe.

"Otherwise," Bedrosian reminded him, "it's just your word against his."

"How's my word with you, Bedrosian? Or you giving him equal billing on that, too?"

"Easy, Lowell. I believe you, but right now Buster Corcoran, a local boy I might add, which is also an embarrassment for the sheriff, is screaming that you kidnapped him."

"Great. He's got a hundred pounds on me, he carries weapons, I don't, and I kidnapped him."

"Luckily for you, he's in the hospital ward overnight for observation. He's kind of banged up. So he won't be at large just yet, but I'd watch out, if I were you."

"It's the guy he works for I'm worried about. Does the name Virgil Malone mean anything to you?"

"*The* Virgil Malone?"

"The one. A real local hero."

"Jesus, Lowell. Why don't you just find me a suspect that

177

everybody in the world loves? That'll really make my life easy."

"Sure. How about Lenny Smith?"

"Yeah. Right. So what about Malone?"

"He's got something going regarding that sinkhole. I need to find out what."

Lowell had promised he'd be careful, and to meet her that night at the Oyster House, on Bay Drive—sort of a halfway point for them. He'd fill her in then. She also had some news for him: the coroner's report, and also a police lab report regarding the piece of glass they'd found near where Tim Cross's body was discovered. It wasn't certain where he'd died yet, which was why the lab and medical examiner's reports were so important.

What happened next, however, was that he got sidetracked. Cecilia Potter had said something to him three nights ago at the church supper at the AME Church. Something about Carla Brewer. That he should watch out for her. He hadn't really had time to take that in just then, with Leonard Smith breathing hot sauce and threats in his face, and Carla watching him like a hawk. Carla had been very brusque with him. Anxious, basically, to get rid of him. Surprisingly unsympathetic, even, to the untimely demise of a rather exemplary young black man. That was strange. All that talk about jobs, and mouths to feed. He wondered.

He wondered if she was listed in the phone book. After hanging up from his call to Bedrosian, he decided to look her up. There were several Brewers, but no Carla, or anyone under *C.* He didn't want to call randomly. In a town of that size, it was too likely to put her (or her friends) on alert. He checked his notes, sticking out of various pockets, and found the little pad that had the notes from the church supper. Ben Tompkins, he'd written. That was the big man who'd hovered over her at the plant. Presumably one of her friends. He wasn't listed either. Anyway, he would be protective of her, just like he was in the parking lot, and at the church. On the other hand . . .

There was another name. Yasha Dromes. The West Indian, possibly Haitian man, who'd been very friendly to him. Maybe Dromes would talk to him. He thumbed through the white pages under the *D*s. Someone had torn the page out. Cursing that particular careless act that film and television directors had thoughtlessly popularized over the years, he dialed Directory Assistance. "Please deposit fifty cents," he was instructed. He didn't have fifty cents. Hanging up in disgust, he got back in his car, turned around, and headed back to Orange Blossom. Yasha Dromes was there somewhere. He would find him.

As Lowell entered town, he remained watchful. Cahill and Corcoran might well have friends looking for him. Not to mention Malone. He decided to stay off Main Street, and use Second Street, just to the south. There were fewer stores (and therefore phones) but the possibility of being spotted by someone unfriendly was less likely here. Luckily, the African Methodist Episcopal Church, he realized, was just a couple of blocks away. It was Friday evening. Sometimes people went to church events on Fridays: choir rehearsals, or community meetings, or lay ministry and the like. Someone might be there who could tell him where to find Dromes. Or maybe the minister would be there.

He heard the gospel music before he was within two blocks: mournful yet hopeful, mystical yet earthy, beautiful, and divine. In Lowell's opinion, there was no one on earth closer to God than those who could lift up their voices like that. He'd always wished he could sing. At least he could listen.

He parked and walked, enthralled. The choir was indeed rehearsing. He went into the church, and stood in the back.

The same large woman as before was leading. The minister was singing lead baritone in his deep, rich voice. The song was "River Jordan." Lowell almost ventured to sing along, but managed to restrain himself. The minister looked up. Farnsworth, his name was, Lowell remembered. The Reverend Farnsworth. The reverend spotted Lowell, recognized him, beamed, and waved, all in one highly efficient motion.

"Mr. Lowell," he called out, much to Lowell's embarrassment. "Welcome back, welcome back! Do you sing, by any chance?"

"Not in your league, I'm afraid." All the choir members laughed. It was a friendly laugh. Many of them were still smiling at him. It wasn't common, even in today's "New South," for a white man to show up at a black church. Let alone twice. And even if one did, they weren't always so welcome.

Farnsworth swept down the aisle to greet him, and Lowell sheepishly met him halfway. "Well, if it isn't to sing, what brings you back to our hallowed halls, Mr. Lowell?"

"Sorry to disturb you." Lowell was covertly studying the membership of the choir for familiar faces as he spoke. He recognized several, but not the persons he was seeking. "I met a gentleman the other evening by the name of Yasha Dromes. I was wondering how I might find him."

"Ah," said the reverend. "This is about that young man, isn't it. Timmy Cross?"

"Afraid so."

"He was a good boy. I'd wanted to speak with you about that, that night, but you seemed busy."

"I was kind of overwhelmed, I think, meeting your whole flock like that, all at once. I don't want to interrupt your rehearsal. Would there be a good time and place to talk?"

"How about after rehearsal? We'll be another hour. Meanwhile, you could try and talk to Yasha. He works at the gas station nights, just on the corner of Palmetto and Pinellas." He pointed. "Two blocks over, three down. It's a small town, Mr. Lowell."

"Yeah. Too small."

The reverend laughed appreciatively, and returned to his choir. Lowell listened to a lively version of "You Got to Walk that Lonesome Valley," and quietly slipped out.

It was one of those rare evenings when the moon was just rising at the same time that the sun was setting. Cumulus clouds billowed to the west over the Gulf, streaked with brilliant orange and red from the sunset. The moon was nearly full, and loomed above the eastern horizon, refracted huge in the dust and moisture-charged atmosphere of central Florida. It was a special night. A dangerous night. Not a night for a white out-of-town private investigator to be alone, associating with black people, in the town of Orange Blossom, Florida.

The gas station was a true gem, probably deserving of a place in the National Historic Register. It was a faded two-story Queen Anne-style clapboard building with a wide porte cochere that had carved pillars supporting each end, and two antique manual gas pumps in between. It had no name, or sign of any kind. There was just enough space for a car to pull in for gas, which Lowell did. In the two big plate-glass windows was an assortment of the most eclectic variety of bric-a-brac and junk—all of it for sale—that he'd seen in years. There were antiques, there were collectibles, there were car parts, truck parts, tires, sewing machines, obsolete small appliances, you name it. Lowell spotted something he'd wanted for some time—a replacement for the missing hubcap from his left rear wheel. He went inside.

Dromes was behind the counter. His face lit up like a birthday cake when he saw Lowell coming.

"Nice shop. This your place?" Lowell asked, upon entering.

"Heyyyy, mon!" Dromes exclaimed, coming around the counter to pump Lowell's hand. "Yeah, yeah, my own little enterprise, be it ever so humble. I own everything but the building, the land, and the stock. So, what brings you back here to the OB? That's black for outback, as well as Orange Blossom," he added with a hefty laugh.

Lowell smiled. "I got it." He liked this man. "I thought I'd try you one more time for that recipe. For the ribs. Also, I can use this hubcap."

Dromes looked out the window at Lowell's car, and his smile widened another foot. "All right! A 1965 Chevrolet Impala that still runs!"

"Most of the time. Badly."

"Yes, I've been holdin' that item for three years, just waiting for you to come along. It's on the house."

"No, it's worth ten. Let me pay, it won't kill me."

Dromes shrugged. He seemed disappointed, as though Lowell had hurt his feelings, maybe just a little. "Make it five, then."

"Deal. Now, about those ribs."

"Maybe someday. But I have to know you better first. What you come back here for?" His voice dropped and he glanced around. "This place is dangerous for you, don't you know that?"

"I'm beginning to get the idea," said Lowell. "What I don't get is, why? I'm kind of hoping someone will tell me what all this business with the sinkhole is all about, for one thing."

"That? That's much ado about nothing. That mon Malone and his cronies, like Dicky Cahill, all just trying to make a buck over there. That's all I know."

"Do you agree with Carla Brewer? That black people's jobs are at stake?"

Dromes sat back. "You want some coffee?"

"Sure. Also I like honey, if you have it. And milk."

"Milk and honey. River Jordan is deep and wide," sang Dromes. "Coming right up." He fetched two steaming hot mugs and set one down for Lowell. It was a Cincinnati Reds mug. "Look," he said. "Ms. Brewer, she is a dedicated woman. She believes in her people, and works hard for us. There isn't a one of us in town that wouldn't lay it all on the line for her. But she's got her weak spots," he went on after a sip. "She's as weak as the rest of us when it comes to love."

"Love?"

"Love. She had the hots big-time for that young fellow who come down here with all those fancy degrees. She's the only other one 'round here went to college, so I suppose that might've been part of it."

"So why was she so down on him?" Lowell figured he knew, though.

Dromes laughed. "You ever know a woman wasn't down on her man?"

"So they were an item, then. I mean, he was her man?"

"No, not exactly." Dromes frowned, and turned away. He picked up an ancient alarm clock and shook it a couple of times. It chimed, then croaked. "No, I don't think he had no time for her, tell you the truth. He was all eyes for that sweet lil' young thing, from over Manatee City."

"Cecilia Potter."

So. The smaller the circle, the more larger circles around it, like a pebble tossed into a pool. "Cecilia seemed to feel it was the other way around."

"Hey. Women. How many women you know who see things straight, mon?"

"Maybe one. But then I don't know too many women. I don't know too many guys who see things straight either."

Dromes laughed. "I can dig it. Now, can I interest you in a nice watch? One of those old windup ones, no miniature nuclear reactors boring tiny holes through your bod with radium or some shit like that. You just wind it up, and—"

"Not yet, thanks. My old nuclear reactor still runs. So what about Carla, then? You think I might be able to talk to her a little?"

"You ask her about her and Cross, you may's well ask her about the price of coffee on the moon. She's not gonna talk to you, mon."

"Maybe she'll talk to a woman." He was thinking of Lena.

"Long as it's not that Potter girl."

"Fair enough. Would you tell me where I can find her, then? Or where a woman friend can find her?"

Dromes eyed him shrewdly. He dug into a drawer under the counter and found a business card: ebony black with gold lettering. He handed it to Lowell. "I don't need this, I guess," he said. "I can call her anytime I want to. Also, I see her at church."

Church. Of course. If all else failed, she'd be there on Sunday, for certain.

"Thanks," said Lowell. "By the way, do you have any old carpentry tools, hand tools, preferably?" He was beginning to get some strength back in his hands, after his old gunshot wound, and was yearning to work with them again.

Dromes did. He had a really nice set of carving tools in a nice oak box, and a beautiful wooden-handled plane.

"Five dollars each," he announced. Lowell would have paid ten. "How about seven fifty?" he asked, smiling.

"For both?"

"For each. They're worth it, believe me."

Dromes gave him a look, and carefully wrapped the two

184

packages. Lowell handed him a ten and a five. "Hey. You all right, for a white boy."

"Thanks. That's what everybody tells me. When they're not trying to kill me."

Dromes let forth a short, sharp laugh, and walked him to the door. "Yes. Well, listen. You take care, mon. And maybe not just around here. I'd watch my own pea patch, if I were you."

"I'll keep that in mind."

Lowell left, pleased with his purchases, but disappointed with his lack of information. He had added another suspect, possibly. But without any more substantive information than he'd already had. And he already had suspects aplenty without needing to be encumbered with another. He looked at Carla's card. The civil rights office was in Plant City. She wouldn't be there at this hour, though. It was Friday night. The sun was already setting.

He considered grabbing a bite at the nearest coffee shop, then thought the better of it. Discretion getting the better part of valor, he decided he'd better head back on down to Manatee, and develop and print the sinkhole shots.

Pulling his Chevy out of Dromes's store, he made a U-turn in the road, and headed west. The last rays of pink and turquoise light still streaked the sky, dead ahead.

He'd just gotten to the outskirts of town when he remembered: the reverend. The reverend had wanted to talk to him, after rehearsal. Spinning the car around, he headed back into town. Two men in a green pickup slowed as they passed him, eyes large and unfriendly as they looked him over. But they didn't stop, or follow him.

Lowell drove back through Orange Blossom, now surprisingly clogged with traffic, this being Friday night. He wondered where they were all going. Church, maybe. Or the nearest country western bar, or rib house. He turned down

Second Street to the AME Church, and pulled over to the curb. Most of the cars that had been parked here earlier were gone, and the parking lot was dark. There was a single light on at the back of the building. There was a small house behind it as well, he remembered, from his prior visits. Probably the parish house. If the reverend wasn't in the church proper, he'd probably be at the house.

Lowell walked along the grassy parking lot to the back, and knocked on the door. It opened.

"Ah, Mr. Lowell." It was the reverend.

"Reverend Farnsworth? Thanks for seeing me. I really love your music, by the way."

"Of course you do, son. Everyone does. Even the most bigoted white people in the Old South who wouldn't let us in their restaurants or schools always loved our music. They even tried to copy it. That's kind of why we tend to discourage white folks from attending our churches, by the way. We feel if they really want to find common ground with us before God, the first step is for them to invite our people into their churches. For the most part, we're still waitin'."

"I'd invite you to mine, if I had one," said Lowell.

"Then you don't believe in God?"

"I didn't say that. I'm not sure what I believe, to be honest. Other than it's pretty clear to me the difference between right and wrong, and between justice and injustice."

"Ah, yes. You are a detective. Investigating the death of that very unfortunate young man."

"His uncle was—is, one of my oldest friends."

The reverend's eyes widened in surprise. "Come in," he said, and held open the door. "Can I offer you some coffee, or soda?"

"Root beer, if you have it. Otherwise, water would be fine."

"One root beer, comin' up."

Lowell sure was being offered a lot of hospitality lately. "Thanks," he said.

He took a plain wooden lyre-back chair that the reverend slid over to him, and sat at the little Formica table in the center of what must be the rectory, he figured. A simple combination office, kitchenette, and meeting room. The reverend brought two root beers, and sat down across from him.

"You like to arm wrestle?"

Lowell declined. "Thanks, but I might win, which would be ungracious."

The reverend laughed. Then turned serious. "What've you figured out so far about this young man's death?"

Lowell decided he could trust him. He was, after all, a man of God. He told him about Cecilia, and her boyfriend, Smith, and the strange goings-on at Florida Fertilizers. He asked the reverend if he knew anything about the activities of Cahill and Malone. The reverend didn't. "I'm not too privy as to the doings of white folks, I'm afraid." Lowell then mentioned the sinkhole.

"Ah." Farnsworth knew about that. "One of God's little messages," he said gravely. "We have not been humble, in his eyes. We have not been respectful of his creations."

"You mean planet Earth?"

"On earth, as it is in heaven."

"I think that's what Tim Cross's thing was all about," said Lowell. "He was an avid environmentalist. That isn't exactly popular, in these parts, is it?"

"No, it isn't," admitted the reverend, looking thoughtfully at the ceiling. Lowell followed his gaze. The ceiling was of hammered tin sheeting, very old, its white paint peeling and flaking. Lowell wondered if Farnsworth was aware of

187

the hazards of old leaded paint. He decided to leave it to someone else to tell him. Besides, Farnsworth probably didn't eat much paint, these days.

"So I gathered, from what Ms. Brewer was telling me," concluded Lowell, seizing the opening.

"Well." Farnsworth laughed. "Carla tends to be a little outspoken at times, and between you and me, a little softening of the spirit would do her a great deal of good."

Lowell wasn't about to volunteer for the job.

"Also," added Farnsworth, almost as an aside, "she's not as popular as she might think, at times. I've had to counsel her more than once regarding humility."

Lowell absorbed that, which got him to thinking about another angle of attack.

"You know, there is someone I'd like to talk to, who belongs to your church. He was here last week with Ms. Brewer."

"Ben Tompkins," nodded Farnsworth. "Yeah, ol' Ben, he's more attached to Carla than a tick to a bird dog."

"He sweet on her?"

"Now that would be a private matter between him, her, and God," Farnsworth said, smiling. "But he'd do anything for that woman, I'll tell you that."

Lowell was formulating an idea as he talked. "He works at the plant, right?"

"Same as practically everyone around here."

"What kind of work did he do?"

"Custodian. What else? A po' uneducated black man like that, what'd you think he be, Vice President?"

Lowell was surprised by the sudden rancor, but shrugged it off. "You never know," he said, smiling.

"Sorry, but jobs for black folks always been an issue around here, as I'm sure Miss Brewer informed you."

"No offense taken. I'm sure you're right." What Lowell

was thinking, now that his guess had been confirmed, was that custodians often knew more about what goes on in a company than the CEO. It's just possible, he thought, that Tompkins knows what the real situation was regarding the sinkhole, not to mention the possible whereabouts of Tim Cross's missing report.

"Any chance you might have an address or phone number for him? He's not in the book."

"Of course he's not in the book, he can't afford a telephone," chided the reverend. "He stays at my home. He takes care of the parish house and rectory on weekends in return for room and board. You don't think they actually pay him a living wage over at the plant, do you?" He had a twinkle in his eye, but Lowell saw the truth in it.

"I see what you mean."

Lowell thought about thanking God for his sudden good fortune. Then decided it would be hypocritical, being as he was an agnostic. He thanked the reverend instead, who by his look seemed to be reading his thoughts.

"He's there now, probably makin' a nuisance of hisself tryin' to help my wife with dinner. Go on, take him off her hands for a while. Down the path, the kitchen door's to the right. Tell Verna I'll be along shortly."

Lowell thanked him, and bade him a good evening. "I will," he said.

Verna turned out to be the leader of the choir, and also the same ebullient woman who'd first welcomed Lowell to the church supper, what seemed like years ago. She ushered him into her kitchen with yet another round of hospitality, stuffing his face with a mouthful of cornbread while Tompkins looked on, half-curious, half-suspicious.

Lowell shook Tompkins's hand, and asked him if he could spare a few minutes. Verna suggested the porch. Tompkins seemed reluctant to go, but did so at her urging.

That left Lowell with only one minor problem: how to get Tompkins to talk. He thought about telling him what had happened today at the sinkhole, and about the dead hydrology engineer. He decided not to, it might just scare him into silence. Then he thought of an angle. Cecilia. If Tompkins was that protective of Carla, he might have a dim view of Cecilia Potter.

"I found something out that might interest you, regarding Carla Brewer's friend, Timothy Cross," he began.

Tompkins frowned. "Yeah, what's that?"

"Are you aware that he was personally involved, in some way, with a woman named Cecilia Potter?"

"Everybody know about that," mumbled Tompkins, "her and that som'bitch Smith, excuse my Turkish. Someone shoulda slapped some sense into the boy 'fore it was too late. I tried to tell Carla, but—"

"But what?"

Tompkins caught himself just in time. "Nothin'."

Lowell changed the subject, for now. "You ever hear of a man named Doc, or Virgil Malone?"

Tompkins snorted. "You mean Gator Malone? I could tell you his career batting average, how many double plays he make, how much money they used to pay him, and that he was one racist som'bitch." He glanced guiltily at the kitchen door, discreetly closed. "Excuse my Turkish."

"Sure. You have any idea what interest Mr. Malone might have in the land around a certain sinkhole that appeared on company property a month or so back?"

"That ain't no secret. He was buyin' the land, last I heard."

"Until the sinkhole?"

"Even recently, far's I know. He's just tryin' to keep it a little under his hat, if you know what I mean. Sinkholes are bad omens to a lot of people." Like Tim Cross, thought Lowell. And Harry Baumgarten.

"So Dicky Cahill works for him, too. On the side, like?"

"I ain't heard that. I do know they been seen together plenty of times. That anything to do with Cahill bein' in the lockup?"

Man, but news does travel fast in a small town, Lowell thought. He also thought about paying Cahill a visit while he was at the jail. Ask him a couple of questions. He decided it wouldn't be a good idea. Back to Tompkins.

"No. That was a domestic matter." Lowell thought it best not to bring Lena's short-lived murder charge into it just yet.

Tompkins nodded. He was lost in thought, then appeared to come to a decision.

"I know about the plans," he said.

Lowell sat forward at once. "What plans?"

"The plans. For Sunshine. I seen them on Mr. Freeman's desk. Them and the reports."

"Sunshine?" The word set off an alarm in the back of Lowell's mind. "What's that?"

"This big project they was workin' on. Mr. Freeman, Mr. Largent, and Mr. Malone."

"Any chance, any eensie teensie small chance in hell—I mean heck," Lowell corrected himself, "that I could get a look at these alleged plans?"

Tompkins appeared outraged. "I couldn't do that, I'd lose my job!" he exclaimed indignantly in a low voice.

"I was thinking of an incentive," said Lowell hastily. "I was thinking of maybe a contribution. Say, to your church."

Tompkins outrage abated considerably. "How big a contribution?"

Lowell thought quickly. He didn't have much money, and wasn't going to get paid very much, either, for this job. It was possible, but only slightly possible, that Lena would come through with some reimbursements. He hated to have to resort to bribery. But he didn't make the world, he thought to himself.

"I was thinking around fifty."

"Hmph," snorted Tompkins, very skillfully concealing his glee. "Ain't hardly worth the risk."

"Well, there is the reward factor," improvised Lowell. "For information leading to the arrest and conviction of the killer or killers of Timothy Cross, esquire."

"I ain't heard about no reward."

That's because there wasn't one. But maybe there ought to be, thought Lowell. Maybe he could scrounge one up. From the Feds, for civil rights violations. Or the EPA, or Sierra Club, or somebody. Maybe the earth was a giant Caesar salad. Anyway, he'd kick in the fifty himself, for now. He took out his wallet. "It's all I have," he said, and showed Tompkins the contents as proof.

Tompkins took the money. "I got that old pickup, behind the church. Meet me there in ten minutes," he said.

It was nearly dark as Lowell pulled his Chevy around next to the battered old Ford. He waited in the car with the windows open to allow what little breeze there was to get in. A mosquito buzzed in his ear and he swatted at it in vain. The minutes passed. A Camaro squealed around the corner and slowed. A teenager hurled a beer can in the direction of the church. Several others laughed raucously, and the car sped on. Lowell checked his watch and began to wonder what was keeping Tompkins. He got out and scanned the area, sensing the hostility out there. He was about to go and look for the old man when Tompkins emerged from the shadows, breathing hard.

"Let's go," the janitor said, glancing around nervously. Lowell didn't argue.

15

Lena Bedrosian had finally gone home to bed after booking Perry Garwood and Lenny Smith, each in separate cells so there would be survivors in the morning. Both men were raging, for wildly differing reasons. She'd informed Perry that it would be up to his friend to get him out, and it was very unfortunate Lowell hadn't bothered to show up tonight. That oughta fix Lowell's wagon, she'd thought to herself between pangs of worry. Lena Bedrosian was not above an occasional act of spite. As for Smith, a seething cauldron of rage, he shouted threats and invective at all within earshot (basically the entire cell block) until he fell asleep, exhausted, his venom spent, at around four in the morning.

Bedrosian had gone home hours earlier. It was nearly midnight, however, by the time she emerged from her bathroom in her panties and nightshirt, ready to collapse. She'd put in a hard day and week, and needed some rest. Also, her husband, Michael, needed some attention. Or felt she did. Not that she had any energy for it, of course. In fact, the only mood she was in was to roll over, curl up, and go to sleep. Maybe kiss the kids first, if any of them were awake.

Lena's husband, Michael, had long since resigned himself to the role of house-husband and primary caregiver to the children. With his part-time, mostly seasonal, work as a tax accountant, the job had fallen to him by default, and he had accepted it with aplomb. "I'll have to introduce you to your kids, though, one of these years," he often warned her. He was a tower of patience, although not above complaining at times. Tonight had been one of those times.

"Dammit, Lena!" he'd groused as she stumbled into the living room, waking him up where he'd fallen asleep on the couch. David Letterman droned on in the background, unwatched. She offed him.

"Sorry," she said. "It can't be helped."

Of course, it was her fault mostly, she had to admit. She'd come home in a foul mood after getting stood up by Lowell, and then having to cope with those two Rambo characters—one of them Lowell's friend and associate, no less, the other a key suspect in the Cross murder whom she was absolutely not yet ready to bring in. Three arrests in one day, in two different counties and jurisdictions. Enough already.

She had just curled up with one of those nice cozy mysteries she liked to read a few pages of before shut-eye (Michael had given up on her, and gone back to watching Letterman in the Florida room), when the phone rang.

She didn't have to guess. It could only be Lowell.

"Lowell, you inconsiderate, subcompetent log of moldy driftwood! Where the hell were you?" she barked before even asking who it was. On reflection, she realized, it could also have been Captain Arlen Jeffries, her superior. That could have been awkward. He'd been known to call her at worse hours than this. Rarely, however, on a Friday night.

It was Lowell. "I'm sorry, Lena. Really. I was in another place entirely. In more ways than one."

"Meaning what?"

"Orange Blossom."

"You are still in Orange Blossom?" she exploded. Michael looked in on her from the Florida room.

"You okay, honey?"

She waved him away brusquely. "Lowell, what the hell are you *doing?*"

"Reacquainting myself with the black community out here. You should try it sometime. I recommend it for consciousness raising."

"Look, I can barely keep conscious at all, at this late hour. What do you want that you were too busy for at ten o'clock, that can't wait the hell until morning?" she shouted. Michael popped his head in again, joined by one of the girls, Jackie, the oldest. Almost eight now. She waved them both away furiously.

"Sorry, Lena. No report in on Baumgarten, yet, I suppose?"

"Jesus, Lowell, I only just got the report on Cross today. Which is what I wanted to talk to you about."

"What did they find on him?"

"Fluorine. Cause of death is still a single gunshot wound to the head. But he had a ton of something called silicon tetrafluoride in his blood."

She could hear him catch his breath. "Was it in his lungs?"

"I don't know," she said, annoyed. "I don't have it in front of me at this particular moment, if you must know. I was about to go to bed, which I would have liked to have done an hour ago, but for you."

"Sorry. I was just wondering if he might have been submerged, before he was shot."

She hesitated, intrigued. "I'll have to check on that. There's more, though. There was a small amount of some derivative of the same stuff that's apparently highly toxic, called hydrofluosulicic acid, both of which are byproducts of phosphate processing. That was in his marrow, though.

He probably wouldn't have lived very long, anyway, they told me."

"Jesus, that is weird." There was a long pause. She could almost hear his wheels spinning. "What about sulfuric acid?" He finally asked.

"What about it?"

"Did they find any of that in his system?"

"No," she replied, annoyed. He was always changing the subject. "Not that I know of. Why?"

"Because that sinkhole is full of it. I'll tell you more to-morrow. Breakfast, Oyster House, nine-thirty?"

"Coffee, Red Top Café," (it was across from the police station) "seven-thirty, and be there or you're off the case," she snapped. Then sighed to herself. Michael was going to love that, she thought. Especially after this. Going to work on a Saturday morning, when they'd planned a day at the beach up at Fort DeSoto.

"I suppose this wouldn't be a good time to remind you of my time sheets and expenses," he said.

"Go to hell, Lowell!" she shouted. She was about to hang up the phone when the door popped open, and three very admonishing and disapproving sleepy faces looked in on her.

"Honey, are you *sure* you're okay?" asked Michael, a note of reproach in his voice.

"Mommy said a bad word," said Sarah, the youngest.

"I'm sorry, I'm sorry, I'll be off in a minute," she told them. Back to Lowell, she snapped, "Now you're messing with my home life, Lowell. The other thing was, it might interest you to know that we've gotten a partial ID on that piece of glass we found, out where Cross's body was dumped."

"So, the body was dumped," noted Lowell. He'd figured

as much. "Want to keep me guessing about the crystal? Or do you want to go ahead and spill it out?"

She swore under her breath. "You can be really annoying at times, Tony Lowell. What it is, is a piece of quartz crystal. The lab is running some further checks. I'll let you know."

"That's it?"

"Anyway, it's all we've got so far. Go ahead and talk to them if you want, and follow it up. Also, we've looked at that photo lab work you did, and I can't say there was anything much there we could use."

"That's because there was nothing there," he protested. He'd checked it very carefully himself before sending it over. Aside from the alligator (which he'd deleted) the only items of note had been the crystal fragment and the sinkhole story. "Is that a complaint?"

"No, merely an observation."

"Are you finally ready to tell me about the paternity thing?"

She exulted. Triumph was at hand. "I'll tell you about the paternity of Cecilia Potter's kid tomorrow."

A pause. "Fine," said Lowell, sounding suitably exasperated. "In that case, I'll save what I found at Florida Fertilizers until then. See you." At that, he hung up. She sat, openmouthed for a full ten seconds, and finally slammed down the phone, irate. Just when she'd gotten him but good, he'd matched her blow for blow. Now she wouldn't be able to sleep all night, wondering. Just to make sure he didn't try anything really obnoxious, like calling her back, she took the phone off the hook. Then she put on her bathrobe, and went out to make amends with her family.

Down on the bayou, Lowell shook his head in incredulity. Women, he thought. Feeling a twinge of remorse, he dialed her back. The line was busy. Damn! Now who was she talking to, at midnight, her girlfriend? Women! He pondered the chemicals in Cross's body, and what they might mean. To ease his frustration, he went downstairs and got out his camera bag. He might as well take a look at today's shots. He hadn't seen anything at the sinkhole, other than the pickup and the yellow fluid, but film and precision lenses tended to capture what the eye failed to see. Of far greater interest were the fruits of his visit to the empty offices of Florida Fertilizers, courtesy of Ben Tompkins.

Entering his darkroom, he turned on the black light, poured the developer, and unloaded the first roll.

The next morning, while children all over America were busy frying their brains watching animated supermorons zap each other mindless, while parents like Lena Bedrosian were supposed to be allowed to sleep in, Lowell and Bedrosian sat glaring at each other over two cups of steaming coffee at the Red Top Café. He'd brought a large brown folder, which he laid on the seat beside him, and ordered a bagel. She had a bran muffin. He had black splotches under his eyes and looked like hell: unshaven, overripe jeans, and black T-shirt cut off at midriff. She looked perfect despite her mood, in a new spring designer outfit from Burdine's: pink-and-mauve flowery blouse, beige flannel jacket, and trim matching trousers. Michael had bought it for her for Easter, the week before.

"Okay, let's deal," he said. "My Soil and Water Report for your paternity."

"Say what?" Bedrosian blinked. Soil and Water Report? One of the missing documents relating to Tim Cross's activities? Lowell's cryptic remark last night had been the first she'd heard about one. Her pulse raced. But she didn't want to give him too much satisfaction. She could bide her time. She was a virtuous woman, and patience was one of the re-

quired virtues. "Not so fast," she said, determined to maintain some degree of control over the situation. If paternity
was what he wanted so bad, he could damn well wait, too.
"Here's the coroner's report," she told him. "In addition to
the fluorine stuff, they found some other interesting things.
There was phosphogypsum under his nails."

"That's the stuff they have piled up all over the place out
there. I've got a rundown on it, if you're interested."

"Don't let me stop you."

He fumbled for his little notebook in his shirt pocket, and
thumbed through it. "Okay. Phosphogypsum, the main
waste product of phosphate mining. It's actually fairly inert,
except for a few traces of uranium and toxic metals." He
paused, recalling the video and what Solano had told him.
"They're spending millions as we speak, trying to figure out
clever things to do with the stuff. Ship it overseas for wall-
board and road materials, that sort of thing. They used to
just dump it in the ocean."

"No wonder my father went broke," she muttered. Her
father had been a fisherman. He had drowned at sea. "They
probably killed all the fish with it."

"This guy Freeman who gave me a tour," Lowell reflected, "had mentioned something they were trying to do
with that stuff. Something about desalination of the coastal
water table."

"That would be a good thing, if they can do that. Salt
water is contaminating half the lakes in Citrus and Her-
nando."

"I know. Anyway," continued Lowell, "this is more evidence Cross was probably dumped from somewhere else.
Maybe they had him in the boneyard somewhere, he tried to
escape, maybe crawling up one of those piles out there, and
they shot him."

"Possible. There's no powder marks on him, which

means he wasn't shot at close range." She brushed a crumb off her lap. "Take a look at what else was in his tissues."

She handed him a list. He read it over. "Mercury, cadmium, selenium, beryllium, lead, aluminum, and arsenic?"

"Plus the normal levels of copper, iron, and so forth. But this," she emphasized, tapping on the bottom of the analysis chart, "is the main event."

"Fluorine," he pondered. "It's a toxic chemical. Freeman told me it comes naturally from the rock out there."

"So what are you saying? This stuff slips through the cracks? On account of everybody is busy clucking their tongues at all the phosphatic gypsum, out on Route Sixty?"

"Something like that."

She looked at the report again. "Funny, you look at all the reports, the environmental studies, the reclamation permits, and plant schematics, and there's no mention of where it all goes. It just disappears somewhere."

"They process it. I saw the processing. According to the industry, all fluorine is processed—recovered, they call it. It's the main ingredient in fluoride."

"The stuff they put in the water?"

"No, they would've—wait a minute!" He sat up straight. She looked at him.

"What? Out with it."

"Cecilia Potter told me Tim Cross had said something about 'toothpaste.' It didn't make sense to her, but he was talking about fluoride. Maybe they were dumping it out there—"

"But if it's so useful, they'd sell it. For toothpaste," she pointed out. "And the drinking-water supply almost everywhere."

"Right. Damn." He pondered. "But maybe there were residual byproducts, like those PCBs, that they couldn't sell, so they just dumped them. He was doing a lot of tramping around out there, maybe he stumbled into a pool of it or something, and got poisoned."

"Maybe they caught him, and injected it into his bloodstream with an umbrella," she suggested sarcastically.

"It's possible."

"Come off it, Lowell, you're really getting out on a limb, there."

He decided to change the subject. "So, nothing about sulfuric acid."

She shook her head. He told her about the yellow stuff in the sinkhole.

"Are you serious?" she asked in alarm.

He nodded.

"We have to get someone over there to do a test," she declared. "Before it all sinks into the aquifer. You're talking about the main water supply for Manatee County!"

"I'm talking about the main water supply for the state of Florida." Her jaw dropped, and she hastily stuffed the opening that resulted with a piece of bran muffin. "I called Solano this morning," he assured her. "You're not the only family man working today. He sounded skeptical, but he's going to go out there himself."

She ignored the barb. "I'll send a patrol with him. You told him about Baumgarten?"

He nodded.

"They're calling it an accidental death, for now," she informed him.

He nodded, not pleased, but not surprised. "Now. Are you going to tell me about the paternity?" he finally asked. "Or were you planning to keep me in suspense indefinitely?"

"Not that you wouldn't deserve it," she opined. "You first. What's this about soil and water?"

Lowell took another sip of coffee. She waited, her fingers

202

drumming. "Soil and Water fits right in with the coroner's report, actually," he said thoughtfully. "But you got the paternity information yesterday during the day. I didn't get the Soil and Water Report until last night. You first."

She almost choked on her coffee. He could be so infuriating at times. It was kind of a macho thing. Playing childish games as a power play was just machismo in disguise. She hated machismo. She got it from the cops at the station, as well as the crooks she investigated, on a daily basis. Lowell she expected to be different. Even though she would never openly admit to any appreciation whatsoever for his differentness.

"I went to a lot of trouble to get at those records," she snapped at him. "They're going to great lengths now to protect those battered women and children and their privacy."

"Maybe not enough," he remarked. "So, who was it?"

"The father of Cecilia Potter's daughter, Natasha—Natasha Potter, you should know—is not Leonard Smith," she told him.

"That's your big surprise? Give me a break."

"It wasn't Tim Cross either."

"No surprise there either. C'mon. Out with it."

"Richard Cahill," she informed him.

"No shit!" He remembered Briana's complaint about child support. "That unbelievable, hypocritical, two-timing son of a bitch!"

"One of zillions," she snapped, irritated that he'd stolen her thunder. "You should talk." She gave him a "meaningful" look as she said it. He fidgeted, wondering how she knew. To change the subject, he told her about Carla Brewer's alleged crush on Tim Cross.

"That's hearsay again," she complained. "Any evidence?"

"I knew you'd say that," he said. He told her about the break-in.

She was appalled. "You broke into Florida Fertilizers?"

"Not actually. Actually, I was let in by the janitor. For a price. The point is, what we found may be very pertinent to our investigation."

She took a large bite of muffin, washed it down with some coffee, and fixed him with a glare. "Such as?"

"Cross was concerned about the aquifer. There were several memos on Freeman's desk, and the Managing Director's, Pierce Something, who doesn't seem to be involved with this thing. Pierce Something had ordered an internal investigation of the sinkhole incident, and it got buried. Maybe conveniently buried. By Tom Freeman, VP of Operations, I had no idea he was such a heavyweight when he gave me the tour, by the way. There was another thing: a Soil and Water Report on one of the sectors that included the sinkhole area, called the Sunshine Sector. According to Solano, the original was positive, there was nothing wrong. But this one basically put the kibosh on a major development project."

She frowned. "Cross had that kind of authority?"

"Basically, yes. He had just not yet chosen to exercise it."

"I don't get it."

"He hadn't found anything wrong, as of January, this year. However"—and here he paused significantly—"take a look at this." He picked up the brown envelope from the seat next to him, opened it up, and took out a photocopy of a cover sheet. He handed it over to her. It had a Florida Department of Environmental Protection heading, and the title "Soil and Water Report" was plainly visible, with references to International Phosphates and some outfit called Malone and Associates, with "Sunshine Sector" on the title page. The author was Timothy Cross, MA.

"This is the Soil and Water Report for a huge land-recovery development being planned for four thousand acres of land owned by International Phosphates, otherwise known as Florida Fertilizers. It's dated March first. It basically kills the whole venture. This is just the cover page. You'll have to go in with a warrant to get the whole thing, it was a couple hundred pages."

"Cross had the power to stop something that big?" she repeated, incredulous.

"He had, and he did."

"Let me see if I've got this straight. He was out there in January, or whenever, doing his usual thing, and everything was fine. He was getting ready, according to Hoyle—"

"Solano."

"Whomever, to approve a zillion-dollar project—"

"Only ten billion or so, but hey, who's counting—"

"And then this sinkhole thing happens at the beginning of February," she continued, "and—"

"That's not all. Something happened in the interim. Cross found something else entirely. An old Environmental Impact Report. I couldn't copy all the pages, but apparently what he found out had to do with some long-ago chemical dumping in the area. Apparently, according to this memo he dug up, there was some huge toxic dump out there from the fifties. A lot of the same stuff they found in his tissues, incidentally. So what if all this old stuff percolated up, all of a sudden, maybe even caused the sinkhole? Say at a very inconvenient moment."

"So you're saying just when they were about to get the green light on this Sunshine thing, he changes his mind, based on this new information?"

"Or on the sinkhole itself. I saw the sinkhole, Bedrosian. It was brimming with what I'm positive is sulfuric acid."

"Let me see if I follow this. So Tim Cross, our Timothy Cross, age twenty-one—"

"Twenty-four—"

"—threatens to ax some kind of big project out there, on account of a toxic sinkhole, after he was about to go and approve it, so they got pissed and zeroed him out?"

Lowell tapped the report. "That's my theory, and I'm stickin' to it."

"So who killed him? Florida Fertilizers? Or is that sort of minor detail beneath the dignity of your brilliance?"

He looked piqued, and tapped the report. "I think you should read this. There are things in this report that FF didn't want known." He slid a stack of large eleven-by-fourteen photocopies from the envelope and pushed them across the table. "I also got photos of Harry Baumgarten's notes. They were in plain sight in his waiting room. I figured that was sort of like public domain, since he's dead."

She cursed silently. She hadn't had a chance to get over to Brandon yet herself.

He took one off the top. "This is from a yellow pad by the phone, in the outbuilding. It should still be there. Take a look at this."

A note was circled, written with a marker, in plain, clear handwriting. "Where is Soil and Water????????" it said.

"He knew about the report, knew it was overdue."

She shoved the papers back. "What the hell good is this? It's illegally obtained!"

"Hey. If you insist on being the only cop in America who's still worried about the Fourth Amendment, get a court order." He slid them back to her. "At least take a look at them while you find a magistrate. It's the weekend, they'll be there at least until Monday. Florida Fertilizers, Orange Blossom, Florida. Right on Tom Freeman's desk, to the left of the globe."

"You are unbelievable."

"Hey, I've been known to smoke pot. That makes me an outlaw. So bust me already."

She was half tempted. "Don't you ever mention pot around me again, in case you're serious."

"Sorry. Only ten percent serious."

"Some things you don't joke about. Such as drugs."

"Would that include alcohol and nicotine?"

"Do you always have to be so argumentative? Why don't you just get me some usable evidence?" she snapped.

He tapped the envelope. "This is evidence."

"None of this is admissible, you realize?"

"Not yet," admitted Lowell. "But I'm working on it. I'm gonna go out there with my friend, Perry Garwood, and stick to the baseball hero like a Band-Aid, until one of those scabs falls off."

Bedrosian curled her lip in distaste. Then her eyes widened a moment in recollection. "Speaking of your friend, Mr. Garwood," she remembered, "I think we better talk."

Lowell had to go and roust out a bondsman he knew, Rick Barsanian, to spring for Perry's bail. Barsanian had been just about to leave to exercise his cigarette boat on Manatee Bay, and wasn't pleased. But he had Perry out by ten-thirty. Lowell was effusive with apologies to his friend for not coming sooner. "On the other hand," he pointed out, showing him the rear exit, "part of a private investigator's job is to keep his own ass out of jail."

Perry was too tired to offer much of a rejoinder by then. "That bastard, Smith, I'm gonna get that man," he finally managed to splutter as they walked out into the morning sunshine. "If only for keepin' me up all damn night!"

"What happened?" asked Lowell, leading him across the

street to the Red Top, which was never closed, even on a Saturday morning when all sensible working people slept in.

Perry told him, over a second round of coffees (for Lowell) and a stale Danish. Bakers, it seemed, also slept in on Saturdays. "Far as I'm concerned, the man is psycho," said Perry. "You look at the total picture, you get caught up in too many details, all that scenery in the background, all those extraneous characters walkin' around. The real action, the main scenario, my man, is front and center. Smith is your man. He's got commando training and a killer's instincts. I should know. You put him in a situation with a girlfriend he treats like personal property, a kid he'd rather not have around, and a naive interloper who shows up full of righteous good deeds and actually has the balls to try and horn in on the dude's turf, womanwise, he's gonna blow, man. It's inevitable."

Lowell told him about the paternity. Perry whistled, shaking his head. "Cahill? No shit? I gotta meet this guy," was all he managed to say for the moment. The caffeine hadn't been able to close the fatigue gap just yet. "It's a scientific proven fact men are no better than lizards, man. Our brains work the same way, they studied the EKGs. Ain't it ironic, we're the ones keep tryin' to dictate moral standards to women."

"What do they think like?"

"You kiddin'? Who the hell knows?"

Just then, Bedrosian came rushing back in, breathless. "Lowell!" she almost shouted, spotting him back in the no-smoking section (always the smallest section, for some reason), with Garwood. "We have to talk," she gasped, joining them at the table.

"Don't tell me. Your cup needs a refill," suggested Lowell amiably. "Perry Garwood, I gather you've met Detective Bedrosian."

Both Bedrosian and Garwood scowled.

"I just got news, I thought you ought to know," she said. She glanced at Garwood and decided he was Lowell's business. "Dicky Cahill just got released. The wife wouldn't sign a complaint, and you weren't there to. They had no grounds to hold him. He, on the other hand, is probably signing one against you right now."

"Or taking out a contract," growled Lowell. Then a thought struck him like lightning. "Christ!" He jumped to his feet, spilling coffee. "Perry, we have to get out there. Briana Cahill may be in serious danger!"

"Easy," counseled Bedrosian. "The wife is at her sister's. According to the sheriff's deputy who works the district, Cahill stays away from there. Apparently this has happened before. Also, they'll be keeping an eye on him the next few days. He goes home—alone—stays out of trouble, that's all they can do. The missus has been counseled, it's up to her to move out, get a restraining order, whatever."

Lowell wondered if Briana would listen to him if he talked to her. He decided he'd probably be the last person she'd listen to. He, after all, had been the catalyst for this latest disaster in her life. And yet, and yet, she'd had the opportunity, a golden opportunity, to dump her husband, and hadn't done so. And she wasn't alone, he knew. That's what was so sad, the way so many women clung desperately to a hopeless life, for fear of having no life at all. Which, ironically, was what they all too often wound up with anyway.

16

When Dicky Cahill was ordered released from the lockup in Plant City, the deputy who gave him back his belongings, Jeff Davis, generously offered him a ride home.

"Man, Cahill, you better watch your ass, you can't hit a woman, you can't hit a kid, you can't hit a palmetto bug without I gotta take you in."

"If that ain't fucked up, you tell me what is."

"I ain't sayin' it ain't fucked up. What I'm saying is, don't you fuck up, or I have to come get you and fill out a lot of state and county reports and do a lot of damn paperwork, which I really hate, by the way—"

"What you want me to do?" exclaimed Cahill. "My woman was messin' around behind my damn back!"

"You mean like you and the nigger chick?"

"Fuck you, Davis!"

"Only in your dreams," said the deputy as he passed a pickup truck on the highway and accelerated to ninety.

"Hoooeeee! This sucker's almost as fast as my T-bird!" shouted Cahill, momentarily enjoying himself despite the mess he was in.

"Don't let me catch you openin' that sucker up, either, Cahill. You are on total probation, for everything but takin' a dump."

"Why stop there? Next time I gotta take a dump, I'll be sure to call you, Davis."

"You do that, I'll be glad to take you in and lock you up with your very own shit can, which I might just flush the keys of down the fuckin' pipe, Cahill."

"Yeah, yeah." Cahill glared out the window. The bitch, he was thinking. The bitch is gonna pay for this. And the som'bitch hippy dude. He's really gonna pay for it. What the hell was his name again? Some kind of private dick. Private dick is right. Briana sure went for it, like she never went for mine. Not in a long time, anyways. Fuckin' whorin' bitch. Fuck that shit the deputy was layin' on me. A woman gets out of line, you put her back, that's all there was to it. They take away a man's rights to keep his family together, next thing, they'll be takin' away his guns. Probably want my fuckin' balls next, he thought. Fuckin' Yankee liberal bureaucrats, tellin' everybody how to live. Fuck them, and fuck you, too, Briana!

They reached Cahill's house in twenty minutes. Deputy Davis made a point of pulling up directly in front to let him out.

"Thanks for the ride, Davis," said Cahill sarcastically, opening the door.

"Try not to need another one anytime too soon, Cahill."

"Yeah, yeah, fuck you, Jeff." Cahill headed for the house without looking back. Davis and Cahill had gone to high school together, been on the baseball team together until Cahill got kicked off for bringing beer to a game, and had been more or less jocular enemies since as long as either of them could remember. They didn't take each other very seriously, as a result.

"Fuck you, too, asshole!" The deputy waved and sped off.

Cahill looked at his house. It was quiet. Too quiet. The

T-bird was still there, skewed across the driveway at an angle where he'd left it after his drunken arrival yesterday afternoon. The image of the detective SOB humping his wife kept replaying again and again in his mind like a movie reel, tinged in red. There would be red, all right, before he was through. They had made a fool of him. Nobody made a fool of Dicky Cahill and lived. Nobody.

"Briana!" he shouted as he walked up the drive. He listened for sounds of the kids, of a washing machine, of the TV, the usual hum and drum of a household's daily activities. Not that he paid much attention to exactly what they were. That was women's work. But this was a weekend! They should be home.

"Bree? Where the hell are you, darlin'?" he shouted again as he unlocked the door and entered the house. "You get on out here, now."

There was no answer. The house was quiet. Filled with a new paroxysm of wrath, Cahill went through the house, kicking open doors, then smashing things, shouting in growing frenzy. They were gone. Even the kids. The bitch had taken the kids—his kids—and walked. He couldn't restrain himself. Picking up the almost new twenty-three-inch color TV he'd bought for Monday night football, he hurled it through the plate-glass patio door into the backyard.

"Fucking bitch!" he yelled into the void. "Fucking bitch!"

He tore through the house, systematically smashing everything he could lay his hands on before grabbing the last of a six-pack of Buds, still in the refrigerator, and collapsing on the sofa. There he sat, glaring into his own black, hate-filled internal void, trying to decide what to do next.

Sheriff's Deputy Jefferson Davis had an unsettled feeling after dropping Cahill off. The man was too out of control, too full of snake venom for his own good. He was liable to hurt somebody. He'd made sure, at the insistence of that woman detective, what's her name, from Manatee, that Cahill's wife and kids were out of harm's way. But it was a small town. Too small. He wouldn't live here on a bet himself, preferring the comfort and convenience of new suburbs like Brandon, his home, any day.

His usual routine patrol was to run down 64 to 39, then up to the crossroads, then swing back along the periphery of the plant property. Something made him decide against it. Something in Cahill's tone, or manner. The man was dangerous, and bore watching.

Davis swung the new Taurus patrol car into the gas station lot on the corner—that nigger's place, he remembered—pulled it around, and headed back the other way.

Yasha Dromes, also working weekends, looked out the window, and watched him go. "Damn," he muttered to no one. Luckily, the Man had other fish to fry this time. Too often in his life, they'd come for him. Usually for reasons solely to do with his skin color, or nationality. At least he had a green card now. He went back to his magazine. He was reading about Jamaica, and what was happening down there. His old country.

When the storm passed over Orange Blossom, the lights went out. Cahill paid no attention. Sitting in the daytime darkness, he lit a Marlboro and sucked the smoke into his lungs as though to caress them, reassure himself that he was still in charge of things, still in control. Except he wasn't.

He went to the phone and dialed a number. "Hello, Carol? Where is she? Look, don't fuck with me, she's your fucking sister, you know where she is. I don't—what? You say what? Look, bitch, I don't care if she's in Timbuktu, you get her ass home here—what? I didn't call you—all right,

213

I'm just tellin' you—oh, hi, Jerry. Nothin', just havin' a friendly little chat with your lovely wife, my lovely sister-in-law. I'm looking for my wife and kids, if you must know, and Carol knows damn well—what? Hey, hey! Fuck you, too, Bubba!"

He slammed the phone down. "Son of a bitch!" he shouted in growing fury. "Son of a bitch!" With a burst of new ferocity, he ripped the phone out of the wall and hurled it through the shattered hole in the window, in the direction of the departed TV set.

There was a closet in the hall where he kept special things. For special occasions. Briana and the kids were forbidden to go near it, on pain of a major whipping. This was one of those special occasions. He went to the closet and opened it. It wasn't locked. It didn't have to be. His family knew better than to risk his fury. Inside was a gun rack, as well as a case full of hunting knives and military knives. He decided on the shotgun: a double-barreled Remington 12-gauge. He had a brand-new box of buckshot somewhere. He found that, and headed for the car, kicking a child's toy into the street, on his way.

He knew where she was. Or thought he knew. Her damn sister, Carol's. She'd gone there before, when they'd had fights. Carol was a tough bitch, not to mention her trucker husband Jerry. Everyone called him Bubba, for good reason. He weighed close to two eighty, and it wasn't fat, either. Cahill didn't care. He'd just as soon blow Carol and Bubba away, too, they got in his way. He'd taken enough shit from them both, especially over the last couple of years, since he started hanging out with Virgil and them. Just 'cause he moved up a notch in class, they couldn't deal with it. Fuck them.

He burned rubber out the driveway, and gunned the T-bird down toward Main Street. He'd just run the stop sign and spun out onto the state highway when he heard the siren behind him.

"Fuck!" he almost screamed, banging his fist on the wheel. It wasn't fair. It was as if the whole world was conspiring to fuck him up. So be it. From now on, it would be Dicky Cahill against the whole world. If they were gonna take him down, a whole helluva lot of them were gonna go down with him.

There was an old towel in the back seat. Quickly he reached back and threw it over the gun and shells on the floor behind the front seats as the deputy pulled him over. Davis again.

Davis approached the car cautiously. His recent required training in dealing with domestic battery, and several real-life situations since, had taught him that domestic violence was the most volatile, most dangerous, situation of all. Cahill was wacko and unstable enough already. Throw in the catalyst of some spat with his wife on top of those ingredients, you had nitroglycerin on your hands. He watched for any sign of sudden or covert movement as he reached the driver's side window. The window slid open just as he reached to tap on it.

"What?" demanded Cahill.

"Dicky," he said. "Where you think you're goin'?"

"Out for cigarettes. Why, that against the law?"

"No, sir. But you passed the 7-11 two blocks back. Doin' about sixty. Now, why do I get the feelin' you haven't listened to a word I was sayin' to you, back there?"

"What? About what?"

Davis shook his head sorrowfully. "You're goin' after her, aren't you?"

"Look, she's my wife, dammit—"

"We already had this conversation, Cahill. I'll put it to you straight. You go anywhere near where she is, you even

215

go on the same side of town she is on, until such time as you get a written invitation from her, I'm takin' you back in."

"Bullshit."

"Not bullshit. You're really gettin' on my nerves, Cahill. I don't care what she did, or didn't do. You keep away from her. Period. Until things settle down, and that ain't gonna be anytime soon."

Cahill knew he was beaten. He decided on another tack. Mr. Cool, calm, and collected. "All right, look, Jeff, you and me go way back. You know and I know I get a little hot now and then, but that ain't what's happenin' right now. I'm just out pickin' up a few things for when my family comes back. Which they're gonna do. So don't you worry about a thing, I ain't botherin' no one."

Davis gave him a long look, and finally shrugged. "All right, Cahill. But you been warned. I'm serious about that. You got too much of a reputation for your own good. You're gonna have to cool it."

"Yes, sir, I'll do that, sir," said Cahill with a military salute.

Davis hesitated once more, then turned and went back to the patrol car, got in at a deliberately leisurely pace, started the motor, and drove slowly off.

Cahill's first impulse was that it was all bluff, and that Davis had better things to do than butt in on a man taking some rightful action regarding his own wife.

On the other hand, he'd been pretty pointed about it. He hadn't really paid much attention to what the deputy had been telling him, but it seemed like the gov'ment, the same fucking gov'ment that kept raisin' taxes and givin' privileges to niggers, was now telling him he couldn't discipline his own wife and kids. Fuck them. He would finish what he set out to do, they didn't have the right to stop him. Or the balls. He started his engine and gunned it, making sure the

216

custom glass-pack mufflers sounded off good. He threw it into gear, and was about to pop the clutch, when the sheriff's patrol car reappeared, right on his bumper.

Davis had decided to ride this one out. Baby-sit, more like. The man was more unreasonable than a spoiled child. A dangerous spoiled child. He definitely bore watching.

Dicky Cahill glowered at his rearview mirror. Boy, wouldn't you be surprised, he thought. To know what I got right here with me. I could swing my hand back here, pick this up, it was already loaded and cocked for just such an emergency, lift it up, and let you have both barrels right in your pimply fat little face before you knew what hit you.

Only problem was, he'd need a new rear window. He didn't want to mess up his car. Plus, he was too smart to shoot a cop, he had to admit to himself. They'd give him the chair for that, it wasn't worth it. The bitch, now that was somethin' else. He'd been wronged by her. A jury, certainly a jury of his own peers, would understand. She had it coming. Just like that O.J.'s wife, out west. That's all there was to it.

But it would have to wait. The bastards weren't going to leave him alone, obviously. So be it. He could wait, too. Let her think she won, that she was safe, that she'd gotten away with it. He'd call her up, make nice to her, invite her home. "Take your time, honey," he'd tell her. "I understand you need to think things over for a while. I can wait." And she'd come around, too. Just like she always did. One thing about Dicky Cahill, he smiled to himself. He knew women.

As he drove back to the 7-11, the smile vanished. Women. Briana wasn't the only one who'd fucked him over. They all had, one time or another. A regular sisterhood of cunts.

Inside, he bought a carton of Marlboros, and a cold case of Buds. Maybe the cops were right, maybe he did need to simmer down a little, and think things through. Maybe he could even forgive the bitch, in time. If she gave him blow jobs twice a day without bein' told to or askin' for nothin' in return, and just basically kissed his ass for a month. Yeah, sure. Maybe she didn't fuck that hippy. Maybe she was just a good sweet mother. Maybe the Gulf of Mexico is really Coors beer.

"That'll be sixteen fifty-two," the clerk told him.

He reached for his wallet. All he had was a ten. "Fuck!" he muttered. He'd have to settle for one six-pack and one lousy carton. Money was tight, even with the extra from Virgil. Virgil, who owed him big, as far as he was concerned. What he'd got so far—and a lot more had been promised, a lot more was coming until that damn sinkhole thing and that meddling kid had got in the way—all went into the car, of course. And the bitch took the rest, for food and shit for the kids. Spoiled little shits, too, got whatever they wanted. She'd bitched to him plenty about money herself. How much of it he spent out with the boys—he earned it, goddamn it, he had a right to some fuckin' enjoyment! And how much he had to pay to that woman. She knew about it, of course. The child support. He was paying four hundred a month to that nigger bitch, just because she didn't know enough to use birth control. Briana was right about that. It was her money, too. Come to think of it, all their problems dated back from that time, when that bastard judge from Tampa had ordered him to pay. Making a white man pay money to a nigger woman. Things had sure gone downhill to hell in the great state of Florida since Dicky Cahill grew up.

Suddenly a great sense of purpose filled him, a sense of inner peace, almost joyfulness. He knew what to do. It had been an omen, that cop stopping him from nailing Briana. It wasn't Briana's fault. Well, some of it was, and he'd still be teachin' her a lesson or two. Make her clean up the mess she'd caused him to make at the house, first and foremost. But he had to admit, was starting to admit to himself, most of it was the nigger cunt's fault. Incredible, how he had failed to see that before. She's the one who'd cooperated with that smart-ass college kid, too. She's the one who was seen talkin' to the hippy detective, probably put the heat on him, too. Be just like her to snitch, just like she snitched about who fathered her baby. Even tried to call it rape, but of course that wouldn't of stuck, not in rural Florida. Bad enough he'd been forced to pay. Now she would pay.

There was no hurry. He'd finish his beer first. And wait until dark. Deputy Davis would watch him, but eventually he'd get bored, or tired, and leave. The sheriff wasn't going to put someone on his tail all night. Not with all them criminals and lowlifes out there, for cryin' out loud!

Once he was good and ready, he'd fix things right, once and for all. There wasn't gonna be no more fuckin' child support, because there wasn't gonna be no more fuckin' nigger woman with her little snotty half-breed twat that he, Dicky Cahill, had paid through the nose for, and wasn't going to anymore, no, sir.

Retribution time had come to Bone Valley. Or Manatee City, to be exact . . .

17

Lenny Smith awoke late in the morning to the sound of metal striking metal. He swore, and rolled over on his cot, sweat causing his clothing to stick to the uncovered mattress. A tick had bitten him in the armpit during the night. He scratched the sore and curled up tight, trying to recover a vague dream involving marvelous weapons, wasting his enemies, and girls that looked like ancient Egyptian goddesses fighting each other over who would get to suck his cock next.

"Smith!" a voice shouted, cutting through the dimness like a Yamaha motorcycle through heavy traffic. "Wake up!" The banging sound was repeated.

"Fuck you," he muttered, and managed to force one eyelid open. It was a cop, a black cop, in fact.

It was Sergeant Peters, a model citizen of Manatee, one that the local white power structure loved to parade as an example of their own forthright open-mindedness and lack of bigotry. The kind of black man Smith especially hated, because they had succeeded in a white man's world.

"Let's go. Up and at it. Rise and shine," commanded Peters.

"What you want, man?" Smith sat up ever so slowly. He had never been prone to rising before noon, if he could help it. When he had driving jobs (less and less often, because he kept getting into fights), he preferred night jobs. He was a night person.

"You're out. Let's go."

Smith's eyes opened the rest of the way without further prodding. "Say what?"

"Hard as I find it to believe, you got a friend. Somebody sprung bail."

A grin slowly spread across Smith's face. Bail! The last thing he'd expected. He'd been inside before. It usually took a public defender with a misplaced need to do good to get him out. That usually took days. He'd only been in overnight. He could hardly believe his luck.

Smith didn't even ask who was his benefactor. His arrogance was such that it didn't matter to him. Everyone owed him, was the way he saw it. So it was irrelevant. He simply had been awarded the rights he was entitled to, as a citizen of the Jew-nited States of America, as he sneeringly called it, Jews being yet another target of his venom. It was just another entitlement.

Cecilia sat waiting for him, her hands curled nervously in her lap. She was wearing a short skirt that had ridden high up her thighs where she sat on the chair. Cops and others with police business passing to and fro couldn't help but look. They assumed she was a hooker. It wouldn't have occurred to them that she was a mother. With a job, trying to keep her life together, trying to take care of her daughter, struggling to maintain some semblance of self-esteem. The looks she was always getting hadn't helped.

Last night she had been alone for the first time she could remember. After what happened outside, her mother had come over at midnight and demanded temporary custody of Natasha. She had wanted Cecilia to come to her place, too, but Cecilia had been unwilling to leave the house.

"What if Lenny calls?" she'd complained. "He might need me, and I wouldn't be here!"

Her mother, Sendra, was furious. "Ceecee, are you crazy? I been telling you from the start that man is no good, and you don't listen. Now he's in jail where he belong, and you should be comin' home, where you belong."

But Cecilia had refused. Sendra, in exasperation, had called her a fool, and stormed out, dragging a tearful Natasha with her. There was no way to explain to her mother that she loved him. Her mother was old, over forty, what did old people know of love? Sure, he was mean to her at times. But that's the way love was, is all. Cecilia's father had been mean to Sendra plenty, too, she remembered. Before he left for good. He'd also been a trucker, and would be away for days at a time, only to come home reeking of stale beer and grease, and beat them both.

Lenny was a lot nicer than that. Wasn't he? Didn't he bring her presents, now and then? And when he did hit her, wasn't it usually her own fault, for talking back, or not having dinner ready, or not having Tasha asleep when he came home? And he knew how to make her feel good, too. Soooo good, the way he knew just where her secret love spots were, when to touch them, how to caress her, touch her hair, make her feel all hot and mushy, and then overpower her, the way she loved to be overpowered, heat and sweat, biting her nipples, tearing away her clothes, going down on her until she dripped, putting two, then three fingers inside her, twiddling her G-spot until she screamed, then rising inside her like a great erupting volcano.

Most of all, though, Cecilia was desperately, terribly afraid to be alone. Lenny was usually there. Sometimes he held her, those sweet times she lived for, every so often when he was in a generous mood (which was rare, she had to admit to herself), his hard muscles like great fortresses to protect her from those demons that haunted her sleep. He was so protective of her, though, (the way she saw it), so jealous, he never let her out of his sight for longer than he could help (unless he himself had another place he'd rather be, another woman he'd rather be with). He loved her, the way she saw it. And she wanted, needed, to be loved.

Tim had loved her, too, though, she remembered. But he was so . . . quiet, so different. It wasn't the same. She missed him, though. Who could have hurt him? she had to wonder again and again. Surely not her Lenny. He wouldn't do such a thing. Not on purpose, anyway. Would he? She shuddered to herself, and her skirt rode even higher up her thighs. Bill Allenson, currently relegated to desk duty, couldn't tear his eyes away. He was almost certain, or maybe it was just his imagination, that he could see just the tiniest glimpse of pubic hair.

At the end, though, it was the loneliness, and the terror that always came with it, that had finally driven her to the bail bondsman, and then the police station. She couldn't bear not to have a man, her man, there to watch over her, and guard her from those nameless terrors that lurked in the dark.

"Hi, baby," she greeted him as he shuffled into the room. Smith stared at her in surprise.

"What the hell you doin' here?" he demanded as the sergeant handed him his property.

"Baby, I just came to get you out," she said, plaintively. She hadn't really expected gratitude. It was an experience unknown to her, other than from her daughter, which was different.

"Shut up, c'mon, c'mon, let's get outta here." He almost shoved her out the door. The cops watched them go, shaking their heads. A pimp and his hole, they figured. They'll be back.

Cecilia braced herself for what was coming, as he forced her into the car—her own little Nissan she'd driven over—taking the keys, and squeezing into the driver's seat.

"I hate these fuckin' little cars," he complained, shoving the seat back as far as it would go, crushing a bag of groceries she'd picked up at the convenience store in hopes of fixing him breakfast.

"Lenny, are you mad?" she wanted to know. She'd messed up, somehow, she knew. She sensed she'd bruised his male ego, somehow, his pride. "I'm sorry, I thought you'd want to be out."

"Shut up, and put your mouth where it'll do some good," he ordered. She knew what he meant. Grateful for the chance to please him, and win back his love, she nestled close to him while he drove, unzipped his fly, reached in, and began to caress him. Soon he was hard. She took it all in her mouth, and began to slide her head up and down, taking it deeper and deeper into her throat.

He moaned, and barely managed to maintain control of the car as he drove. He grabbed her by the hair, and forcefully guided her motions. "Slower, goddamnit!" he grunted. "I'll come when I'm good and ready!"

When they got home, he began to beat her. She whimpered, screamed a little but not too loudly, so as not to disturb the neighbors. She was certain she had it coming. Wasn't he telling her as much? And the pain was no worse than usual. The bloody lip would heal, the bruises around her eyes, on her neck and throat, on her arms and buttocks. She'd tried to protect herself one time, throwing an arm up to block his rain of blows. He'd nearly broken it for her that time, seizing it and twisting until she shrieked.

"Who was it?" he kept demanding.

"Who? What you talkin' about?"

"The man. The som'bitch out in the yard last night? You fuckin' somebody behind my back?"

"No, baby, no!" He hit her in the mouth.

"Who was he?"

"I don't know." She couldn't restrain her tears anymore. This was wrong. It was one thing to mess up. But he was blaming her for something she didn't even do. "I don't know who he was."

"This honky who's been sniffin' around your pussy. Who he?"

She flinched and choked back a scream as he hit her again. "I don't know! A detective. He tryin' to find out what happened to Tim."

He hit her on the head with his open palm, making her hair fly. "I thought I told you not to mention that name again."

"But that's why he was here!" She sobbed.

He had her by the hair now. He threw her head back and let go, walking away, brooding. "Go fix me some grits, ho'. Don't you know I'm famished?"

Fighting back the tears, she got the key and went back out to the car, carefully picking up what was left of the eggs, the package of bacon now half open, the spilled milk and juice.

Inside, Smith's rage settled down, and a sense of calm came over him. So, he thought. The detective. Has the balls to be watching him. Him, Leonard T. Smith! But that wasn't the honky who got picked up out there last night. It was somebody else. An Indian dude. He'd seen him before somewhere. The guy gave him the chills. He was going to have to deal with this. Too many people sniffing around his hole. Literally.

And what about the kid, the dead one? Why they care so

much about him? He wasn't even from around here, and didn't amount to nothin'. Just another Oreo. Like that cop who let him out. Speaking of kids, where the fuck that little bitch?

"Ceecee," he growled as she came back in the kitchen. "Where's the kid?" It was Saturday, he remembered. She'd be here. Or actually, out shopping with her mother, at this time. He usually let them go, just so they wouldn't whine all day at him. Also it gave him some time to be in the house by himself and collect his thoughts without some woman harping at him every minute. But he didn't like the fact that she wasn't where he expected her to be.

Cecilia looked in the door from the kitchen, where she was heating up the griddle. "She with her grandma."

"Good riddance."

She brought him a mug of coffee, hoping to please him again. He took it grudgingly. She knew how to make coffee just the way he liked it. She'd learned the hard way. He'd thrown her first cup in her face, giving her first-degree burns that time, for making it too weak. "Do I look like a schoolboy?" he demanded. "Am I some kind of wimp, to you?"

"No, baby, I'm sorry," she'd whimpered, and gone back to try it again. Her friends, what few she was allowed to have, couldn't believe she would stay with a man like this. But some of them were in the same kind of situation. You didn't just up and leave a man like Lenny Smith. And he took care of her. A girl like her needed taking care of in a place like East Manatee. You never knew who might come along, otherwise. . . .

As the caffeine coursed through his veins, Smith remembered another grievance. Regarding the girl. "Yo, bitch!" he called as she returned to the kitchen. "Maybe it's the kid's father who been sniffin' around here, not just some honky detective."

She could hardly believe it, that he would think she still cared a whit about Dicky Cahill. Up until now he'd never shown the slightest interest in Natasha or in who her father was. Other than the way he looked at her sometimes, the child was so pretty and innocent, it made Cecilia fear for her little girl.

"What difference it make anyways?" she demanded, with a boldness that surprised them both.

"I'll tell you if it makes a difference or don't," he said, a new tone of menace in his voice. He threw his fork and napkin aside, got up, and walked toward her. Her eyes widened, and she backed against the wall. Usually, she wasn't afraid, even when he beat her. Not deep down terrified, like she'd been, all alone last night. Now she felt afraid.

"Baby, what you gonna do?"

"I'm gonna find out how come there's some mother-fucker dude hangin' around my house and my woman, and you ain't tellin' me about it. And I'm gonna find out where you gettin' the money to feed that little snatch—"

"Welfare, baby!" she lied.

He slapped her. "Didn't I tell you I didn't want no woman of mine on no welfare?"

"But you never give us money! You always take my check, and I need to get things for her!" she protested.

He slapped her again. She was numb now, he couldn't hurt her anymore, she thought. She was wrong. He seized her arm and began to twist.

"Now," he said, his voice a deep and menacing snarl, "you are going to tell me what's goin' down round here, or I am going to break your fuckin' arm."

She screamed, and held on. He twisted harder. "I don't

know!" she cried. He twisted relentlessly. "I hate you," she moaned. She'd never had the guts to say it before. It felt surprisingly good, even amidst all the pain. He let go, shocked, and at that moment she knew how to hurt him back. She'd simply keep lying, and tell him what he least wanted to know.

"All right. It was Cahill," she breathed, gingerly flexing her arm.

He struck her. "Cahill!" she repeated. "Dicky Cahill."

He couldn't believe it. "That honky asshole som'bitch? You made nasty with him again?" He turned away, his guts churning.

She almost laughed. "That's right."

"But why?" he demanded, shaking her.

"Because he told me if I didn't, I'd get fired. Just like the first time."

"Jesus Christ!" He threw up his hands. If that didn't beat all. Fucked again by her boss, just to keep a fuckin' job. She'd already had his damn baby. This was too much. Unless . . . then another thought dawned on him.

"He been payin' you?"

Her eyes widened. She had lied about it, hidden the support checks, mostly used them for food for Natasha. If he knew about the money, he'd just spend it on gambling or something. She couldn't tell him. No matter what, she told herself. She couldn't tell him. Must not tell him. Natasha's life could be at stake. She steeled herself, and made the bravest decision of her life. She would not tell him, even if he killed her.

Lenny reached out and touched her hair softly, almost gingerly. She closed her eyes and stood her ground, waiting for the blow to come.

That was when the kitchen door crashed open, and Dicky Cahill walked in, a Smith & Wesson .38 held cold and steady in both hands.

18

Perry, with Bedrosian's support, managed to convince Lowell they should take his four-wheeler. Assuming it hadn't been ripped off. The Impala would be a marked vehicle by now. At least it wouldn't be like entering town waving a banner, shouting "Lowell's back!" he'd pointed out. Lowell couldn't argue. They found the Cherokee untouched where Perry left it the night before, in Cecilia's neighborhood. Or more accurately, Leonard Smith's neighborhood. For some reason the locals had left it alone. Maybe word about the Indian renegade who had taken on Smith had gotten around. Two teenagers were eyeing it in something akin to awe when they arrived, and stood deferentially by as they drove away.

They drove in silence, the tension mounting as the miles ticked by. As they neared Orange Blossom, Perry stared balefully out at the stacks of phosphatic gypsum that began to appear along the side of the road.

"Son of a bitch," he muttered, mostly to break the silence. "Son of a bitch."

Lowell looked at him. "What?"

"This is some heavy shit, bro'."

"Yeah. It's called toxic waste. They have no place to put it anymore, so they stack it here."

They drove on, past the decreasing clumps of pines and oaks, into increasing evidence of mining activity. They were nearly there.

"This whole thing is about water," said Perry after a while. "You know how fragile the water table is in this state, man? We got only one source, the fucking Floridan Aquifer, sitting right underneath Disney World. Our water supply lies at the mercy of Mickey Mouse! We have no mountains, so there's no runoff. No rivers flow into Florida from the north. They only flow out, to the east, and west. It rains a lot. But in short bursts, that run off into the sea, full of cigarette butts, and soda cans, and gasoline, and pesticides. Every acre they pave, there's that much less soil to absorb what's left. And a lot of what's left is polluted, man, and people changing the oil in their engines, millions of gallons just get dumped in people's backyards. Where's it gonna go, except into our aquifer? They shouldn't even be doing heavy industry, or raising cattle in this state."

"Cattle?"

"They've been moving here in droves, from east Texas. Cattle ranchers, man. They're doing the same thing here Chico Mendez tried to stop in Brazil. It's cheaper, more grass, more water. Except that they are sitting right on top of the state's one and only aquifer, and each head of cattle is dumping a shitload of waste material into this sandy, porous soil, every day. Every fuckin' day, bro'. Now our water is getting polluted by cow piss!"

"Tastes like it."

Lowell was thinking. Worried about Briana. He and Perry needed a plan of action. It had taken all of his powers of persuasion to convince his friend not to bring along an arsenal of heavy weaponry, as it was. No point giving Sheriff Pearson yet another reason for pulling them in. Luckily, Bedrosian had done her utmost to pave the way. The sheriff's department was savvy enough not to take any complaints from such as Corcoran or Cahill too seriously.

They passed the pay phone where Lowell had stopped and turned back the day before. "You say there've been two killings, now?"

"Two deaths."

"Both related to this water thing?"

"Maybe. Maybe one was done by a jealous lover, maybe the other was an accident. It may all be coincidental. That's the problem. There's too many damn possibilities."

Perry frowned. "You got a point. You ever consider the possibility of this being a serial killer?"

Lowell shook his head. "That's way off. There's no pattern, in that sense. First of all, those are usually sex related. Here we got two men, one white, one black, one young, one old, one drowned, the other shot, it doesn't follow."

Perry shook his head. "Those serial killings. Those aren't just about sex. Those are warfare, man. Class warfare. That Danny Rollins, up at Gainesville? He was poor white trash, and all those girls—all those victims. They were middle class. Gettin' an education. They were way too good for him, and he hated them for that more than anything."

Lowell thought about that. Perry had a point. Both of the victims, in this case, had been educated professionals.

"Unh-unh," he said finally. "You could make a case, but not a good one. Serial killings are, ultimately, acts of insanity, whatever the courts may rule. Those guys are psychos. In the case of Tim Cross, the pattern is a logical one. It has to do with business, or love. Dicky Cahill, for example—has an illegitimate child with a pretty black woman, has to pay child support, the girl has a new boyfriend who's violent, then a suitor comes along, who pisses off both men. A lot of possibilities there. Not to mention another jealous lover—"

"What's your point again?"

231

"The point is, Cahill may be a raving, racist, double-crossing, unscrupulous, violent son of a bitch. He may also be a killer. But he's not psycho."

They passed the fertilizer factory. The stacks were emitting a few fumes, nothing much. The parking lot was empty. It was Saturday morning, Lowell remembered. A time when people with actual jobs and families and such took the day off to go on picnics, or wash the car.

They drove on into Orange Blossom and pulled into the parking lot at the local library to go over their plans. Lowell wanted to go straight to the Cahill house and check up on Briana. But Perry reminded him about discretion and valor, and so forth. "She's at her sister's, the lieutenant said. Only person's gonna be there is the man himself. And unless you've changed your ways, it'd be best let the cops handle him. Or me," he added.

Lowell thought about it. "Let's find Malone. He had his goon pull a weapon on me out at the sinkhole, I think he tried to get me killed, and he's definitely into something nefarious. I want to know what," said Lowell.

"If he did all that, why ain't *he* in jail?" complained Perry. "Never mind, don't answer that, I know already. He's a celeb."

"Also, there's no proof."

There was a pay phone by the entrance to the library: a small, squat brick building. Lowell went to it, inserted a quarter, and dialed information. The operator answered, and asked how may she help him.

"For Plant City. May I have the number for International Phosphates?"

"Main number, or Personnel?"

He thought a moment. "Main number, please."

There was the usual pause, followed by the computerized voice that slowly, ever so slowly recited the number, then informed him: "You may complete this call by inserting fifty cents." Lowell dropped in two more quarters, and the phone rang.

"International Phosphates," a surprisingly urbane female voice said.

"Yes, um, I'm trying to reach a Mr. Malone, a Mr. Virgil Malone. I believe he works for Public Relations?"

There was a pause. "Sir, are you referring to Doc Malone? The baseball player?"

"Right. I believe he's connected with the company in some way."

There was another long pause. "Sir, he's not in our directory, and I'm just the weekend receptionist. You'd have to call back on Monday."

"How about at Florida Fertilizers?"

"No, sir, I checked the computer. I believe he's done some promotional work for us, but he's not an employee."

"Hmm. You wouldn't happen to know where he might be reached?"

"You could try the Reds," she suggested.

"Thanks, anyway." He hung up in chagrin. It wouldn't be of much help to call the Reds. He was retired, and even if they had his number, they wouldn't give it out. Perry was busy studying a lizard climbing the library wall.

"So did you find him?"

"Nope."

"Now what? Wait here until he needs a book?"

Lowell laughed. Perry could be very funny at times.

"We-e-ll," reflected Lowell, "we could start with the phone book, but it seems like everyone around here is either too poor or too rich to be listed."

"Yeah? That's right, with his celebrity status, he's probably got an unlisted number."

"Probably. Although this isn't L.A." Lowell suddenly

slapped his thigh furiously. "Shit, what the hell is the matter with me?"

"You've suddenly realized you're brain-dead?"

"Malone. Malone. I've been thinking 'Virgil.' The baseball player. He's 'Malone and Associates.' Of course. Jesus!"

Perry looked at him blankly, and followed as Lowell stormed into the library.

"Tim Cross was working on a report involving International Phosphates and another company. Malone and Associates. It's got to be our Virgil's company."

"I'll buy that."

They hurried past a curious librarian to the reference section. Lowell yanked down the phone books from the shelf. "You check the white pages. I'll check the yellow," he directed. Perry nodded. Lowell decided to start with real estate. Then he'd go on to investments.

He found him, almost right away, under "Malone and Associates. Virgil T. Investment Brokers and Developers." The address was on Tangerine Way, in Plant City.

"Nothing under residential," said Perry. "And if it's a business, they'll probably be closed, this bein' Saturday," Perry pointed out.

"You have a better idea?"

Perry didn't.

"Then Plant City, here we come," said Lowell. They got into the Cherokee, and headed north. The air was heavy with moisture, as the sun reached its zenith overhead. Clouds were piling up thick and white just to the west. They were going to be in for a rare but vital spring thunderstorm.

Lowell had a copy of the local street map, courtesy of the JC's, from his first visit. "Should be second light, left, then second right," he said.

Perry nodded, turning onto an almost empty main street, then a small side street. They found the address just as the storm hit. There was a rush of ozone, and the sudden smell of orange blossoms. They got one quick good look at the building and grounds of Malone and Associates, Investment Brokers and Developers. Then a sheet of water covered them, obscuring the small but elegant Moorish building set back from the road.

"Now," said Perry, "comes the fun part. We sit in here and sweat, or we get out and go in. Either way's about the same. Either way we get soaked."

"Let's give it a few minutes," suggested Lowell. "It's always best to make a good impression when dealing with business types. And two soaked water rats don't cut it."

Perry sullenly agreed to wait it out. The rain had a cooling effect, and they were able to open their windows an inch or two without getting the car drenched. As the minutes passed, however, the storm intensified. Thunder and lightning were crashing all around them. It grew as dark as if it were twilight, or an eclipse. Lowell wiped on the window, which was quickly fogging up, trying to see out through the rain.

" 'Patience is the best remedy for every trouble,' " he muttered after a while. As though to remind himself.

"Say what?"

"Nothing. A quote. From Titus Maccius Plautus," Lowell explained.

"Say who?"

"Forget it. A Roman playwright, from around two hundred B.C."

"No shit."

"You see any cars out there?" Lowell asked.

Perry wiped a clear space on his own window, then on the windshield, and squinted out into the storm. He had better vision than Lowell, both had acknowledged. An Indian thing, or something.

"Don't see—wait a minute. Over beyond that row of poplars." He pointed at an area toward the back of the building, behind a decorative windbreak. "Three cars. Maybe more in back."

"A lot, for an off day," said Lowell.

Perry squinted again. Lowell wished he had his camera, it had better opticals than he did.

"Let's see. You got one sea green Mercedes," reported Perry. "You got one black Lincoln Town Car."

There was blinding flash instantly followed by a huge bang, followed by a loud crash as a large tree branch fell into the parking lot from a besieged magnolia next to the building. The builders had enough class, Lowell noted, to leave the tree alone when they built the place. Most builders, and nearly all developers, wouldn't have bothered. They'd have bulldozed the tree, for convenience, so they could get their backhoes and cranes and flatbed trucks in there without hassle.

"What about the third car?" Lowell was getting frustrated. Sweat was pouring down his brow, further blinding him. He couldn't see a damn thing.

"Wait a sec', it's too fuckin—there. Yeah." Perry looked at Lowell, questioning. "A blue Ford pickup."

Lowell frowned. Who had he run across with a vehicle like that? Probably about a million people. It was standard cracker.

"No sign of a red T-bird?"

Perry shook his head. Lowell felt a hollow in the pit of his stomach. He wished Cahill had been here. Better the devil you know, especially in the presence of a witness. And that meant that he was out there somewhere. Which could be very bad news for Briana. He cursed at himself under his breath.

"What?" demanded Perry, hearing him.

236

"Briana Cahill. He's gonna go after her."

Perry looked at him gravely. "What do you want to do?"

"I don't know the sister. I don't know where she is. Shit!"

"So what do you want to do?"

"I guess we have no choice. We're here." Lowell sighed. "In any case, I think this is going to be quite a meeting."

The rain let up for a moment. Perry squinted at the building. The large ten-pane windows were covered by white Levelors. "You sure you want to go in there?" he asked. He had a bad feeling himself. He didn't like being without his weapons. Although, if it came down to it, he could make an effective lethal weapon of virtually anything. Including his bare hands. Still, bare hands weren't much good against an assault weapon.

"I can hardly wait," said Lowell.

The rain began to subside. They opened their windows, breathing in the ozone, the moisture, the steam already rising from the pavement, while the thunder receded.

Smith recovered from his surprise at Cahill's sudden intrusion almost immediately.

"Well, well," he murmured. "If it ain't the Big Bad Wolf."

"Fuck you, Smith," snapped Cahill, moving quickly over to Cecilia and seizing her, his gun pointed to her head. "I'm taking her."

Smith shrugged. "She's all yours, man," he said, his voice calm. In a sudden move, faster than Cahill would have believed possible, he was out through the open dining room window and gone. Dragging Cecilia with him, Cahill rushed to the window and stared out, just in time to see Smith roar away in his Firebird.

Cecilia was almost serene as she felt Cahill's grip tighten

around her neck, watching her man make good his escape. At least, she thought, there wasn't no bloodshed on her account.

Cahill watched Smith run for it, and almost laughed out loud.

"Chickenshit," he'd chuckled.

Cecilia couldn't see him breathing stale beer and cigarette smoke down her neck from behind. She was glad of that.

"He gonna get you," she said.

Cahill had gotten to East Manatee before lunch hour was over. He'd never actually been there, but he knew the address. He'd sent enough checks there, that was for shit sure. Fifteen Sycamore Place. He'd stopped at a Citgo convenience store near the center of town, bought a cold Bud, and asked where Sycamore Place was. The pudgy white teenage girl behind the counter had never heard of it. A balding black customer had. He gave Cahill a bemused look, and told him how to get there. If the honky wanted to cruise the toughest block in East Manatee, that was his problem.

Cahill pulled his red T-bird directly up in front of number 15. Figures, he thought to himself. A goddamn slum. She probably spends my money on crack or some shit, and lives here. With some kind of nigger gangster, he'd heard. Great. He'd take care of him, too. He reached into his backseat for the shotgun, then changed his mind. It would be too visible. Someone was liable to call the cops, or maybe just start shooting. He'd heard they carried automatic weapons around here. Sheeit, even he and his buddies didn't have but one or two of those. They were a lot of fun for poaching gator. You shined a light out there, caught the glint of their eye, and blasted them into little pieces of bloody stew meat. It was a blast for real.

He had a handgun under the seat, a plain old-fashioned .38 Smith & Wesson revolver he kept for just such emergencies. A regular cowboy gun, for a regular cowboy, he chuckled to himself. Stuffing it under his Hawaiian shirt, he got out, pressed the autolock button on his key chain. It emitted the familiar loud bleeping sound, announcing to the neighborhood that Dicky Cahill had arrived, his car was secured with a big-time antitheft device, and not to fuck around. A couple of local teenagers watching from a nearby doorway contemplated hitting it immediately, just to teach the stupid honky a lesson. But it was broad daylight, a weekend, and at least one of their mothers was nearby.

Cahill silently climbed the porch steps and peered in the front window. He saw her, talking to the big nigger, Smith. He knew him, of course, from work. A mean motherfucker, and dangerous. Walking softly, he went around to the back of the house, to the kitchen door. He could hear arguing inside. He tested the latch. It was locked. But the door was flimsy, and rotten. One swift kick with his cowboy boot was all it would take. All it had taken.

Inside, now alone with her long-time enemy, Cecilia's terror returned. It hit her like an instant nightmare, her man gone, and this demon, this white devil here in his place. It was lucky for him he had caught Lenny unawares. Bad luck for her, though, she knew.

She tried to bluff.

"What you want?" she gasped. He was choking her.

He tightened his grip.

"Why, I'm here to see my daughter, darlin'!"

"You ain't never even spoke to her in six years. Why you want to see her now?"

"To let her know she's half-white, darlin'. Maybe one day she'll want to move up in the world."

Not that it worked that way, they both knew. He was just

239

jerking her around. He could tell she was frightened. Home alone, he thought. Nice work, Cahill. As always, your timing is outstanding. This might even be fun.

"She's not here," Cecilia told him, feeling a deep sense of relief at that knowledge. In spite of her fear for herself, she took some solace in knowing her daughter was safe.

Unfortunately for her, that was the answer Cahill liked best. "Good, then you and me can have a nice friendly chat without bein' bothered by nobody."

She felt his grip loosen, and seized the opportunity. The downstairs lavatory was right behind her. Twisting away in a sudden motion, she was free. Diving for the lav, she was inside before he could react. She slammed the door in his surprised face, and twisted the finger latch. She knew this moment of safety would be a fleeting one. But it would give her time to think.

On the other side of the door, Cahill laughed. "Now, c'mon, darlin'. You know I'm gonna get you. Just open the door, and I won't have to break it down. It's less messy, you know?"

She hesitated, knowing he was right. "Go away!" she wailed. "Please!"

He very casually stepped back, lifted his foot, and kicked the door open. Just a little swift kick with his steel-tipped cowboy boot, was all it took. Cecilia's eyes flew open as did the door and Cahill was grinning at her, casually twirling the cylinder of his handgun. She backed away.

"You're a feisty one," he said, moving toward her. "I kinda missed that."

"Keep away from me," she almost screamed. "Lenny, he be comin' back any minute with the cops!"

"Nah," laughed Cahill. "You know better'n that. I don't think he cares enough for you, anyway, tell you the truth. C'mon, darlin'. I just thought you and me would have a little reunion. Then maybe take a ride to the country. You like the country, don't you? I got a nice place out there, we could spend some time together." He reached out and yanked her blouse open. "Just you, me, and the gators."

She screamed. He gave her chin a little chuck with the gun. "Easy, now. None of that. Ain't nobody gonna do you no harm, girl. You just relax and enjoy it. Maybe I'll even give you another little pickaninny. Then you can go on welfare, collect some real money."

She slapped him. In spite of the gun. In spite of her fear. She'd simply had enough. She almost knocked the gun away from him in the process. He recovered from his shock quickly, and reacted the way he always reacted: with immediate, full-bore violence. He slugged her with the butt of the pistol, on the side of her head, and she fell to the floor.

He knelt beside her, in sudden consternation. He hadn't meant to knock her cold, just meant to punish her. He wanted her awake and alert, to enjoy what he was going to do to her. He wasn't some necrophiliac. He wanted his women looking at him while he fucked them. He wanted to make them whimper, and moan, and beg for more. Not just lie there like a lump of meat. He checked the window. There was no sign anyone in the street had heard them. But he'd better get her out of here, he decided.

She still had a pulse. That was good. But she was breathing erratically, and blood was seeping from a deep gash on her skull. Shit, he thought. Maybe he'd better just finish the job, and go. He pointed the pistol at her head. She stirred, and groaned. Her eyes fluttered open. He lowered the gun. He wasn't ready to just kill her in cold blood like that. He really hadn't thought it through, he realized. Always acting on impulse, he often found himself halfway out the door before he knew where he was going. All he wanted was to get her financial monkey off his back. Maybe he could make her sign a paper or something. That boyfriend of hers, Smith, worked at Florida Fertilizers. When he bothered to show up. Maybe he could put some pressure there, make him pay.

Checking the street once more, he didn't see anyone. He got some twine from the kitchen, and tied her hands and feet, and stuffed a filthy lace doilie from the telephone table in her mouth. He went out to the car, started the motor, and pulled it into the driveway. Gingerly avoiding the motorcycle and other debris, he drove across the grass and around to the back of the house. Leaving the engine running, he went in through the smashed kitchen door, lifted her up, and carried her out the back. He loaded her like a sack of potatoes into the car, and slammed the door. He knew where he'd take her now. He had a special place, perfect for occasions like this one. . . .

Leonard Smith had driven mostly on adrenalin—first during his flight from Cahill, who had scared him more than he was willing to admit to himself, then as a clear plan of revenge settled in his mind. Okay, mother fucker, he thought. You got my woman. Now I am gonna get yours.

He got to Orange Blossom around two o'clock in the afternoon. A storm was brewing. He could smell the ozone in the air. It was hot, and still. There was no one in sight. Everyone was indoors, hunkered down in front of their TV sets and air conditioners. Or off at a beach or lake, somewhere. That was good. He had looked Cahill's address up before coming into the town. It was in the phone book. He stopped at Yasha Dromes's gas station and got directions. Dromes knew that to be a lily white neighborhood. Somebody, thought Dromes, is in for trouble.

Smith found the house with no trouble, and decided to lie low until dark. He didn't want to be seen going in. Then he

242

noticed that the garage door was wide open, and led to the house. The inside door would pose no problem. Why wait? He pulled his Firebird into the garage. Deep in its shadows, he could get out of the car unobserved, and enter the house before anyone, inside or out, was the wiser.

He decided to close the garage door, with his car inside. Best no one driving past, or coming home, be alerted to a strange car on the premises. That's when he noticed that the inside door was off its hinges. Someone, he realized, had run amok here. Too bad. He would like to have done the honors himself.

He went inside, and surveyed the damage. Damn, he thought. Somebody hit this place big-time. He wondered who, and sat down to wait. Cahill would show up sooner or later. And when he did, he would kill him.

Six blocks away, in another part of Orange Blossom, Briana Cahill and her sister Carol were having an argument. Carol and her husband wanted her to stay put, Dicky was still out there somewhere.

"The sheriff can't watch him every minute," Carol reminded her.

"But I need things. He won't dare go back there now, in broad daylight."

"How do you know he's not home?"

"Because I've been ringing the phone off the hook. I've never known him to let the phone ring. He's too afraid he'll miss a call from one of his big-shot buddies."

"He should've bought an answering machine, then," said Carol.

"Him? Too damn cheap."

Briana was fretting, because she missed her belongings. She'd left in such a hurry yesterday, she hadn't been able to pack much for herself or the kids. They were all clamoring now, for this toy, that item of clothing, even their toothbrushes, although Carol had insisted they had plenty enough of that sort of thing in the house. The clothes were the main problem. Carol's kids were teens now, and Briana's preschool age. Also, Carol was what she laughingly called "full figured," while Briana was as slim as a model—for which Carol was never going to forgive her, Briana knew. Carol had put on weight with each child; Briana had stayed so thin she didn't even believe she was pregnant the first time.

"I just need to go over there for a minute," she insisted. "Jerry can drive me."

"He's at the game."

"Then you can drive me. You're a pretty good bodyguard," she laughed.

Carol glowered. "Is that supposed to be a compliment? Another one of your little references to my weight?"

"No, I didn't mean it like that at all. Come on, Carol," cajoled Briana. Carol was so damn sensitive! "All I meant was you are smart, and quick on your feet. Dicky's afraid of you."

That part was true. Dicky always acted cowed in her presence. He wasn't used to women who talked back, was Carol's theory. Briana took too much crap from him, and she let her know it whenever she could. Like now.

"I know, I know, you're right. But please, we need stuff, he's not going to be there—or at least if he is, we'll see his car, and just keep going. Please, Carol. Please?"

Carol relented. "Fine, you win. But I have to get Becky to watch the kids. And only for a minute. In, out, that's it."

"Thanks, sis," said Briana, and gave her a hug. Southern country Irish weren't big on hugs, but Carol took it with aplomb. She extricated herself, and went to tell the kids.

"All right, then," grumbled Carol, returning from the living room. "Let's get it over with."

The storm had actually regained its strength, and was still raging in Plant City. Lowell, out of patience, had been about to get out of the car outside the offices of Malone and Associates when his friend Perry stopped him, his head tilted, listening.

"What?" snapped Lowell.

"Wait," whispered Perry. "I heard something."

Lowell hadn't heard a thing, except thunder. Maybe it was nothing. Maybe it was one of Perry's Native American innate superior sensory awareness things. Perry really did have acute senses, he had to admit. But a lot of that had to do with commando training.

Rain continued to pour, obscuring the entire vicinity. Lowell hunched down in frustration.

"There's somethin' not sittin' right here," Perry said.

Lowell frowned. He could never tell with Perry whether he said things like that for effect, or whether they were for real. But on principle, he had to agree. Perry was usually right. They sat in silence, and waited.

The thunder abated. The rain continued steadily, showing no sign of letting up.

"Must've fallen two, three inches already," noted Perry.

Ten more minutes went by. Both of them were getting overheated, and restless. Perry relaxed a little and reached for his shirt pocket, now soaking wet with perspiration.

"Mind if I smoke a number?"

He meant pot, and extracted a joint. Lowell shook his head. "Come on, Perry, you said yourself we have to keep alert, here."

"It helps me keep alert."

"Yeah. But that's not all it does."

Perry paused, shook his head, and blinked. "Yeah," he admitted. "I think I'm hallucinating already, as it is."

Lowell didn't want to wait any longer. "Ready?" He reached for the door handle. Then he, too, heard a sound.

Lowell turned instinctively. A devilish, blurred face was staring at them through the passenger side window, blurred and distorted by the rain like a carnival mirror, water pouring down the nose, running off the chin, dripping from the hair. Then he recognized the face through the rain-smeared window: the sad face with the five o'clock shadow.

19

When Briana Cahill's sister, Carol O'Brien, pulled up outside the Cahill residence, Carol felt something was wrong, right off.

"It looks weird," she said.

"Yeah, well, no shit, Dicky's been there, I'm sure. But he wouldn't stay around. Without me he's a little baby, afraid of the dark."

"Dicky Cahill? Your Dicky Cahill?" Carol reacted, incredulous.

"My soon to be ex, Dicky Cahill," corrected Briana.

"I don't know, honey. It just looks weird. I wouldn't go in there."

"I'll only be a minute, come on, Carol, if Dicky was there his car would be in the driveway. He couldn't bear to put it away where nobody could see it, and behold what a cool hombre he is."

"Yeah, but—"

Briana opened the door. "I'll be right back," she promised, and hurried up the walk.

Carol watched her, her apprehension increasing.

Briana used her key to open the front door, and felt reassured to hear the lock click open. Then she stepped in, and saw the destruction.

"Oh, my God," she moaned. "Oh, my God."

She walked through the house in a trance. It had to have been Dicky, she knew at once. She saw the gaping jagged hole in what had been the back patio door, and stifled a scream. The house was now wide open to the wind and the rain. The floor was wet. It had been raining on and off all day. Get out, a voice shrieked, inside her skull. Get out now! She turned to run.

Then she screamed.

White girls in the rural South had been instilled for two hundred years and more with a clear, distinct vision of their worst possible nightmare. Despite all the socialization and integration that had taken place, the easing of prejudice, the relaxation of restrictions, still the most deep-seated fear of white daddies for their pretty white daughters remained the same, and had been driven home again and again—the dread of the big, black cock. And the man who wielded one.

Smith was that nightmare. There he stood, rippling with power, black, and menacing. In her own house. She managed to scream again before he seized her and covered her mouth with his huge viselike hand.

"Don't," he warned her.

Outside, waiting in the Ford station wagon with the engine running to keep the air-conditioning going and radio playing, Carol hadn't heard the scream. But as the minutes went by she began to worry. Turning down the radio, she got out of the car and walked slowly toward the house. Her heart began to pound in her chest. Something was wrong.

"Briana?" she called. She reached for the door handle. It had a finger latch as well as dead bolt, and had automatically locked when Briana had gone in. She rattled the latch, and pressed the doorbell. "Briana, you all right?"

Inside, Briana's eyes were wide with fear. Smith pulled her forcibly into the kitchen, toward the garage door. He whispered in her ear, "Don't even breathe. I ain't gonna hurt you, lady. I didn't do this to your house. Your old man prob'ly did it. And he's the one I want."

Briana wanted to believe him. She wanted desperately to believe him.

"I ain't gonna hurt you," he said again. "I ain't interested in gettin' the chair for doin' a white woman."

He shoved her into the garage. "Get in the car," he ordered.

Outside, Carol called once more, then turned and ran for the station wagon. Briana was in trouble. Dicky must've hidden in there, hidden in wait for Bree, and stupid her, to let her sister talk her into taking her there, letting her walk right into the trap! She had a girlfriend on the next block. She'd call the police from there.

Fighting back her own fear, she jumped into the station wagon and turned the key. She pumped so hard the engine wouldn't start. She'd flooded the carburetor. "Oh, no," she whimpered. "Oh, God, please start!" The engine finally caught and sputtered, and rumbled back to life. Tires squealing, she tore off down the street, praying for all she was worth.

Inside the garage, Smith saw her go, through the side window, as he pushed Briana into the driver's seat of his Firebird, got in behind her, and shoved her over.

"What do you want me for, then?" sobbed Briana, trying to cling to the smallest thread of hope.

"I tol' you. Your husband. The one who fucked my woman, and give her a chile. He with her right now, you know that?"

"No!" She gasped, and covered her mouth. "Let me go, please, he won't come here. But the cops will. My sister will be calling them any minute!"

He knew she was right. He checked the window, and

started the engine. "Then I'm gonna have to take you," he told her. "Until we can do a little trade."

Her heart sank. But then the tiniest glimmer of hope crept into her thoughts. This man might actually play into her hands. If it was Dicky Cahill he wanted, Dicky she would give him.

"I know where he'll go," she managed to say, her voice trembling. "He's got a place he goes, up on the Little Manatee River. I'll tell you how to get there."

"No, that's all right," said Smith. "You just show me."

He put the car in reverse, and pressed the door lock. "Don't try to get away," he warned her in a tone that sent a new wave of fear down her spine. That's when he showed her the gun. She recognized it from Dicky's collection: a 9-mm Beretta. Now her fear gave way to sheer terror.

As Smith backed out of the garage, the thunderstorm that had been roving the Tampa Bay area for much of the day struck in full force.

Twenty miles away, Lowell and Perry made their moves simultaneously. Lowell nailed Buster Corcoran with the door, throwing it open, staggering him as he rolled to the ground, and kicked out with one of his old wrestler's moves from high school. As the big man went down, Perry was on him. Corcoran was wearing a disguise of sorts—a woman's wig that flew off as they rolled and tumbled, each trying to get a grip. Lowell saw the weapon before Perry did. Corcoran had a handgun—what looked like an old police special.

"Look out!" he shouted. It was too late. Perry had made a critical mistake. Despite all his bravado—his boasts, his claims of a nefarious background, of covert "terminations"—at heart, he was not a first-strike killer. Corcoran was. And so, just when he had him, Perry hesitated, and

Corcoran did not. He shot Perry at close range as Lowell, five feet away, was still scrambling to his feet. Perry groaned and struck back with all his considerable remaining force. It was called, in self-defense terminology, a startle response. He struck Corcoran in the windpipe with three fingers, and both men collapsed onto the rain-soaked pavement as the storm raged on.

Lowell pulled Corcoran aside and checked for breathing. There was none.

"Perry!" he shouted, pulling off his shirt to tie the wound. It appeared grave, but Perry was still breathing. Lowell ran for the building, some fifty meters away.

"Call the paramedics!" he shouted as he burst into the room. There was a meeting going on. There were four of them: Virgil Malone, Tom Freeman, and Mrs. Jessup were there, together. Jack Largent, the PR man from International Phosphates was with them. Lowell, still dazed, had to search his memory a moment before remembering who Largent was. They had heard the gunshot. No one moved. In exasperation, Lowell scanned the room. It was a small conference suite, with a rich Berber carpet, white walls, off-white Levelors on the windows, and simple, expensive white Danish furniture with leather cushions and arm rests.

Lowell found a phone on a desk by the door. He dialed 911. "Hello?" he shouted, into the phone. "I'm calling from five sixty-three Tangerine Way, Plant City. There are two casualties in the parking lot, one possible fatality, one with a gunshot wound. Get an ambulance out there, and hurry!"

He turned to face them. They all looked as though they'd been whipped.

"What happened out there?" Largent managed to speak first. Ever the PR man. He was probably already thinking of damage control, Lowell figured.

Lowell turned to the door. "Nobody leave," he ordered.

"I've got to take care of my friend. You have a first-aid kit in here?"

Mrs. Jessup was the first to move. She hurried to the rest room and came back with one of those little white metal boxes the Red Cross distributes. Lowell seized it, and was out the door.

"Where the hell'd Corcoran go, dammit?" Largent shouted after him.

"You asshole," snarled Malone, revealing an entirely new side to his character. "That's the other casualty out there. Corcoran may be a tough hombre. But he's also stupid. Mr. Lowell, there, he may be a meddling thorn in the side of business and commerce. But he isn't stupid."

Lowell ran back out to the parking lot. He had already begun administering first aid when he noticed something else chillingly wrong. He spun around, realizing with cold certainty what he'd overlooked as he'd come rushing back to his friend. Corcoran. Corcoran wasn't dead. Corcoran was gone. Lowell couldn't search for him, he had to keep his friend alive. But he felt terribly vulnerable, there on the wet pavement, rain still falling, receding thunder still rumbling, and a possible killer lurking somewhere out there—maybe close by. There was nothing he could do about it. At least he had the—shit! The weapon. Corcoran's weapon had been left on the pavement, next to the body. In his concern for Perry, he hadn't given it another thought, until now. The gun was gone as well.

The ambulance arrived in seven minutes. Lowell held his friend's head, struggled to breathe life into his lungs, tried to staunch the flow of blood. His own tears joined the sweat from his brow and the rain from above, pouring down his face.

The paramedics were good. They did what they could. Lowell was torn. He wanted to go with his friend to the hospital. But as they were loading him into the ambulance, Perry opened his eyes for just a moment. "Lowell?" he whispered.

Lowell gripped his hand.

"Get those bastards, will ya?"

Lowell nodded. "Sure I will," he promised.

The ambulance raced away, siren screaming. Lowell turned and walked back to the offices of Malone and Associates. He had unfinished business to take care of.

He went back in. Twenty minutes had passed, maybe more, and no one had moved. Mrs. Jessup brought him a cup of coffee, with a reproachful look. Almost like a peace offering. He wondered how Mrs. Jessup fit in, until he saw her clutching Freeman's hand.

Lowell noticed a large wall chart on a pulldown roller against one wall. Freeman was covertly trying to close it.

"This is a private meeting, Mr. Lowell," he said feebly as Lowell strode over and yanked the chart back down for a look.

"This the Sunshine Project?" he asked. "I read the Soil and Water Report on it. If that report was where it was supposed to be, namely at DEP in Tampa, then you people are out of business, right? But it wasn't, and you aren't. Yet."

They looked at each other—Mrs. Jessup, Tom Freeman, Largent, and the affable Malone, America's baseball hero. "Fuck," muttered Malone.

"Where'd he get it?" Largent wanted to know.

"What difference does it make?" growled Malone. "He got it. He's been out there, he knows."

They hadn't seen Corcoran, Lowell learned in relief. Corcoran had headed for the proverbial hills. "Call Manatee City Police," he told Jessup. "Ask for Lieutenant Bedrosian."

She backed away in alarm.

253

He turned back to Malone and Associates. "Corcoran is gone," he informed them. Malone's expression returned to its usual good cheer, but Lowell sensed consternation on the part of Largent, and open fear from Freeman. Freeman was going to fold soon, he knew. Whatever face card was holding up this paper castle was about to fall out, and the house of cards would then collapse.

"We don't know what to do about you, Lowell," Largent finally said. "We'd like to press charges, but there are complications." No shit, thought Lowell. "On the other hand, we need to make it very clear to you, that you don't go barging onto company property, into private property, with impunity."

"So you admit you've been trying to hide something?"

Largent glowered. "Don't wise off, Lowell. People like you always think you have the right answers to everything. You paint a picture of us as the bad guys, we're the ones contaminating the environment, we're the ones killing the spotted penguins, or whatever. Well, let me tell you something. We have as clean a record as any industry, we care about the people around these parts—none of whom would even appreciate what you're trying to do, by the way—"

"What am I trying to do?"

"You and that black kid, he had all the answers, too. Shut down a whole industry, put nine thousand people out of work, just because a little acid spilled."

"You kill him for that?"

The question came out of nowhere, and threw Largent into an instant rage. He grabbed Lowell by the shirt.

"Listen, you bastard, don't you ever accuse us of something like that again. We run a clean, legal business. There is nothing we do, are doing, or have done, that can be construed in any other way, and we had nothing to do with whatever happened to some meddling investigator who stuck his nose in the wrong beehive. Much," he added, "as we grieve for his family, and regret his passing."

He sounded like a politician, thought Lowell. "It was your beehive, though. Right?" he queried, going for the thumbs, and removing a surprised Largent's hands with ease. "He was on his way to Plant City to see you, the night he was killed. Wasn't he." It wasn't a question. Lowell only had Cecilia's word on that, but the bluff worked.

Largent sighed, loosened his tie, and sat down. "Look," he said. "It's not easy, keeping your head above water in this business. We've been good citizens down the line. We've played a major role in feeding the world. And we've had to fight every step of the way, ever since the environmental people came along, screaming about all the gypsum stacks, and ugly holding ponds and the damn smell of ammonia and sulfur everywhere. Industry isn't pretty, and that's the truth. But we've done our best. You see some of those parks and golf courses out there? Former mining sites, all of them."

"I know. They look great. Use lots of your fertilizers, too, I'll bet, to keep 'em so green like that." Further polluting the water table, he thought, but didn't add. "But anyway, you didn't do any of that restoration voluntarily."

"Not at first. But we love our communities like you love yours, and we've tried hard for the past two decades to make things better around here."

"So what about Cross then?"

Nobody spoke. Lowell turned to Malone, who'd been pretty much silent up until now. "He was going to eighty-six the Sunshine Project, wasn't that it?" He got up, went over to the wall, and examined the chart. It was a detailed, full-color illustrated layout of an entire planned development. "Your big showcase reclamation plan. What, four thousand acres of former phosphate minings, a planned community, industrial park, two lakes, two golf courses, three housing developments, the works. Nice! It was all set, you'd jumped through every hoop. Then this kid comes along."

Malone smiled, his eyes glittering, and shook his head.

"There had to have been preliminary plans, EI Reports, tentative approvals along the way," continued Lowell. "You said this was in the works for years. Why did he suddenly turn on you like that? Or was the DEP against you all the way?"

"Not at all. The problem was"—and at this Largent turned away, and gazed out through the gray tinted window—"that damn sinkhole."

"Cross saw it coming, didn't he? He must've found, what? A huge underground plume of chemicals. Stuff like sulfuric acid and ammonia and heavy metals that your predecessors had covered up out there years ago, just hoping it would go away, in time. But it didn't go away, did it? Except into the aquifer. Of course, we all know better now. But it was pretty much an inconvenience for your planned city here, having that down there."

"Where'd you get that information?" demanded Malone, his smile fracturing, threatening imminent collapse.

"We didn't know about those plumes!" protested Freeman. "No one from today's management team had any knowledge—"

"It began to leak, was that it?"

"No—!"

"And Cahill's job was to cover it up again, but it kept leaking, didn't it? And eventually, Tim Cross found it, like he inevitably would. They found fluorine in his blood. Among other goodies. Care to explain how that happened?"

Freeman shook his head, took off his glasses, and wiped his forehead. "That was an accident. He took a serious dose of a highly potent fluorine extract during one of his inspection tours. We did what we could for him."

"That was big of you."

"He had no business down there!" blurted Largent.

Lowell ignored him. "Well, in any case, he knew trouble was just waiting to happen, tried to warn you guys, tried to do it right, give you a chance to make corrections before filing his report. So you put him off, maybe roughed him up a little—"

"We did no such thing!" insisted Freeman.

Malone lit a cigarette, turned and gazed out the window.

"Look, Mr. Lowell," said Largent, "nobody's asking you to do anything against your will. But I think you should get the whole picture, before you start pointing fingers."

"Why don't you cut the bullshit," said Lowell, "And start by explaining what happened to Tim Cross?"

"I think maybe you should leave now," said Malone. "You're wasting your time, and ours."

"Thanks, but I'm just getting warmed up." Lowell turned back to the chart, studied it a moment, then once again faced the others. "So where were we? Oh, yes. Let me see if I can picture it," he resumed as they stared at him, faces ashen. "The plume, the old chemical plume, must've broken through the walls of one of the caverns where it had been stored, somewhere deep beneath the surface out there. The first leak eventually drained the cave out, probably into the aquifer, leaving a big underground hole. Boom. The earth falls into the cave. Sinkhole! Then some water trickles in from the water table above. No problem. Baumgarten comes out, sees the water, it's fine, he writes a routine report. Interesting, but no problem, right? So he leaves. Then, uh-oh, what's that? A leak? From another old plume, still lurking, lurking, nearby. Seeping, seeping into the new hole. Not water, this time. Something worse. Much worse. Acid. And all those other wonderful things that had been dumped down there." He looked at them. They were looking away. "How'm I doing?" he asked.

No one bothered to answer.

"Then Cross gets wind of what's going on," Lowell continued. "He had no choice now but to hold up the Soil and Water Report. But you weren't finished yet, were you? You got hold of the report, somehow, and buried it. And him along with it." He reached into his jacket pocket and produced a copy of the cover sheet he'd photocopied after his meeting with Bedrosian. "Problem is, I got a copy."

Malone smiled. "Illegally obtained, of course."

"Yes," agreed Lowell, with a smile of his own. "By you."

Malone's smile vanished quicker than a pick-off at second base. Largent shook his head and put his hand on Malone's arm, cautioning him.

"So that was why Cross was going to shut down the Sunshine Project," explained Lowell. "And why, out of courtesy to you, he hadn't yet filed the report. He wanted to give you a chance to offer a cleanup proposal. That's why he was coming up to your meeting, wasn't it?"

"It would have cost millions," sighed Freeman, looking ready to collapse. "We just don't have that kind of capital anymore."

"The EPA would have helped."

"Not that much. They'd just try to make us pay."

"Look, you've got it all wrong, Mr. Lowell," Largent sighed. "We are not gangsters. We didn't kill anybody."

"Maybe." said Lowell. "Meanwhile, poor Harry Baumgarten, the state hydrologist, must've been mighty surprised to see all that acid that had leaked into his sinkhole since his last visit." No wonder Solano had insisted there was no problem, he thought. There hadn't been, until the plume began to leak.

"You can't put that on us," insisted Malone. "Baumgarten rubber-stamped the whole thing, it was routine."

"Until he suddenly found himself with a major problem—sulfuric acid where there'd been none before. No wonder he'd panicked."

"That proves it could have been suicide, then," pointed out Largent. "Or an accident."

"That," admitted Lowell, "is true. It could have been."

A moment later, Mrs. Jessup, who'd slipped out of the room while Lowell was holding the floor, returned.

"I called the police," she told them. "About the shooting." She looked at Malone. "We had to. The paramedics would have to report it anyway. It's required."

Malone nodded, looking indifferent.

Largent was suddenly insistent. Defensive, a whining note creeping into his voice. "Listen, you have to believe us. We had nothing to do with what happened to either of those men. I don't like it any more than you, whatever Cross's politics or color, he had a right to live. And he was right about the damn sinkhole, we're working around the clock trying to contain it."

"When were you planning to call in Natural Resources and the DEP, not to mention the federal EPA?"

"You're right, we tried to keep it in-house, and that was wrong. But we had a billion-dollar project at stake. It was our last hope for turning this company around. As you may be aware, the fertilizer market has been shaky for several years. We've taken a hell of a beating."

"I'm not too impressed by your decision that your company's welfare is more important than twelve million people's water supply."

"We had no idea it was going to be that serious. We have every intention of calling the EPA," insisted Largent. "First thing Monday morning."

"Maybe you'd better not wait that long. You're also going to have to talk to the cops about Harry Baumgarten."

"Yeah." His expression showed considerable distaste for the task at hand.

"They're going to want depositions from all of you." No one looked too pleased about that, either.

"Great," muttered Largent, sounding bitter. "Now we have not one but two deaths we're going to have to explain to the board. Sunshine is going to go down. All those years, all that investment. For nothing."

Jessup clutched Freeman's arm and gave him a woeful look. Freeman spoke up. "Not necessarily!" he interjected, a hopeful tone creeping into his voice. "We can close off that hole. I've been thinking about how. If we pour in enough cement, it will—"

"Shut up, Freeman," snapped Largent. Even Lowell wanted to strangle him. Then there'd be three murders.

Malone had been silent for some time. He stubbed out his cigarette, turned, and faced Lowell. "The man you want," he said, "is Dicky Cahill."

Lowell sat back on the nice white leather couch, not unlike the one in his own studio, and put his feet up on the adjacent lacquer coffee table.

"Cahill, your own private hit man?"

"I never authorized that. He's a loose cannon. You've seen that. He and Corcoran . . ." He hesitated a moment. "You say Corcoran is dead?"

"I was under that impression. Turns out I was wrong. He's gone."

Largent was on his feet. "What do you mean?"

"He attacked my partner and me in the parking lot. Both of them went down. But when I went back, he was gone."

The others looked at one another.

"Shit!" muttered Malone. "There's no telling what he'll do. As for Cahill, I knew I made a mistake the day I brought him in on the Sunshine Project. He was supposed to see to it that Cross was dealt with, got what he needed, but was kept out of the way. Maybe his idea of how to do it was murder. If so, I never intended that. I'm a legitimate businessman. Besides, I got a public image. You think I'm gonna blow that?"

"And Corcoran?"

"Hell, the two of them were two peas in a pod. Hated black people, too, or anybody with more education than third grade. Me, I played ball with blacks, some of them were great ol' boys. Frank Robinson, Tony Perez, Ken Griffey. I'm no damn racist."

Just then the phone rang. They looked at each other, the Sunshine People. Finally Jessup answered it. She listened, and looked at Lowell.

"It's the police," she said. "For you."

20

Bedrosian had hurried home for a quick lunch of Campbell's tomato soup and her usual Wheat Thins, and to change into a fresh, cooler spring outfit from JC Penney's—a beige single-button cotton-blend jacket and slim skirt in herringbone. She'd begun to rely on the low-priced department and budget stores. Her current family budget was pretty much limited these days, which worked out all right because that enabled a celebratory occasion, now and then, when Michael would surprise her with a new accessory from Arpel's or something off the rack but nice from one of the Sarasota boutiques, for a splurge.

Lena had made a quick excuse to her husband—now glued to the TV—gotten back in the squad car, and hurried back to the station. At least she'd managed to placate Michael and the kids with a promise she'd take them out for pizza tonight. The kids were busy with their grandma, and Michael was busy watching the NCAA basketball tournament and probably wouldn't even notice she was gone until then. Otherwise they wouldn't have spoken to her for a week.

There were some things that were nagging her regarding the Cross case. It was still way too wide open, and she had to admit to herself she was worried about Lowell. He'd gone off half-cocked back to Bone Valley with his crazy friend, Cochise. Meanwhile, she'd finally gotten a look at the newest photographs he'd left her. He'd dropped them off two days earlier with Allenson at the desk. But Allenson still harbored some bad feelings both for her and private investigator Tony Lowell going way back, and hadn't bothered to go out of his way to pass the photos on to her. He'd tossed the envelope on her desk along with a ton of miscellaneous paperwork and forgotten about it. She'd found it last night, just as she was leaving, but she was too tired then to look at them. Forensics had just reported that morning that they'd made a positive ID on the little piece of glass. It was from a watch crystal. More specifically, a Rolex. They were waiting for a call from a Rolex expert in New York regarding which model might have had a beveled crystal like that. The call was due in any minute. Meanwhile, she'd gone over the coroner's report on Cross again. He'd had a watch on, and it had been intact. Cahill'd had a watch too—hell, everybody had a watch. But it was something she'd wanted Lowell to look out for. "Watch out for," she'd thought about telling him, but neither of them was in much of a mood for joking lately.

She'd been going over Leonard Smith's inventory when the news came in about Cecilia.

Out in Plant City, the storm had finally receded, and the late-afternoon sun shone momentarily through a break in the clouds, before vanishing again. Inside the offices of Malone and Associates, Largent and Malone shrugged helplessly as Lowell walked over and took the phone receiver from Jessup.

"Lowell here."

"Lowell? It's Bedrosian." She sounded breathless. "I'm

calling you from Cecilia Potter's house. We just had a Signal Twenty-four over here."

"Meaning what?" Lowell hated police jargon.

"We got a call from a neighbor. It seems somebody with honky cracker written all over him just abducted Cecilia Potter. Somebody who drives a late-model red T-bird."

"Christ." He glanced at the others. They seemed frozen in place.

"You okay?" she asked.

"Yeah. How'd you know to call me here?"

"I'm a detective. Plus, it was in Baumgarten's notes you gave me. Malone and Associates. It seems they'd paid him a visit. And it also happens I just picked up a police report of a shooting at that address you're at. Your friend Perry Garwood's name came up."

"How is he?" asked Lowell quickly. "The ambulance just left a little while ago."

"Stable, they told me. I figured you might be involved."

"Why me? I don't own a gun."

"Good point. But you seem to attract people who do. What the hell happened out there?"

"I'll tell you later," he promised.

"There's something else," she said quickly. "Smith is out."

He took a deep breath. "Great. I guess all in all that makes this a memorable day for life, liberty, and the pursuit of happiness. How in the name of Jesus, Mary, and Joseph did that happen?"

"Don't be sarcastic, Lowell. She's the one got him out."

"Cecilia?" The utter dismay those words caused flooded through him. He closed his eyes tightly for a moment. "Aw, man," was all he could say.

"We have an APB out on Cahill," she started to tell him. "We'll find him."

He was worried about Perry. But Perry was a survivor. He was worried more, right now, about Cecilia. And the child! "Where's the girl, Natasha?" he demanded.

"She's all right. The grandmother has her."

"Cahill just kidnapped a woman," he informed Malone and Associates, still holding the phone. "Where is he?"

They looked aghast.

"Why are you asking us?" demanded Largent indignantly.

"Gotta go," said Lowell to Bedrosian, and hung up.

"Lowell—wait!" Bedrosian shouted into the receiver. Too late. She listened to the dial tone for a moment, in exasperation. Then paused a minute to go over her notes and thoughts. She'd wanted to tell him about the crystal. And the message—Cross's cryptic message he'd written on the front seat. She had a theory about what it meant, and felt it might be important.

Lowell turned to face Largent, Malone, Freeman, and Jessup. "All right," he said to them. "I'm going to ask you once. Where's Cahill?"

They looked at each other. Malone was sweating even more. "He has a fishing shack," he finally said. "I'll take you there."

Lowell turned and headed for the door. "Now," he said.

Malone looked at the others. "Wait here," he told them.

Freeman glanced at his watch. "But it's late. That's going to take hours, and it'll be dark before—"

"Wait here," repeated Malone.

Freeman nodded, his face ashen. Largent's expression lockjawed into its blankest MBA inscrutability. Freeman and Jessup clutched each other's hands. Malone gave Lowell a tight-lipped smile.

"Let's go," he said.

265

Back in her office, Bedrosian hung up the phone. Forensics had just called with an answer regarding the Rolex watch. It was a very special watch, it turned out. To be exact, one of kind. Only one person in the world owned a watch like that, and it was now extremely urgent that Lowell be informed as to who it was. It was an All-Star Game Most Valuable Player watch, given at a New York Baseball Boosters Banquet to go along with the trophy, car, and usual perks that Virgil "Doc" Malone had won one memorable summer a couple of decades back, at the peak of his career. She hit the redial button.

Jessup and Freeman looked at each other as the phone rang. They stared at it, frozen, paralyzed with indecision. It rang six, then seven times.

"Answer it, for God's sake," Freeman finally pleaded.

Bedrosian hung on. "Come on, dammit!" she swore into the receiver.

Jessup finally answered, unable to bear listening to the ring any longer. Too many years as an office receptionist, perhaps, had conditioned her to respond to a telephone like a mother to a baby's cry.

"Malone and Associates," she said in her not-quite-pleasantest office tones.

Bedrosian almost exploded through the line at her. "Where's Tony Lowell? I have to talk to him!"

She was taken aback. "He's just left, I'm afraid."

Bedrosian nearly cursed her out, managed not to. "This is Detective Lieutenant Bedrosian of the Manatee City Police Department. I was just speaking with him. Where did he go?"

Jessup looked at Largent, then Freeman. "It's the cops

again!" she whispered. "They want to know where Lowell went."

Largent shrugged bitterly.

"What should I tell them?"

"I don't give a shit what you tell them," said Largent, and walked out.

Jessup looked at Freeman helplessly. He threw up his hands.

"Lady, this is extremely urgent!" insisted Bedrosian. "What did he say when he left? Was he going to the hospital?"

"All I know," Jessup finally said, "is that they went up the Little Manatee River, somewhere. To a fishing shack. Dicky Cahill's place. I think it's out in the middle of nowhere."

"They? Who'd he leave with?"

Jessup hesitated. "Mr. Malone," she finally said.

Bedrosian slammed down the phone, and pressed a button on the intercom. "Allenson, where's Baker?" she shouted.

The sergeant took his time answering. "He's off today."

"Where's the chopper? I need it now."

"It's in the hangar, but—"

"Who's authorized to fly?" she demanded.

"Well, let's see, there's Captain Jeffries, there's Peters—"

"Get Peters!" she shouted. "On the double! And call Sheriff Pearson up in Hillsborough, we are going to need backup!"

Malone and Lowell sat in silence as Malone drove his olive green Range Rover. The clouds had dissipated now, and the late-afternoon sun slanted low above the tree line, delivering one final discharge of heat before yielding to evening's coming chill. The canopy of oaks and magnolias gave way to open meadows and scrub. Both men were sweating. Malone was driving fast. Too fast. Lowell instinctively reached down to check his seat belt as they took a curve at sixty. He felt something metallic wedged deep between the seat and console. Looking down he recognized the object at once, and closed his fist around it quickly. It must have fallen down there, and been thought lost. Well, now it was found. With a quick glance at Malone, he surreptitiously pocketed it: a Rolex Oyster chronograph watch. With a broken crystal.

Lowell gave Malone a quick, furtive look. Now for the first time, he saw the other Malone. The one known as Gator. That was when he knew where the nickname came from. It was the grin. An alligator always had a grin on its face, even when it was about to tear yours off.

As the car accelerated along a straightaway, Lowell gripped the seat in front of him, and suddenly remembered something else. The message Bedrosian had found on Cross's car seat. It wasn't gibberish at all. It hadn't said "Sushi." What Cross had tried to write was "Sunshine."

Malone turned off Highway 39 onto a dirt road, then onto a narrow two-track road. There was water ahead—a river, running wild, swift, and green.

"Where are we?" asked Lowell, trying to sound casual. It felt more like Vietnam, suddenly, than Florida. There was thick woods and mangroves you couldn't even see through, huge oaks, ficus and mangoes, undergrowth and overgrowth so tangled it would strangle a boa constrictor. The sun had fallen behind the trees now, and the density of the canopy would bring an early nightfall.

Lowell felt a strange, tingling sensation at the back of his neck he couldn't explain. As though he were being watched. He kept glancing back, but there was no one in sight.

"The Little Manatee River. We keep an airboat down here, we're gonna need it. The river's too shallow and reedy that far up for a V-hull."

Lowell nodded. Airboats, primarily designed for use in the Everglades, were driven by a large airplane-type propeller mounted in a wire cage on the stern deck. They could go anywhere there was water. Other boats couldn't.

There was a narrow sandy parking area that led to a small wooden dock protruding into the river. Another car was parked nearby, half in the bushes. A somewhat rusted white Pontiac Firebird. Lowell didn't recognize it. But a casual hand on the hood indicated that the engine was still hot. That bothered him.

The airboat was carefully covered with a large tarpaulin, and tied down at the dock. There were two smaller boats: a ten-foot skiff with a twenty-five horsepower Johnson outboard, also moored to the dock on the same side, and an aluminum canoe up on the riverbank, with paddles and cushions stowed beneath. Malone parked the Rover, and they got out. The air reverberated with the sounds of spring in the Florida wild—frogs, waterfowl, insects, and small predators, all vying to live. Lowell had been up this river once before, by canoe, but never this far. It was one of Florida's many wild and scenic rivers, as endangered as all other things of such exotic wildness and beauty. He remembered that his motivation that one time, ostensibly to try his hand at wilderness landscape photography, had been to see it while it was still there.

Lowell looked at the water, dark and foreboding. "Do manatee come up here?" he suddenly asked as Malone untied the tarp that covered the boat. He hoped they did. Gators tended to avoid manatee like the plague, for some reason. Some thought it was fear.

Malone was also staring at the river, and the dock, frowning. He'd given up his pretense at jocularity some time ago. He gave a small shrug for an answer. His mind was on something else. "Cahill's boat's gone," he said. "He's there, all right."

Lowell nodded, and said nothing. Malone hadn't commented on the car. Which meant that he either assumed it was Cahill's—that Cahill had a backup vehicle (what car did Briana own? he wondered)—or that the car belonged to someone else entirely. Maybe just a local who shared the dock, out fishing. Yet he had a gnawing feeling he had seen a car like that somewhere. That he should know whose car it was.

"Give me a hand here, will you?" requested Malone, tugging on the tie-line. "I hope you have a plan when we get there. The guy's a nut case."

"Yeah," said Lowell, untying the next line. "But he works for you."

Lowell pushed the boat free from the dock as Malone started the engine. In moments, they were heading upriver into the gathering darkness. There wasn't a house, another vessel, another person in sight. A huge heron flew past them, chasing bass or mullet. Lowell thought he saw an alligator basking near shore in the last shaft of waning sunlight to find its way through the trees. If it was—they'd been moving too swiftly to be sure—it was a fifteen footer, at least. Bad news. They moved out into more open water, and Malone opened up the engine. The boat was fast. But it was also loud, Lowell realized. It would telegraph their arrival by at least five minutes.

"Watch out for animals!" Lowell shouted. "It's getting hard to see out there."

Malone didn't even bother to reply.

As the airboat disappeared around the next bend in the river, and the sound of the big prop engine gradually faded away, silence fell once more on the area of the dock. Then, as though at a signal, the wildlife resumed their clamor. A new noise could be heard—a rustling, rattling sound. Suddenly a plastic tarp in the back of the Range Rover was thrown off, and the rear door was kicked open. A very large, very hot, and very angry man climbed out, breathing in the steaming air. Corcoran. He stared with a mixture of melancholy and malevolence upstream, in the direction the two men had just gone. Malone, that bastard, hadn't even come looking for him, hadn't mentioned him once. It was like he'd been written off. That was a mistake that bastard was going to regret very soon. Corcoran had more than one score to settle, the way things were coming down. So be it. Sad, though, things had to turn out this way.

He walked to the river's edge, and flipped the canoe over with one huge boot, almost casually. The outboard was locked, but the noise would probably tip them off, anyway. The canoe was much, much better. Corcoran didn't have Indian blood, but he knew Indian ways. And he knew where they had gone. Cahill's. He had a score to settle with that asshole, too: letting him be trigger man on the black kid when it was Cahill who hated blacks so much; acting like the big shot, using his weight on the job to push him, Corcoran, around, insinuating that he had more sway with Virgil than he, Buster Corcoran, who'd introduced them, did. Corcoran had known Virgil from his brief stint in the minors—Virgil's brief, disastrous stint as a manager. They'd both retired from baseball around the same time, for similar reasons. But now—now he felt like an empty beer can. Malone had sucked him dry, put together this deal that left him out, given him the dirty work, and now, so close to payback time, he'd dumped him, tossed him in the gutter. Acted like he never knew him.

It was payback time, all right. But not the payback either of them, any of them, had dreamed about. Deep down, he'd known all along that the good life was not going to be for him. He'd never got a break, not once, in all his lousy, miserable life. Well, if they thought they could use him, and then when things got heavy just cut him out, let him take the heat, they were going to be very surprised, and very, very sorry. Sometimes all that was left was revenge. But in a way, that would be a relief. That was something he could understand, act upon. Pretenses of goodwill, promises of riches and glory, always left him empty. This, what he was going to do now, would have to satisfy him. And it would. Just like it always did.

Corcoran welcomed the oncoming darkness. It would be his friend now. His only friend.

Cahill came in by road from the south side, on which bank the cabin had been built. There was no access from the north except by water, which was why he usually used the boat. Malone's boat, whenever it was offered; but otherwise, his trusty, now-battered old Boston Whaler. The road he'd discovered almost by accident, but it made sense. The builder of the cabin, back in the twenties, had built the road to get in materials, and later to bring in supplies, by land rather than by water. It had become overgrown, but the original oystershell tracks had survived, and Cahill had cleared the small trees and underbrush that had gradually filled in, until he had a serviceable track that ran south to a small dirt road in Manatee County, which led to a two-lane paved road a little bit to the west, which ran south to Duette, and Route 62.

The sun was nearly down, the sky prematurely blackened by another imminent cloudburst, by the time he pulled the T-bird down the dirt road to the small turnaround he'd painstakingly carved out of the woods. More like jungle, actually. The road was muddy and rutted, gullies washed out by the recent rains, and difficult going. He nearly got stuck several times, and regretted not having a four-wheel drive. He hated getting his T-bird mucked up like this, which was why he rarely came here by road, except in the dry season. Which this was supposed to be. But this was an emergency.

Cecilia had sat silently beside him. She was still bound and gagged, and she had not struggled. Possibly the fact that he had a pistol aimed at her the whole time helped in that regard. And now that they had reached his cabin, or "shack" as he liked to call it, she could scream bloody murder as far as he was concerned. No one would hear her. He told her as much as he yanked the doilie from her mouth.

She gasped, not speaking, as he got out, opened the door on her side, and roughly pulled her from the car. She looked at the cabin and was filled with fear anew. It was little more than an assemblage of boards and logs, haphazardly thrown together but somehow standing for untold years, unpainted, poorly maintained, up on stilts above the frequent floods, trees looming over it from all sides, the dark, foreboding river beyond. Full of snakes, and gators, and other terrors she knew not what. She trembled.

"Please," she begged. Not even knowing what to beg for. "Please don't hurt me."

Shoving her in front of him, Cahill reached the steps up

to the deck that surrounded the shack, and felt a renewed excitement watching her coffee brown legs, exposed up to her panties, her ass so firm and young and fine, as she climbed the stairs ahead of him. He was going to have some fun now, he decided. Yessirreeee. She had been too good to resist before, even though it had cost him. This time, it was going to cost her.

Because he was so intent on Cecilia's ass, so tantalizingly close to his face as they climbed the stairs, Cahill failed to notice something still plainly visible in the waning light: his Boston Whaler, tied to the piling at the river's edge.

The door was yanked open even as he reached for it, and Cahill found himself staring at the business end of a very deadly weapon. He recognized it at once: a Beretta 9-mm pistol. He had no time to ponder whose it was.

"Well, well, well," said Leonard Smith, reaching out and seizing Cahill's own gun before he could react, then yanking Cecilia into the one-room shack behind him. "So we meet again, boss. Looks like it's a regular party."

Cahill's eyes widened in fear. Then he received a second shock as Smith roughly shoved him into the room. His wife, Briana, was sitting there as though she'd been waiting for him. She didn't look like she was glad to see him. A sense of utter betrayal swept through him. The bitch! he thought. The bitch, she's run off with this nigger. Not tied up or nothin'. He would kill her now for sure, he vowed. And by her expression, he could tell she knew it. Good.

"Briana, you fucking—" began Cahill, until Smith slugged him behind the ear with the butt of the pistol, knocking him to the floor.

"Shut up," barked Smith. "Or you dead meat."

Cahill, on his knees, the pain searing through him, his vision clouded, believed him. The humiliation of being put down by a damn nigger under his employ was overwhelming. Especially watched by two women he'd known carnally. No matter they looked scared shitless. If he survived this, he decided right then and there, no one else in this room was going to. It was that simple.

The airboat continued to race upstream, cutting through pads of lilies, dodging jutting stumps like ancient giant teeth, a tight-lipped Malone at the wheel, straining to see ahead. Darkness would be coming on fast now. Spanish moss clawed at them like soft old fingers as they swept beneath long, overhanging boughs of oak and cypress, mango and ficus.

"Better shut it down!" Lowell shouted. The river was narrowing. It would end in swamps soon. The shack couldn't be too much further.

"What?" Malone shouted back. "Can't hear you!"

"Shut it down. He's going to know we're coming!"

Very reluctantly Malone slowed the boat to a crawl, and finally shut off the engine. The silence swept over them like a tidal surge. The woods at the river's edge loomed above, black and ominous.

"So what's your plan?" demanded Malone sarcastically. "We swim?"

Lowell pointed at a hummock just visible along the river's edge, around a sandbar up ahead. "There."

An old, only marginally (if at all) serviceable fisherman's rowboat was tied to a stake on the sandbar. It had two battered but functional oars stowed under the single wooden bench. The airboat's momentum brought them to the spit, and Lowell pulled off his Nikes, seized the airboat's bowline, hesitated a moment, and jumped overboard. He waded over the sandbar, pulling the boat behind him. Something black and menacing slithered away across the water. He ignored it. The rowboat was half-beached. He tied the airboat to the stake, pushed the rowboat into the water, and scrambled aboard.

"Let's go," he said.

Malone, annoyed at getting his Haggars and Docksiders wet, reluctantly followed suit. Lowell recognized the body language, and thought of Bedrosian. He wondered what she was doing now, and regretted not having asked for her assistance. But then, he hated asking anyone for anything. Especially Bedrosian.

Lowell rowed. Malone navigated. "It's just around another bend, I think, then a quarter mile or so."

Lowell rowed faster. The sense of foreboding that gnawed at his insides intensified as darkness fell. . . .

21

Smith brusquely shoved the two women onto the battered vinyl sofa that stood under the wide multipaned window on the far side of the room overlooking the deck and river. The sun was just setting, illuminating the river with brilliant blue and pink hues. Under other circumstances, it would have been beautiful. Instinctively, Briana and Cecilia drew away from each other, in mutual fear and suspicion. Cahill had crawled into the corner, and was covering his head with both hands, knees drawn up to his chin. Briana looked at him, cowering like this, and had never feared or loathed him so much as now.

Smith was clearly enjoying his superiority. He roamed the single-room shack, switching on every light he could find.

"So, bitches. Either one of you want to take the honors, and blow this motherfucker's skull off?"

Both women shook their heads vehemently.

Smith laughed. "Okay. Guess I'll just have to do it. After that, though, I don't want to be the one who has to do all the work. All right, girls?"

Cecilia suppressed a sob. Briana just bit her lip and held her breath. Both women were silently praying now, each in her own way.

"No!" whimpered Cahill. "C'mon, Smith, don't do it, please!"

Smith walked over and kicked him in the head. Cahill groaned, and toppled over against the wall. Cecilia and Briana both screamed at the same time.

Out on the river, Lowell and Malone heard the screams.

"Jesus," muttered Malone.

Lowell looked at him, wondering if he was armed. He wondered how he felt about that himself just now. Cold, righteous reasoning was one thing. Hard, desperate reality was something else. He sensed that his faith, his beliefs, were about to be tested.

The now brightly lit fishing shack was directly ahead. He rowed faster.

The Bell police helicopter swept north along Tampa's East Bay shoreline, reflecting the fiery glow of the sun setting out on the Gulf of Mexico. Swooping past Cockroach Bay, it turned east at the tiny hamlet of Gulf City into the mouth of the Little Manatee River. Joe Peters, one of Bedrosian's best and longest-time supporters and allies on the force, was a little rusty, but competent. He'd been a chopper pilot in Nam, but since then, the younger Baker had done most of the flying. Peters radioed the Hillsborough sheriff's department to let them know his purpose and approximate destination, and concentrated on the controls. Bedrosian gathered her thoughts, and her weapons. They had their standard police 9-mm pistols, and a Remington 30-06 sniper rifle. There was also a shotgun, a rocket launcher, which she couldn't see much use for, and a tear-gas grenade launcher, which she might need, she decided. She'd apologize to Lowell later, if it came to it. If he was still alive.

She hoped he was all right. She was worried. He had a way

of rushing into things headlong. Or was *headstrong* the right word? Maybe both. That poor little girl's mother, Cecilia. That's who she was mostly worried about. Maybe she was just a hooker. Her lowlife boyfriend Smith was certainly a likely candidate for a pimp. But according to the women at the Health Center, Cecilia had been a caring and diligent parent to the child. She'd even given up alcohol during the pregnancy, they'd confided to her: something they counseled all mothers to do, and woefully few did. The father, however. Now, he was something else. White trash. And yet, he'd paid support. Most trash of any color didn't bother to do that. Maybe he wasn't all bad, then. She surely hoped so, for the girl's sake. For both girls' sake. She picked up the rifle, though, just in case, checked the clip, and released the safety.

Twenty miles upstream, Dicky Cahill's fishing shack was rocked by a loud, searing scream that trailed off ever so slowly into a lowering moan. The voice was male. Two female voices immediately followed, with recurring shrieks.

Smith backed away, staring openmouthed while Dicky Cahill writhed in agony on the floor, clutching his face, gasping and moaning.

It had been instantaneous, and overwhelming. Smith had walked over to Cahill, full of confidence, ready to finish him off. He'd aimed the gun at him, then hesitated. Smith, apparently, for all his bravado, wasn't quite the seasoned killer he'd made himself out to be. This wasn't like taking someone out in the ring, or on a battlefield. This was cold blood. The man was sittin' there cryin' like a baby, for chrissake. Maybe those two women wouldn't think he was such hot shit after all, he just shot him like that. Maybe he should make him crawl. Like out the door, down the steps, and swim for it. Take his chances with the gators and moccasins. Yeah, that was a much better—

That was as far as his thoughts had gotten him. Cahill, encouraged by the moment of respite, seized the opportunity to resort to something he'd never actually thought he'd use. He'd stolen it from Freeman two months ago. It was supposed to be evidence. He'd heard that kid Cross had stumbled across this stuff in one of the holding ponds, and had requested a sample. Freeman, misunderstanding, had gotten some from the recovery tank: a twenty-three percent solution of hydrofluosulicic acid. The most corrosive chemical agent known to man. Very effective for killing rats and roaches, it is also the principle chemical used to fluoridate water. Cross had very foolishly put his nose close to the little vial and taken a whiff. It had nearly killed him. And, as Freeman had nervously confided to Largent (which conversation Cahill had overheard) might have eventually, even so. In the confusion that followed, Cahill had quietly pocketed the vial, and no one had thought to ask for it later. What it did was eat through the cell linings, through the tissues, until it reached the bone. Then it would slowly, pervasively, eat away at the bone. A whiff might take a long time, and the doctors might not even figure it out. A splash in the face, though . . .

Smith had given Cahill his chance. The vial was in a little leather loop, in his belt. Smith hadn't noticed it, or cared, having taken away his gun. Cahill was hunched over, so Smith couldn't see him surreptitiously grope at his middle, feigning a pain in his gut. He managed to work the little rubber stopper off, and grip the vial in his left hand.

Smith had apparently made up his mind. He came closer, and leaned over. "Okay, motherfucker," he started to say. At which moment Cahill struck like a rattlesnake. The hand flew up, intent on flinging the contents of the vial full in Smith's face.

The women were in hysterics at what happened next. Even Smith was sickened. Smith, a trained commando, had been too quick for him. With a reflex reaction to Cahill's sudden motion, his boot had flicked out, caught the upswinging vial, and knocked it straight back into Cahill's face. And now, seeing the results, he decided to put the poor bastard out of his misery, even though he deserved what was happening to him. He picked up the gun, Cahill's gun, and almost casually looked over at the two women, cowering in terror.

"Shut the fuck up," he told them. Then he shot Cahill with a quick burst of fire.

Outside, Lowell and Malone, who had heard everything, quickly tied up to the pylon on the far side of the house, away from the stairs. Both were silent. They knew what they were up against now. Their only chance was surprise.

They didn't speak. They didn't have to. Lowell pointed up to the deck above, and began to climb the weather-smooth wooden pylon, shinnying like a sailor up a mast. Lowell had done this before. Malone watched him with momentary admiration, then pointed at the stairs. He would take the conventional route.

Malone climbed the stairs silently, cautiously, like a base runner girding himself to steal second.

Inside, Smith turned his attention to the women.

"I tol' you shut up," he ordered. Their shrieks and sobs seemed only to intensify.

Then a slight movement out of the corner of her eye caught Briana's attention. She concealed her reaction as Virgil Malone, looking very much the business executive, stepped silently into the room, directly behind Smith. Reaching behind his back, the baseball hero produced a small Browning pistol from his waistband.

Smith's problem at that moment was that the violence that usually stimulated him had this time turned him off. The sight of Cahill, his face ravaged, his skull blown apart, had begun to nauseate him. He felt the gorge rising in his throat, and turned to run for the railing outside to throw up.

Malone shot him in the forehead. Smith fell over backward, almost head to toe with Cahill, an expression of surprise on his face.

Lowell entered the room, pushing past Malone. The women looked at him, and fell into each other's arms. The sense of relief in the room was tangible, you could almost touch it. Lowell let out a deep breath. Malone was very businesslike. He knelt by Smith, then Cahill.

"Wheeeeyew!" he said, and turned away. He and Lowell both spotted the vial at the same time. Lowell was faster, and got to it first. Taking a handkerchief from his pocket, Lowell carefully wrapped it up. Malone looked at him benignly. "Better let me take that," he said, reaching for it.

Lowell looked at his hand still holding the gun. As Malone's sleeve slid up his arm, Lowell noted the white tan mark, where a watch would usually be. Malone had obviously been very attached to that watch, he thought. He hadn't even tried to replace it.

"This is evidence," he said, eyeing Malone with a new and chilling awareness. Gator Malone, he thought.

"No shit," said Malone. "I don't know what you had in mind, Lowell. But this should wrap up your case pretty good."

Except for Corcoran, Lowell was thinking. He'd been troubled by the big man's disappearance in the parking lot, and had been unable to do anything about it. He went to the large jalousie window and looked out. He'd heard a sound outside. A sound of gunwales bumping pilings. It was unmistakable to those who knew boats. He gestured for silence, and nodded toward the deck outside. Malone understood.

Malone moved to one side of the door, Lowell to the other. Malone still gripped the Browning, and held it ready, barrel up the way they did on TV. Lowell tried to shake his head no. Malone ignored him. That was when Lowell knew for certain.

Briana chose that moment to retrieve her husband's gun. Cecilia watched her, eyes widening.

Outside, in the darkness beneath the shack, Buster Corcoran held his finger under a crack in the floorboards. Something was dripping down. He sniffed, then tasted it. Blood. It didn't take an Einstein to figure out what had happened. Only problem was, he didn't know who was left. The shack above had suddenly fallen silent. Shit! It dawned on him. He'd been discovered. He could hear floorboards creaking above. People walking on their toes. In two different places. No, three. By the door, and on the other side. Shit! He cursed to himself again. He'd lost his only advantage: the element of surprise. Whoever had prevailed up there was ready for him now. There was only one thing to do. Get out, and get out now.

The Whaler would do nicely. The engine was still warm, he'd checked. One quick pull, and it would start. Quickly, silently, he freed the lines and swung the bow around, facing downstream. He'd have but one shot at starting it, then a scant few seconds to get out onto the water and the cover of near darkness, around the hummock just downstream to the left. Mist was rising from the river. That would help. He heard footsteps padding softly on the flooring above, then the outside deck, and stairs. Climbing as quickly and silently aboard the Whaler as his bulk would permit, he steadied himself and the boat, luckily flat bottomed and very stable, and yanked the cord. With his massive strength, all it took was a flick of the wrist, and the engine roared to life. In a moment, he was racing for safety, and what he hoped would be freedom. Revenge would have to wait.

Above and behind him, Malone ran to the rail and managed to fire five shots before emptying his chamber.

"What the hell are you doing?" shouted Lowell, coming up behind him. "There's been enough shooting here."

Malone paid no attention, and stopped to reload. "I think I winged him," he stated matter-of-factly.

Lowell went back inside to check the two women. With a look of reproach, he gently took Cahill's pistol from Briana's now trembling hands. Both women reached for him, and he lifted them together from the sofa, almost simultaneously, an arm around each one. Each burst into tears. "I would've killed him if Mr. Malone hadn't," wept Cecilia. "He would've deserved it." She meant Smith, of course.

"Probably no one would blame you. Much, anyway. But it's best you didn't," he told her, and put the gun in his pocket.

"Damn," they all heard from Malone, slamming in from the deck outside. Releasing the women, Lowell walked over to where Malone stood staring out the window into the darkness and mist.

"You had Cross killed, didn't you," said Lowell. It was a statement, rather than a question. "Corcoran was your hit man, but you gave the order."

"Excuse me?" Malone's chronic grin wavered at that. "What are you talking about?"

Lowell looked at him, pale under the naked kitchen light. "Then you got rid of Baumgarten."

"You have proof of that?"

"Corcoran." said Lowell. "You tried to shut him up—eliminate the last witness." He reached into his pocket and pulled out the Rolex. "Recognize this? You must've busted it the night you dumped Cross's body."

"Where'd you find that? I've been lookin' everywhere."

"In your car. Under the seat. I assume you didn't take the Rover to do the dirty work, so you must've dropped it on your way home. Or taken it off, and forgotten about it. I'm sure you had a lot on your mind."

"Give me that." Malone turned the Browning on Lowell now. Lowell took a step backward, and Cecilia grabbed one arm, Briana the other.

"What are you gonna do, kill us all? You can kiss the Hall of Fame good-bye, I'll tell you that!" Lowell warned him.

"Yeah," said Cecilia. "The great Doc Malone. Just another lousy lowlife killer, deep down."

"Shut up." There was a thumping noise coming from downriver, just audible over the noise of the departing Whaler. A chopper. A brilliant searchlight cut through the darkness downstream, coming closer. Bedrosian. She must be searching the river. Bless her uptight little soul.

Malone looked out the window and swore.

"It's the police," Lowell informed him. "It's over, Malone."

Malone shook his head. "Outside," he ordered. He pushed Lowell out ahead of him, onto the deck. The chopper was directly overhead now, its police lights flashing with authority. "Get rid of them!" barked Malone, shoving the Browning into the base of Lowell's spine. Lowell thought about Cahill's gun in his pocket, and thought the better of it. He halfheartedly tried to wave the chopper away.

Bedrosian trained the searchlight on them, and knew something was wrong right away. She nudged Peters. "There!" she shouted. She lifted her field glasses and recognized Lowell's wry look, squinting into the harsh light, the lines of tension in his face. She noted Malone's hand low behind Lowell's back, and construed at once what was happening.

"We got a hostage situation," she informed Peters.

"I can't see where to put down," Peters shouted.

Bedrosian made a decision. She reached for the rifle. She'd probably only get one shot, she knew. She'd have to make it a good one.

"Bring it around," she ordered Peters. He looked at her and his eyes widened, but he obeyed.

"What are they doing?" rasped Malone, behind Lowell. "Tell them to back off, you got it all under control, whatever it takes."

Lowell obliged him. "Go!" he shouted into the night sky. "I got it under control!"

Yeah, right, thought Bedrosian. She focused the searchlight so as to blind Malone, raised the rifle, took her time, and fired a single shot.

Malone yelled and dropped the pistol, which Lowell wasted no time grabbing. He'd express his resentments to Bedrosian later for treating him like William Tell. Then thank her. Malone clutched his shoulder. Bedrosian couldn't have done it better, he would grudgingly have to admit when asked.

Up in the chopper, Bedrosian carefully put the rifle back down. "That should do it," she said, utterly calm. Then she nearly threw up.

"Where the hell'm I gonna land?" complained Peters.

Panning with the high-powered beam, Bedrosian scanned the clearing Dicky Cahill had cut for his parking space and turnaround. She trained the light on Cahill's red T-bird and shouted down to the house:

"Move the car!"

Lowell looked, and got it right away. He turned to Briana. "Can you move the T-bird?"

She nodded. Dicky had let her drive it exactly once, one time at a party, when he was too drunk, and Carol's husband had forcibly taken the keys from him. "Briana drives, or you don't go home," Jerry had said. Cahill had known better than to fight Bubba. She ran back into the shack, dug the keys from her late husband's pocket—being careful not to look at him—and ran down to the parking area. She got in and started the engine, quickly backed the car around, and drove it a hundred feet or so back down the access road. Peters gave her a thumbs-up, and brought down the chopper.

Lowell ushered Malone to the two waiting cops. "Name's Virgil Malone. You may have heard of him. Batted three hundred lifetime. Now he's a big zero."

Bedrosian looked him up and down under the harsh floodlight. "You looked better in the razor commercial," she said.

"This is the real Malone," said Lowell.

"Is the woman okay?" asked Bedrosian, looking up at the shack.

"Yep. Both of them."

"Both? Oh, brother." Her eyebrows raised as she saw Briana and Cecilia come out of the shack together, arms around each other. "And Cahill?" she asked.

"Dead."

"Why does that not fill me with grief?" she remarked.

"It's an honor meeting you, sir," Peters said to Malone.

"Maybe I could get an autograph some time? At your convenience, I mean." Peters shook the great man's hand eagerly, then backed off after a blistering look from Bedrosian.

"What're we supposed to charge him with, exactly?" asked Bedrosian, taking Lowell aside.

"Three counts of murder, two of conspiracy to commit murder, how the hell should I know? I'm not a DA," said Lowell.

"It won't stick, you know it won't stick!" promised Malone with a confident smile, scorn edging into his voice. "That was self-defense in there. Any jury will agree."

"He's lying," spoke up Briana. "We saw it."

Cecilia nodded. "That's right. He shot Lenny in col' blood. He didn't have to."

Bedrosian looked at the two women, and turned to Peters. "Read him his rights," she said. "Just in case." She turned back to Lowell, questioning. "He killed Cross, too?"

"Corcoran was the trigger. You must've just passed him out there."

"We'll get him." She turned to Peters. "Joe, when you're done talking baseball, call the sheriff and put out an APB on this guy Corcoran. Buster Corcoran, I believe is his name."

"It was Corcoran and Cahill!" shouted Malone. "You can't stick that on me."

"Both of them worked for Malone," explained Lowell. "They did his bidding. Wanted to suck up to the big hero real bad, I guess," he added, with just a glance at Peters. Peters blushed. "But Malone was there."

"What's going to happen to me—to me and Cecilia?" asked Briana, joining them.

"You're free," said Bedrosian.

Briana looked at Lowell, who looked away. Cecilia hung back, still shaken. She had no better reason to trust cops—

or men—Lowell figured, than anyone else around here. He went over and gently led her to the helicopter. "They'll take you home," he assured her. "You got my word on that."

Peters reluctantly read Malone his rights under the chopper blades while Bedrosian took Lowell aside. "We got a case on this guy for Cross, or does it all hang on Smith up there?"

"You got two witnesses on Smith. And I'm pretty confident Corcoran will plea bargain and turn state's evidence, for whatever that's worth."

"Where's this Smith person?"

"Upstairs. Him and Cahill. It went down pretty bad for old Dicky boy."

"He was a louse."

"Yeah." He told her what had happened.

"Jesus." She winced. She looked at Lowell. "And you? You got off without a scratch as usual?"

"Right," he said with a smile, in spite of it all. "That's my reward for leading a virtuous life."

"Give me a break," she growled.

Lowell turned serious. "What's the news on my friend Perry Garwood?"

"He's expected to make it," she told him. "Lost a lot of blood, but no vital organs were hit."

"Thanks for checking," he said relieved.

"Any time." Lena was anxious to get home now, take a long, cleansing bath, forget about this day, and make love to her ever-patient husband. She would think about what happened here, though, maybe later, when Michael was holding her, and it was safe.

"Okay, Lowell. How did you know it was Malone?" Bedrosian asked as they walked back to the waiting helicopter. They would take everyone in by air, then have the sheriff send deputies for the bodies and vehicles later.

"The watch. I found it in the car, and remembered something about that fragment we found."

"Which was?"

"The bevels. The crystal was cut with little diamond-shaped bevels. As in baseball diamond?"

"Yeah, yeah," she said. "I get it. I've actually seen a baseball game."

He pulled the watch out and handed it to her. "Anyway, I believe you'll find this was his. He must've broken it carrying Cross that night. It probably came loose, and he took it off in his car, maybe it fell off, and he didn't miss it until later. Probably assumed it was out in a field somewhere."

"I knew it was his watch. That's what I wanted to tell you when I called earlier," she said. "Also Cross's message. What he wrote on the seat, was—"

"Sunshine," he finished.

She looked annoyed. "You knew?"

"Hey, it's my job."

"I tried to tell you before, but you hung up," she said. "You were in too much of a hurry to go rushing off and get everybody killed."

"Touché." He fought back the fatigue that was coming over him as they walked across the grass. "So Carla Brewer's off the hook, I assume?"

"Yeah. She just got over the top about jobs, was all. She even apologized about it."

"Not to me." Lowell sighed.

"Nobody's gonna convict Malone, you know," Bedrosian warned him, as they reached the helicopter. The others were waiting inside. "He's way too popular."

"Yeah," said Lowell. "He hit three sixty-five one year, with thirty home runs. You're probably right."

"Still, you gotta do what you gotta do," she sighed.

Epilogue

Summer comes to Florida every year, whether the Floridians like it or not. People mostly go into hiding, turn on their air conditioners, dodge between lightning bolts, or head for North Carolina. It's good for those with kids in college, though. Like Tony Lowell. His daughter, Ariel, came home from Syracuse—home for her being Palm Coast Harbor across the state, where her mother, Caitlin, lived. (It had been his home, too, once, in that his father had been chief of police and he'd been raised there. But the house where he grew up had long since been razed in favor of a parking lot for a video parlor). He'd gotten to see Ariel briefly, during his trip cross-state to pay his respects to Ernie Larson, after Ernie's return from Philadelphia.

"The funeral was nice," Ernie had assured him. "Marsetta is taking it pretty good, for a mother."

Lowell had nodded, not knowing what to say.

"This woman showed up from out your way, named Carla Something. Seemed nice. You know her?"

"Not really," said Lowell. "I've met her."

Two weeks later, Ariel had called him from Caitlin's and promised she'd be over to the Gulf to see him before long. Then she was off to L.A. Seems she'd met someone new at school who'd gotten her a summer job as a production assistant. On a movie.

"Oh, brother," said Lowell.

"What was that?" she asked.

"Nothing, honey. Go on."

She told him the rest. How her friend was a film student, how he was well connected, how he had an uncle or something in the industry who lived in Sherman Oaks, nearby.

All Lowell could think of was, whatever happened to photojournalism? But he knew better than to ask.

"So you'll be over here pretty soon?"

"Of course, Dad. But not for long," she warned him. "Just long enough for a nice visit. I'm dying to tell you about my school year. What's new with you, by the way?"

"Oh," he said, rechecking a diagram he was drawing of his intended stateroom on the schooner. "Nothing much."

"Sounds boring," she said.

"I can't wait to show you the schooner," he told her.

"Now, that," she said, "sounds like fun. See you soon, Dad." She hung up.

Well, he'd reflected. At least he'd managed to avoid the temptation of asking her about her mother. He still ached for Caitlin at times, he had to admit to himself. They'd gotten along wonderfully that one sizzling reunion a few years back. They were still friends. But distant friends. They were, they both had been forced to realize, irrevocably different.

Today, a week before the Fourth of July, had been a scorcher from the get-go. Lowell gazed out from his back porch at the scaffolding that still enclosed the schooner. It was like the surrounding mangroves; it had been there so long it seemed to have grown there. The water sparkled invitingly. There were no thunderheads in sight.

He would have liked to go for a sail in his little sloop, but he had promised to take Perry to the beach. He hated beaches. He'd thought Perry did, too. But that was before the injury, and Lowell kind of felt he owed him. (Actually, he did owe him, but he was still waiting for Bedrosian's invoices to clear city bureaucracy). Perry was recovering well, just as Lena had predicted.

Lowell got out the Impala and drove to town. He considered stopping at the Clam Shack for a brew, along the way, but decided it could wait until he'd collected Perry. Perry had given him grief for quite some time, after the shooting—mostly for ditching him at the hands of those diabolical medical doctors.

"What did you want? For me to operate? Besides, you told me to!" Lowell had reminded him. "You said to 'get those bastards.' That's a direct quote!"

"Well, I didn't mean it," complained Perry. "What's more important, friendship or catching some lousy killer?"

"You have a point." Killers, it seems, were a dime a dozen, these days. But friends . . . friends were hard to come by.

Perry, however, had an idea of how Lowell could make it up to him. It seems Lowell wasn't the only one with women on his mind. On the day Lowell drove him home from the hospital, Perry broached the subject.

"You remember the lady with the kid? The one that SOB Smith was living with?"

Lowell wasn't about to forget. "Cecilia Potter," he said.

"Yeah. Man. She is nice."

"Yeah." Lowell thought so, too. But he gave Perry her number anyway.

Feeling self-conscious and a little foolish in swimming trunks, Lowell picked Perry up at the rehab outpatient clinic at Manatee Hospital. They were going to meet Cecilia and Natasha at the beach, plus an alleged "friend" for Lowell.

Perry was all set. He had sunglasses, a Hawaiian shirt to cover his still-ugly scars, a baggy orange swimsuit, a gaudy multicolored beach towel, a huge ghetto blaster, and a cooler. He seemed uncharacteristically nervous, though. Lowell ribbed him. "C'mon," he said. "Now's the fun part."

Perry stashed his cooler in the trunk, and climbed in. Lowell already had a cooler. "This was supposed to be my treat," he complained.

"Fuck it," said Perry. "We'll need both coolers before we're done."

He was right.